The Steep Cost of Fate

By Tempie W. Wade

The Steep Cost of Fate

By Tempie W. Wade

This is a work of historical fiction/fantasy. While some of the names in this book are the same as real-life historical figures, the actions and words of the characters are strictly figments of the author's imagination and any resemblance to actual events, places, and persons, living or dead, are entirely coincidental.

Paperback ISBN: 978-0-9600257-8-7
E-Book ISBN: 978-0-9600257-9-4

For more information, please visit www.TempieWade.com

The Steep Cost of Fate

By Tempie W. Wade

Book Five

The Timely Revolution Book Series

The boundaries which divide Life from Death are at best shadowy and vague. Who shall say where the one ends, and where the other begins?

- Edgar Allan Poe

July 5, 1781
Beechcroft Estate
Williamsburg, Virginia

  She looked down in horror and disbelief at the crumpled
and lifeless body of her cherished lover on the steps of
their home. She was still shaky and weak and the blood
that streaked her inner thighs formed a puddle where she
stood; her gown still wet from where she gave birth just a
few short hours before. She took slow, deliberate steps
until she reached him, fell upon her knees and took his
precious face in her hands. His eyes were fixed, locked
open, as if he were about to say something to her, to tell
her that he loved and adored her as he had done so many
times before since they had become one, but he could
not; Duncan was gone.

  His battered and bruised physical form remained, but
his spirit, his life force, and that wonderous inner light,
the thing that made him who he was, had been cruelly
and needlessly extinguished. The love of her life, the

father of her children, her reason for being, was no longer of this world, and nothing in this fucked up world mattered to her anymore. She traced the angle of his jaw and searched his sweet, handsome face, trying desperately to will the life back into his eyes, but he remained still. Her heart shattered, and her tears fell in a deluge, like a torrential downpour from a terrible storm on a hot summer afternoon.

She gently pulled his head onto her lap, rocking him as she softly whispered tender affirmations of love and stroked his face, her own will to live rapidly leaving her.

"I am coming with you, my love!" She wept and kissed the cold, blue lips that refused to acknowledge her as they had never done before. "I will not live this life without you, not now, and not ever."

She slid her hand down the length of his body and reached for the small dagger that she knew he always kept concealed in his boot. Maggie gripped it tightly, pulled it to her breast and pointed it upward to her own throat, ready to slash her own jugular vein, just to be with him; ready to join him in the next world, whether it be Heaven or Hell—it did not matter, as long as they were together...it was a fate she had already willingly surrendered to without giving it a second thought...

...until that British, son of a bitch, opened his mouth.

He rushed to her side when he realized what she

intended to do, caught her by the wrist and peeled her fingers away one by one from the hilt. Once he had taken the weapon away from her, he looked down at it and shook his head disapprovingly. "I am afraid I cannot let you do that, my dear. The children need their mother and a dead bride is of no use to me." He tossed the blade into the yard, went back down the steps to his horse and shouted, "Kill the men, take the supplies, burn the house and do what you will with the slaves! That Scottish bastard is dead, and there is no one here left to stop us!"

Infuriated by his words and actions, and even more enraged that he had kept her from joining her love, Maggie closed her eyes and slowly lifted her chin. The utter devastation and rage washed over her like a tidal wave, the contempt came forward, and seized control of her mind and body. She rose from her knees and clenched her fists tightly, as her face contorted in unadulterated hatred aimed at the one man standing before her that had taken away her entire world.

The gold in her eyes flashed red and she spat, "I wouldn't be so sure about that!"

1 CHAPTER ONE

Seven Months Earlier
The Beginning of December 1780
Beechcroft Estate
Williamsburg, Virginia

The family was enjoying their last supper together before Lady Aurnia and Logan departed for Scotland the next morning. One of the ships from their company would be making its regular run back to London, and they were sailing back on it.

"Are ye sure ye don't want to stay on a little longer?" asked Duncan, moving the food around on his plate with his fork. "It seems like ye just got here."

Lady Aurnia reached over and took his hand. "As much as we would love to, I cannot leave yer brothers in Scotland unattended for too long. God only knows what kind of shape the stronghold is in by now."

"Just promise you will come back soon," said Maggie, sipping her tea, the morning sickness getting the better of her.

"I do hate to leave ye like this, Maggie," she replied. "Sick, and with three little wee ones already. Ye have your hands full and I feel like I am deserting ye."

"We will get her through it," said Gabe, smiling at his mother-in-law. "We did before, and that was without a full staff."

"Gabe is right, we have more than enough help, but it won't make us miss you any less," said Maggie.

"Don't worry!" Logan glanced over at his mother. "All of her grandchildren are here. Wild horses couldn't keep this woman away for very long."

"Well, if my sons back home would take wives and give me some additional grandchildren, I would have something to keep me occupied," she retorted and cut him a scathing look.

Logan picked up his glass and used it to hide the grin on his face.

"It is a shame we are not all in one place," said Duncan, having laid his fork aside.

A wave of nausea slammed into Maggie and she leapt from her chair to go in the other room to be sick.

"How many times is that today?" asked Logan, scrunching up his nose.

"Five or six," replied Quinn, "that we have seen."

"Are ye sure she was this ill before?" asked Lady Aurnia, worriedly.

"Aye, the entire first few months. It was a difficult time to say the least," said Duncan with a sigh.

"I thought she was dying when they showed up at the house in New York," added John. "I have never seen anything like it before in my life."

"Poor thing," she said. "I was nowhere near that sick with any of ye."

"It seems ALL of her symptoms are exaggerated," added Quinn with a smirk.

"What do ye mean by that?" asked his mother.

Gabe chuckled. "Well, let's just say that if you think Maggie and Duncan are amorous towards each other now, just wait a few weeks when the sickness goes away."

"Are ye serious?" asked an astonished and somewhat disgusted Logan. "Worse than they are now? How is that even possible?"

"Oh yes!" John nodded with an amused expression on his face. "It makes for the most interesting dinner entertainment."

Maggie returned to the room and reached for her cup. "I am so sorry. I really have not missed this part of being pregnant."

"They say the sicker ye are, the healthier the baby...or babies," said Lady Aurnia. "Just try to remember that to get ye through the worst of it."

"Well, if that is true, we must have the healthiest children in the world," replied Maggie, dryly.

The next morning, they said their 'goodbyes' to Lady Aurnia and Logan on the dock just before they boarded the ship.

"I wish you could stay." Maggie hugged Lady Aurnia tightly. "Having you here is almost like having my own mom with me."

"Oh Maggie, ye are more my daughter than any one I could have given birth to. I will miss you too. Take care of my grandbabies...all of them." She smiled and touched Maggie's stomach.

They both brushed their tears away before Lady Aurnia moved over to embrace Duncan.

"I will miss ye, Mother!"

"I will miss ye too, son!" She pulled back from their hug and touched his face. "I am so proud of ye. Ye are a good husband to Maggie and a wonderful father to your children. Yer own father would be so proud of the man ye have become."

"I hope so," he whispered. "I still think about him and miss him every day."

"So do I, son, more than ye will ever know. Ye take care of Maggie and my grandchildren. We will see each other as soon as we can."

Logan hugged Maggie. "Take care of my brother and keep him out of trouble."

"Oh, I will," she replied.

Logan wrapped his arms around Duncan. "I will miss ye, brother. I won't miss ye and Maggie keeping me awake at all hours of the night banging your headboard against the wall, but I will miss ye."

"Ye are just jealous," teased Duncan. "Take care of everyone," he said, seriously.

Lady Aurnia and Logan said their 'goodbyes' to the rest of the family before they boarded the ship and waved to all of them as they pulled away from the shoreline.

"It's not going to be the same here without them," said Maggie, leaning against Duncan. "I am going to miss them."

"Aye, so will I. I did not realize how much I had missed them until they came here," he said softly.

Maggie felt a pang of guilt for being the cause of his sadness. "I am so sorry, Duncan, I feel like I took you away from them."

"Nay!" Duncan took her face in his hands. "Do not ever think that. The choice to come was mine and I would make the same one over a thousand times to be with ye. My life is with ye, wherever that may be."

Maggie felt a strong rush of emotions and her tears flowed uncontrollably.

"None of that," he whispered, brushing the wetness from her face with his thumbs. "I cannot bear to see ye cry and ye know it."

"I can't help it," she said and sniffled.

He kissed her and wrapped his arm around her shoulders. "Come on, let's get ye out of the cold and in front of a nice, warm fireplace with a cup of hot tea."

Gabe, Quinn, and John followed them back from the dock to the house and as soon as they returned, they all gathered in the drawing room. Duncan tucked a blanket around Maggie's lap, kissed her nose, and took a seat next to her on the sofa, draping his arm around her.

"Since we are all here," she said, "there is something we need to discuss."

Quinn handed Maggie a cup of the tea he kept continuously brewing on the stove as she continued what she was saying.

"How far can the fog that protects the house in Scotland be extended outward?"

Duncan and Quinn exchanged puzzled looks.

"We have never tested it," replied Duncan. "We always just kept it around the woods surrounding the stronghold and in that immediate area."

"I'm sorry," said John. "I know I am very new to all of this, but what sort of 'fog' are you referring to?"

"One of the spells that we use to protect the home in Scotland creates a fog that we are able to raise so that no one can see through it except those who wear the mark," explained Duncan. "It keeps strangers from stumbling across us accidentally. It is not perfect, and does not conceal us completely, but it does help a great deal. When the Fae blood in our family line was stronger, generations ago, it kept everyone away from us, but its strength has diminished greatly over the years with the watering down of the power in our blood."

"Why are ye asking, Maggie?" asked Quinn.

"This area is about to come into play with the war. What I know, and the rest of you don't, is that after John was captured and Benedict Arnold escaped by the skin of his teeth, he went to the British army and they made him an officer."

Maggie watched John's face cautiously for his reaction.

"What? That man?" He became very annoyed and agitated. "What rank did they make him?"

"If I remember correctly," replied Maggie as she cringed, "Brigadier General?"

The repulsive look on John's face said it all, and he huffed in disgust.

"You were saying?" Gabe encouraged her to continue.

"He has been given a small army and he will be making a move on Richmond. The city will be wide open by the time he gets there. He will be more than a little upset and he will lay waste to it."

"What does that have to do with us?" asked Duncan.

"Arnold will get there by pissing and burning his way up the James River from the coast. I cannot remember all the details of where he starts this, but we are close to that point. Our house backs up to one of the tributaries, and we cannot take any chances with the lives here on the estate. The British will also occupy Williamsburg sometime this year, taking food, slaves, and bringing devastating diseases here with them. While we are not in town, we are a little too close for my comfort. Williamsburg is going to take a major hit in the upcoming year, and we need to protect ourselves as best we can."

Maggie looked at John. "I know your loyalties must still lie with the Crown, but they do not win this war, and we cannot allow anything to change that outcome. If we do, we risk changing the world I was born into and possibly my own future...or past...or present...or everything." She raised her palm to her forehead. "God, I am even confusing myself now. I am going to have to start making flow charts."

John was silent for a moment, before he sighed. "My only loyalty now lies with this family and I will do whatever is needed to protect it."

"Thank you, John," she said, gratefully.

"Ye think the fog will protect the entire estate when that time comes?" asked Quinn. "That is an enormous amount of ground to cover."

"Yes," said Gabe, "but you also said the stronger the blood, the stronger the fog and if that is true, Maggie's blood should be more than enough to do the trick."

Maggie looked to Duncan, confused. "Is Gabe right about that?"

"There is only one way to find out," he replied.

"Well, I guess we won't know until we try. The time for us to close up our ranks and take care of our own is rapidly approaching," said Maggie, pulling the blanket tighter around her, her eyelids drooping.

"Ye look tired, my love." Duncan caught her cup and set it on the table just before it slipped from her hand. "Why don't ye take a nap?"

"I will in a little bit. Why don't you, Quinn, and Gabe go see what will be of assistance in the collection? I need a word alone with John."

"Alright, but then ye get some rest," he ordered and kissed her.

"I will," she promised.

The others departed and left Maggie and John alone.

"Come and sit next to me," she said and patted the sofa. John came over and joined her.

"How are things going with the tribe?"

John smiled. "Very well, actually. I feel like they have really taken me in as one of their own, and they are a wonderful group of people. I must say, I do appreciate the touches you added to my new abode. Having an actual bed has been nice and it makes it feel like home."

"I am glad you like it there." Maggie blew out a deep breath. "We have not really talked about the events surrounding your 'death.' I am sure you have questions, and I am happy to answer the ones that I can. You spent a great deal of time in the army and it is not so easy to just walk away from that—your entire life for that matter."

John looked into the fire, lost in thought as he considered what to ask. "You said that you were doing your best to not change what was meant to be, but you were the one that brought Benedict Arnold to me. You convinced him to betray Washington and join your cause."

Maggie shook her head. "No! That is the one thing that I did not do. You see, according to my history, Arnold did indeed betray Washington, and I knew that you would be the one he reached out to. I also had a fair amount of knowledge of how and when, and I used that foreknowledge to make the deal with Clinton to save Gabe, knowing it was already in motion. All I had to do was intercept what was already on the way to you, and make it APPEAR I had a hand in facilitating it. I merely carried a letter that was already en route to you, nothing more. I did not convince him to betray his country or change anything else, except your death of course."

"How DID he manage to escape?" he asked. "I am thoroughly confused about that."

Maggie made a face. "I am fairly certain you have Peggy to thank for that." She reached for her cup on the table.

John looked at her questioningly. "Peggy? What did she have to do with it?"

"She had a fit of hysteria that gave him the time he needed to get away. History was never sure, but after getting to know her, I am fairly certain that she faked it long enough for him to make his getaway. That woman is a great deal smarter than she has ever been given credit for. If Washington had laid hands on Arnold, your sentence would have never been carried out. He was more than willing to trade you for him, but Clinton would not give over the traitor. I spoke to Washington just before your execution, and he was still holding out hope until the very end that they would. He did not want to carry out your punishment; no one on the Continental side did."

John looked perplexed. "Why were you speaking to Washington on my behalf?"

Maggie took his hand. "We were not completely sure our plan was going to work. This was before the Wilson incident, and before we knew Nathaniel was there. I actually went to him directly to beg for your release, but he would not do it."

"But, if he had, that would have changed the future."

"I know, but I was willing to risk it to see you safe. I am afraid I just could not let you go. You mean too much to me."

John closed his eyes and kissed the back of her hand. "I am not sure what I did to deserve your love, but I am thankful for it each and every day."

"What will become of Arnold?" he finally asked.

She shrugged. "Nothing. Washington never gets his hands on him, he ends up leaving the country after the war, and being marked the most famous traitor in history. Even in the year 2018, a disloyal person is still referred to as a 'Benedict Arnold'."

"And how does history record me?" he asked cautiously.

"Very favorably," she said and smiled. "You are known as a hero to all of England, especially the ladies. As I recall, it was with great pomp and circumstance that your remains were…. or rather, will be, exhumed and relocated to Westminster Abbey."

"Westminster Abbey?" asked an astonished John with a twinkle in his eye. "My remains were laid to rest in Westminster Abbey?"

"Well, they won't be now, I suppose!" Maggie giggled. "I remember a tour guide telling the story. The ceremony was…will be…. quite grand, with the ladies of the town draping your mahogany and gold sarcophagus with garlands of greens while reciting poetry. They will even send a myrtle tree along with your remains back to England. You would have...well, will, love it."

"I must say that I am a little disappointed that I will miss it." He laughed.

"You haven't missed it yet. It won't happen for about another forty years."

John shrugged. "Well, at least my name will be on the marker. Maybe I will go visit it one day, if I am not too old to get around by then."

Maggie pushed the blanket off her lap, set down her tea, and stood. "I have something for you."

She went to her desk drawer, pulled out a newspaper, and handed it to him.

"Nathaniel thought we might want to see this, so he sent a copy of the Gazette reporting your 'death.' James Rivington was even kind enough to publish one of your poems after your untimely demise. You were a well-known, well-loved gentleman to both sides until the very end."

John looked up at Maggie, then down at the paper in his hand. "Would you look at that?" he said and smacked it.

"I won't even mention the droves of women weeping and wailing over your body on the day of your hanging. You would have been very touched."

He laughed softly just as a wave of dizziness hit Maggie out of the blue. He caught her just before she fell.

"Upstairs for you," he ordered, picked her up, and carried her to the bedroom.

John laid her down, tucked her in and kissed her on the forehead.

"After all this time, I finally got you back in bed," he said with a wink. "Get some rest."

"Thank you, John," she said, rolled on her side and closed her eyes.

Duncan was standing in the foyer looking around when John came out of the bedroom.

"Where's Maggie?" he asked.

"I just brought her up," he said as he quietly closed the door. "She almost fainted."

"Is she alright?"

"Yes," he replied, as he came down the stairs. "She is resting."

Duncan looked up toward the bedroom worriedly. "Christ! I hate how sick this all makes her. I wish I could take it from her somehow."

"I guess you are going to have to quit getting her pregnant...and you know what causes that," teased John, and slapped him on the back.

Duncan shook his head. "I could not stay away from that woman if my very soul depended on it."

2 CHAPTER TWO

They all studied the map on the table in front of them, as Maggie ran her finger around the perimeter.

"We need to raise the fog along the riverbank… here. That should deter anyone sailing along the property line from trying to come ashore, and it should be enough for now. When the time comes for most of the army to move into town in the summer, we can enclose the entire property and seal it off."

Maggie folded her arms and looked to Duncan. "How exactly does this work? Do you say the spell once and it is covered forever?"

"Nay," replied Duncan. "The fog is the thickest when the spell is performed, but it does eventually start to fade, and when it does, we will perform it again to re-strengthen it."

"But that is with our blood," added Quinn. "If ye are the one who does it, there is a good chance it will be much stronger and last a great deal longer."

"How do I even do this? Surely, there is more to it than reading a few words," asked Maggie as she sat down.

"You have to focus your energy on the task at hand," said Duncan. "It is like when ye do the fertility touch that ye do and ye wish it to happen...it just has to flow through ye. This is also one of the spells that can be done by more than one person at the same time, the same way Quinn and I joined together to put the fire out here at the house, so we will be able to walk ye through it."

Maggie groaned, and leaned forward, her stomach churning. "If I can manage the ride to the riverfront."

Duncan came to her side and rubbed her back. "Quinn and I can attempt to do this ourselves. Ye should not be out in the shape ye are in."

"But we need it to be strong, Duncan. We cannot take any chances here, so I will find a way to manage."

"Ye will need to practice beforehand," said Quinn. "It does take a little perfecting, but ye can learn the basics here in the house."

Alastair appeared in the doorway and came into the drawing room with a steaming cup in his hands. "Auntie Maggie, I think ye need this." He handed her the tea.

"Alastair, you are my hero." She ruffled his hair and kissed the top of his head. "Thank you. How did you know this was exactly what I needed right at this moment?"

He smiled and shrugged. "I just felt like ye did."

Maggie sipped the tea. "Well, your feelings are spot on."

Quinn came over and put his arm around his son. "Where is your sister?"

"She is helping Hettie in the kitchen."

Gabe shook his head. "I had better go check on her. I am not sure how much 'help' she is actually being," he said with a chuckle and headed off.

"Speaking of concealing things," said Maggie, "John, I am more than a little concerned about Arnold being this close to your proximity. It is time that you started changing up your look."

"My look?" he asked. "What do you propose I do?"

"You can grow a beard," she suggested.

John made a face and moaned. "Those things are so uncomfortable."

"I know," she said, "but, not as uncomfortable as a rope around your neck."

"If ye start dressing like the tribe members, it is less likely anyone will pay any attention to ye," said Duncan.

John sighed. "I suppose you two are right."

"It won't be forever," said Maggie. "Just until the war is over and things settle down a bit."

"It is a small price to pay," he replied.

Alastair looked towards the door. "The babies are awake. I will let Cecile and Cora know," he said and skipped off towards the hall.

Maggie looked at him strangely and called out, "Alastair, how did you know they were awake?"

He shrugged. "Ye rest, Auntie Maggie. I will make sure they are taken care of."

Maggie turned to Quinn. "You are noticing this as well, right?"

Quinn nodded. "Aye. Ever since we returned from New York, he has taken it upon himself to be the caretaker of everyone. I think he took the instructions to be the 'man of the house' while we were gone a little too literally."

"No. It is more than that, but I cannot put my finger on exactly what it is. It is almost as if he has a sixth sense when it comes to everyone around him," said Maggie. "But whatever the case, he is also still a little boy, and he does not need that kind of responsibility at his age."

"Ye are right. I will speak to him."

After supper that night, the adults retired to the drawing room.

"Alright!" Duncan stood in front of Maggie, "The words to create the fog are a chant. Ye just repeat them over and over until the fog begins to form."

Duncan said the words to Maggie, then made her repeat them back, until she had them committed to memory.

"Okay, here goes nothing," she said nervously. Maggie began the chant and did not stop until a small puff of fog finally floated from her palm, but then dissipated.

"Hey, I did it!" She smiled and pointed to her upheld hand, pleased with herself.

"Nay, ye did not," said Duncan, folding his arms, a serious look appearing on his face. "Ye created enough to cover your hand, and that's hardly enough to cover this estate."

Maggie frowned, and scrunched up her nose at him, annoyed. "It was my first time...I am a 'fog virgin', give me a break."

"General Arnold isn't going to give us a break if he finds all that we are hiding here," he scolded.

"You are very cranky today," she retorted.

"Bet I can guess why," mumbled Gabe with a sly grin on his face.

John and Quinn looked at him inquisitively.

"Maggie's sick," he explained, "too sick for their... 'regular activities' in the bedroom."

"Ahhh!" said Quinn and John in unison, a look of understanding washing over their faces.

"Frustration will do that to a man, or so I hear. Personally, I make sure things do not get to that point," announced John. "It's not good for you to keep things bottled up like that."

Duncan cut his eyes back across at the three of them with a scathing look.

"Ye should rest now anyway, brother," goaded Quinn, "ye know how she will be in a few months. Ye will need all of your strength to try and keep up."

Maggie attempted to hide her grin by pressing her lips together and covering them with her hand. She looked to the side and feigned a cough.

"Can we not discuss what goes on between me and my wife tonight? We have more important things to deal with," grumbled Duncan and gritted his teeth together.

Maggie leaned back against the chair and cleared her throat. "So, what am I doing wrong?" she asked to change the subject that was an obvious sore spot with her beloved.

"Ye are not concentrating. Ye need to focus and feel it through every part of your body."

"Alrighty!" Maggie straightened up, closed her eyes, rubbed her hands together, and took in a deep breath. Concentrating, she said the words over and over in her mind until she could feel the ebb and flow of the magic throughout every cell of her being before beginning to recite the words in a low, repetitive voice. Maggie popped open one eye when she heard everyone around her sputtering and coughing and was surprised to find the entire room engulfed in a thick, heavy fog.

Gabe and John moved to the nearest set of windows and threw them wide open to help clear out the room.

"Is that better?" she asked Duncan, sarcastically.

He and Quinn went to the opposite side of the room to open the doors that went out into the garden.

"Much!" He smiled and waved his hand in front of his face.

"Look at this," said Gabe, calling them over to the window.

The fog moved in a steady roll straight up the left side of the path leading to the house.

Quinn turned to Maggie. "Use your hands, focus on the movement, and see if ye can make it shift in a different direction."

Maggie nodded, narrowed her eyes, and willed it to turn to the left. They all watched in amazement as the fog slowly made the turn and headed along the outer perimeter of the drive.

"That is amazing," said John, "but we can see through it, so how does that help us?"

"WE can see through it," corrected Gabe. "The MacGregor mark that was placed on your back gives us the ability."

"Really?" said John in utter astonishment. "That is fascinating!"

"Is it thick enough?" asked Maggie.

"Aye," said Duncan. "It is stronger than anything we have ever been able to create ourselves. Ye did very well, my love!"

"Good! Can I go vomit now?" she asked and looked around for a bowl.

Duncan came to her side and helped her to sit down.

Quinn moved to the center of the room and waved his hands to form a circle and directed the rest of the fog outside of the house to clear the air.

"So, does the mark give us the ability to create the fog as well?" asked John, curiously.

"Nay, the Fae blood is what gives the person the power to wield the spells we were given. The mark lets ye see through it, since the only people who would ever receive it would be the ones who would never betray the family or their secrets. It was a gift from the Fae."

"Well, then, John should be able to create it as well," Gabe pointed out.

Quinn pulled the windows closed. "Aye, he should. What do ye say John? Do ye want to give it a go?"

"Maybe later." He grinned and pointed to the window. "I think we have enough right at the moment."

"You know," said Maggie as she wiped her face with a handkerchief she kept handy, "it probably wouldn't hurt to give John a little lesson on the ins and outs of being a part of this family, now that he has had time to process some of this information."

"That is a good idea. It is best if ye know what is normal for us and what to be on the lookout for as strange. Gabe and I can take care of that," offered Quinn.

Maggie leaned against Duncan and he looked up. "While ye do that, I will get Maggie to bed. She needs some rest."

Maggie washed her face while Duncan stood against the doorway and watched her. She wiped her mouth with a clean towel and came over to kiss him.

"Gabe is right! You ARE frustrated," she said, leaning her forehead against his chest. "I'm sorry. I know this isn't easy on you."

"I will survive," he said with a smile, and tucked a strand of hair behind her ear. "It is a small price to pay for the gift ye are giving me. I just hate seeing ye so ill."

He helped her over to the bed. "I am not so fond of it myself," she said, as she laid down and curled on her side to face him. He stretched out next to her and stroked her forehead as she pulled him into another kiss.

"You are not the only one feeling a little neglected, you know?" she said.

He wrapped his arms around her and kissed her on the nose. "I know, but ye need rest and we will make up for lost time when ye are feeling better."

After Maggie had fallen asleep, Duncan went back downstairs to the drawing room. There was a little bit of the fog left in the corner and Quinn was instructing John on how to control it. He stood at the door and smiled at the wonderment on John's face.

"He's a natural," said Quinn, as he came over to join Duncan.

"Good! We will need all the help we can get before this is all said and done."

"How's Maggie?" asked Gabe.

"It didn't take her long to fall asleep. Her body needs to rest as does her mind. All of this worrying is not good for her or the bairn."

A few days later, Maggie, Duncan, Gabe, Quinn, and John rode out to the riverbank. Gabe stayed with Maggie at the point closest to the house, while the others rode out to the furthest positions away, until they covered the entire property line along the water. Once everyone had time to get into place, Maggie looked to Gabe nervously. "I sure hope this works. Here goes nothing."

She held up her hands and began the chant. As the fog rose from her palms, she extended her arms and directed a steady stream to the left and then to the right.

Gabe stepped back and watched the rolling movement of the mist.

"That is unbelievable," he said to himself, a look of enchantment upon his face.

Soon, the others did the same, until a solid wall of haze had formed and rose from the ground about fifteen feet high.

"I think it's done," said Gabe to Maggie, stepping back to inspect the wall.

She stopped the chant, leaned over with her hands resting on her knees and promptly vomited.

Gabe came to her side and handed her a handkerchief from his coat pocket when she was finished.

Maggie wiped her face and moaned in misery.

"Let's get you home, sweetheart," he said sympathetically and helped her onto Onyx before climbing on behind her and taking her back to the house.

They were the first ones to arrive, so Gabe got her settled comfortably on the sofa, and wrapped up in a blanket with a cup of hot herbal tea.

They heard the others come through the door laughing and in a jovial mood.

"And?" asked Maggie.

"A complete seal along the bank from one end of the property line to the other. If we need the ship, we can meet the captain at the riverfront and open a spot at the dock just for him," said Quinn.

Duncan came over and kissed Maggie. "Ye did a wonderful job, my love. I am enormously proud of ye."

"I feel much better now that it is done," she said. "We will keep an eye on it, but this should get us through Arnold's little escapades over the next couple of months."

"How do ye feel after the spell?" asked Quinn. "Did it tire ye out?"

"No, not at all," she replied. "Well, no more than I already am anyway."

Duncan smiled and kissed her just as Hettie appeared at the door.

"David Percy brought the mail in for you, and there is someone here to see you." She pointed back to the foyer with her thumb.

"Who is it, Hettie?" asked Maggie.

"Well, he says he's Colonel Asheton's nephew."

"My nephew?" asked Gabe, standing up, a thoroughly confused expression on his face.

"Uncle Gabe!" exclaimed a voice from the doorway.

"Wyatt?"

Wyatt came over to Gabe and gave him a huge hug.

"Aunt Maggie!" he said, leaning down to kiss her on the cheek. "It is so good to see you!"

"Wyatt! What on Earth are you doing here?" Gabe stared at him blankly.

"I couldn't come to America without seeing my favorite aunt and uncle, could I?"

Gabe introduced his nephew to Duncan, Quinn, and John.

Duncan shot Maggie a puzzled look and a message.

Is this the nephew from the whorehouse?

Maggie rolled her eyes and nodded.

"Wyatt, why…" started Gabe, just as there was a loud banging at the door.

"Well, this is a popular place today," said Maggie, sarcastically. "Who can that possibly be?"

Quinn walked over to the window and pulled back the curtain.

"Soldiers!"

"What?" asked Maggie. "Why would they be here?"

"I will find out," said Duncan, and kissed the top of her head.

Duncan went to the front door as Wyatt quickly looked around. "I need you to hide me, Uncle Gabe," he whispered in a panicky voice.

"Why would I need to do that?" asked Gabe, suspiciously.

"Just hide me... PLEASE!" he begged. "I will explain everything later, but they cannot find me here."

Maggie shook her head and pointed Gabe in the direction of the hidden room. Gabe popped open the door and shoved him inside, along with John, just before

Duncan came back into the drawing room with a British officer.

"Maggie, this is Captain Jones."

Captain Jones tipped his hat and bowed.

"My apologies for the interruption, ma'am, but we are looking for a deserter. We have reason to believe that he may have come here since you and Colonel Asheton are well acquainted with the young man."

"Who are you looking for?" asked Gabe.

"I believe he is your nephew, sir. His name is Wyatt Asheton. Have you by chance seen him?"

"No, we haven't seen the little nitwit," mumbled Maggie and rolled her eyes.

Gabe shot her a stern warning look. "A deserter, you say? There must be some mistake. My nephew is not in the army."

Captain Jones pulled out a handful of paperwork from the inside of his coat pocket and handed it to Gabe.

"He is now. He signed up in England and was sent here last month. He missed roll call three days ago, the next encampment over, and has not been seen since. We can only assume he will try to contact his family here in the Colonies."

Gabe looked over the pages in his hand as his face grew solemn and his jaw tightened.

Maggie held her hand up to her mouth and grabbed Duncan by the leg, who had come to stand in front of her. He looked down and she pointed to the table for him to grab a bowl for her to be sick into… and he moved just in time.

Captain Jones looked on in disgust.

"Forgive me, Captain," said Maggie when she was finished. "Pregnancy sickness has not been kind to me."

"Oh, I see," he said. "Congratulations, I suppose?"

Maggie laid her head back against the sofa.

"We have not seen him," said Duncan as he took the bowl away.

"Then, you won't mind if we search the house?"

"Not at all," replied Maggie. "Help yourself but forgive me if I do not give you the personal tour. I only ask that you do not bother my help or wake our triplets in the nursery."

"Of course!" He nodded before he stopped and turned to her, wanting to clarify her words. "Did you say 'triplets'?"

"Yes, and if you wake them, you take them, Captain," she said with a shake of her finger.

The Captain's eyes widened as he quickly came to the realization that this expectant mother was not one to be trifled with. "Understood, ma'am."

"I will escort you," offered Gabe and he held out his hand to show him the way.

Once they had left the room, Maggie turned to Duncan. *Warn Hettie to mention nothing of our visitor.*

He rose, moved silently to the kitchen, and returned a few moments later with more tea for Maggie.

Done.

They sat in silence until Gabe and Captain Jones returned from their search.

"I am happy to report that your children are sleeping soundly," said Captain Jones. "Again, my apologies for the intrusion. You will send for us if he turns up? There is a fog rolling in off the river, and it is making our search a great deal more difficult."

"Certainly," replied Maggie as she watched him go.

Gabe and Quinn watched from the window until the soldiers were out of sight. Duncan closed the pocket doors and Gabe popped open the door to the secret room. He grabbed Wyatt by the collar and dragged him into the middle of the room.

"What the hell is wrong with you? Not only do you desert the army, but you bring them to our doorstep, putting everyone here, including a houseful of children, in danger? What do you have to say for yourself?"

Wyatt shrugged his shoulders. "Uncle Gabe, I am in love."

3 CHAPTER THREE

"Oh, good God in Heaven!" exclaimed Gabe. His nostrils flared, and the skin around his shirt collar quickly turned bright red; he reached out his hands towards Wyatt's throat. Managing some restraint, he rested a hand on each shoulder instead, patting them forcefully while gritting his teeth. "You are WHAT?"

"I am in love," said Wyatt, grinning like an idiot. "I joined the army for a girl I met in Edinburgh."

Gabe stared at him in disbelief and his hands slowly inched up towards the boy's neck until Quinn took his husband by the shoulders, put forth some much-needed effort to pry his hands loose, and pulled him away.

"Maybe you should enlighten us," said Maggie.

Wyatt happily nodded. "Her name is Chastity. I met her when I was in Scotland. She works at a brothe…respectable establishment," he corrected himself, looking to Maggie warily. "She is the most wonderful girl ever and I cannot wait to make her my wife."

"How did that put you in the army?" asked John, having become completely enthralled in the story at this point.

"Well, she didn't think working for my brother was a proper job for me to have, so she said that I needed to prove to her that I was responsible enough to marry her."

Duncan held up his hand. "Wait! This girl works in a whorehouse?"

Wyatt looked to Maggie, then down at his feet, as he covered his mouth and turned his head. "Maybe?" he mumbled under his breath and hoped that she did not hear.

Maggie narrowed her eyes and shot him a dirty look.

"I will take that as a 'yes'," said Duncan. "So, the girl, who works in the whorehouse, doesn't think that being a bookseller is a reputable and responsible occupation?"

Maggie looked at Duncan.

I am guessing Chastity is not so chaste either.

I would take that wager.

"Well, she said that I shouldn't be working for someone else, especially not my brother, so I asked myself, 'who is the most responsible person that I know?'...and that was you, Uncle Gabe. You did very well for yourself as an officer and, respectable women do fall all over themselves for your attention, so I thought it might be a good choice for me."

Gabe closed his eyes and rubbed his chin furiously, trying to process everything that his nephew just told him. "If you are being so responsible, then why did you desert your new occupation?" he asked, enunciating each word for added emphasis.

"Well, it wasn't as much fun as I thought it was going to be."

Gabe's mouth began to twitch, and he looked as if he were on the verge of hyperventilating, the vein on the side of his head starting to visibly throb.

John grabbed his shoulder and handed him a large glass of whisky. "Drink it!" he ordered.

Gabe downed the whole glass in one swallow with his eyes wild and fixed on Wyatt the entire time.

"What made you think it was going to be fun?" he whispered angrily and slammed the glass down on the nearby table so hard that it caused Maggie to flinch.

"I thought we would just come over here, put on a good show, march around a little bit, fire off a few guns for the colonists, and then go drink it up in the taverns with the women the rest of the time," replied Wyatt, indignant.

Gabe balled up one of his fists and raised it to his own mouth. "You do know there is a war going on, right?" were the only words he managed to get out.

"Well, I do NOW," Wyatt replied, seemingly annoyed. "To hear everyone talk in London, this was an easy job. We would just sail over here, give the colonists what for, and it would be all over with. But then, when we got here, they had us working all hours of the day and night, in the rain, the mud, and people are getting sick and dying, for goodness sakes. No one mentioned that might happen. No, the army life is not for me...so I just left."

John took a seat and placed his hand on his cheek, half-baffled, half-amused at the boy's reasoning. "You do understand they hang deserters, don't you?" he asked. "I can assure you from personal experience, it is not a pleasant position to be in."

"Oh no, I don't think so," said Wyatt. "They just make you go back to the army if they find you."

"NO, YOU MORON!" exclaimed Gabe. "They HANG deserters...without asking a single question...ON THE SPOT!"

Wyatt turned his head slowly, dumbfounded. "They do?" he asked timidly.

"YES! THEY DO!" shouted Gabe.

"Oh!" said Wyatt, looking down awkwardly and scratching his head. "I guess I misunderstood that part."

Gabe was about to hurl himself at Wyatt, but Quinn caught him by the shoulders and stepped in to prevent him from strangling the boy.

"Quick question!" Maggie waved her finger around in a circle in the air, above her head. "Is Chastity waiting patiently for you back home? With your parents perhaps?"

"Well, no. They have not met her yet; after all, she is still working," he said. "I mean, we are not married yet, and I am not supporting her. She told me to come and get her when I was a rich man; she would be waiting with bated breath right there at the… 'establishment' for me."

Quinn leaned close to Gabe and whispered, "Are ye sure that the two of ye are related?"

"I think his parents dropped him on his head a few hundred times," said Gabe, pouring himself another whisky and downing it.

John had lowered his chin to his chest and his body quivered from the laughter he attempted to keep under control. He looked up, thoroughly entertained by the absurdity of the boy's ignorance. "So, what exactly is your plan now that you have quit the army because I am certain they won't mind. After all, they are so understanding about matters of the heart. I am sure if you simply explain your reasoning to them, they will…" he stopped, unable to finish his sentence because he was snickering so hard.

Wyatt looked up at the ceiling, thoughtfully. "I haven't decided yet. I mean, of course, I need to go get Chastity, but I do need a job, so I was hoping I could become a partner in the shipping company with Uncle Gabe and Aunt Maggie. That would please my bride-to-be, and since we will want to start a family right away…"

"Wait! You want to procreate?" asked Maggie in disbelief.

"Oh yes," he said with a nod, "we will want lots of children."

Maggie pressed her forehead to her palm. "Have you ever actually BEEN around a baby?" she asked.

"No, but how hard can it be?"

Scratching the back of her head, Maggie got up, hearing Hettie, Cora, and Cecile in the hall with the babies, and opened the pocket doors.

"Bring the babies in here," she called and pointed to the middle of the room. "This is Wyatt, and he will be taking care of them for the rest of the day."

Hettie came in and handed him Kendric in one arm, as Cora put Alanna in his other. Cecile stood there and held Morgan out, waiting for him to take her.

"I only have two arms," said Wyatt. "What do I do?"

Maggie patted him hard on the back. "Figure it out! After all, how hard can it be?" she said and smacked him on the back of the head. "You idiot!"

Alastair came into the room and took Morgan as Kat ran to climb onto Gabe's lap.

"I have her, Auntie Maggie," said Alastair.

Maggie dug her finger into the middle of Wyatt's chest. "This seven-year-old boy is more responsible than you, and you want to take a wife and have children? You will be extremely lucky if we find a way to get you out of the country with your head still attached to your shoulders."

A wave of dizziness hit Maggie and she wobbled slightly. Duncan caught her from behind, just before she turned her head and vomited into a nearby bowl.

Wyatt's face went pale and he struggled to hold onto the babies who squirmed and giggled.

"What's wrong with you?" he asked.

"She's pregnant," said Gabe, taking Alanna from his arms, as John moved to take Kendric.

Gabe pointed to Maggie. "That's what women who are carrying babies do for nine months-they vomit. It gets you ready for when the baby comes out and does the exact same thing."

"Do they all do that?" asked Wyatt.

"YES!" everyone shouted in unison.

"Does the family even know you are here?" asked a flustered Gabe as he bounced Alanna.

Wyatt looked down at the floor and shuffled his feet. "I left them a note," he mumbled under his breath.

"What about Henry?" asked Maggie, wiping her mouth and setting the bowl on the table, before collapsing on the sofa. "Did you leave him a note too, telling him what a horrible brother you are to leave him in a lurch when he is just trying to make an honest living? You know, he depends on you and he trusts you, although for the life of me, I cannot figure out why."

Easing down in a chair, Wyatt made a face as the smell from Maggie's sickness hit him. "I may not have thought this completely through." He turned to Gabe, a look of desperation on his face. "Uncle, I may need your assistance."

Kat came over and climbed up on the sofa next to Maggie and leaned against her.

Maggie looked down at her and stroked her hair. "Can you heal stupid?" she whispered.

Kat only shook her head.

"I didn't think so."

Maggie gave Wyatt a good once over. His clothes were dirty; it was obvious that he had not had a decent night's sleep in a while, and she could hear his stomach growling from the other side of the room. The mother in her could not help but feel sorry for him.

"Where have you been the past three days?" she asked, her tone somewhat softened.

"Mostly walking around trying to find all of you," he said, with his head down, looking ashamed and defeated.

Maggie shook her head. He was in the body of a man, but he was still, very much, a kid, and she still had a soft spot for him.

"Go to the kitchen, get Hettie to get you something to eat, and then she will show you up to one of the bedrooms so you can get cleaned up."

He looked up at her and smiled appreciatively. "Thank you, Aunt Maggie," he said gratefully; he held his nose and kissed her cheek on the way out of the drawing room.

"What are we going to do with him?" asked Duncan.

"I have no idea," she replied.

"The army will be back," said John seriously, "and if they find him here, they will not be as kind and understanding as you are."

Maggie was already in bed that night when Duncan came into the bedroom. "Everyone settled?" she asked.

"Aye, the babies are asleep, and the oldest child is all tucked in the spare bedroom."

"That boy!" groaned Maggie. "I have no clue what to do with him."

Duncan undressed before he slipped into bed and Maggie curled against him.

"You see what going to whorehouses gets you?"

Duncan chuckled softly. "Don't be so hard on him. Ye can't fault him for falling in love."

"Love, my ass!" scoffed Maggie. "I wonder how much his last 'loving' trip to Chastity cost him. Do you suppose she gives him a discount or still makes him pay full price?"

"I wonder how many men she has told to come back when they were rich?" Duncan laughed, unable to hold a straight face.

"Every damn one of them, I'm sure!"

The next morning when Maggie and Duncan came down, Wyatt was already having breakfast.

"Good morning," he said and smiled happily, with a mouthful of food.

"Sleep well?" asked Maggie.

"Yes! The bed here is much more comfortable than what the army provides, and the food is a tremendous improvement."

Hettie set another plate in front of him and beamed. "This boy sure can eat," she said with a grin.

"I think I may have fallen in love with you, Hettie," he said, stuffing another piece of food in his mouth and looking up at her adoringly.

"You sure do fall in love a lot," mumbled Maggie.

"What shall we do today?" he asked, enthusiastically.

"YE will not be doing anything except confining yourself to the house," replied Duncan. "As long as ye are here, we are all in danger."

Wyatt looked deflated. "So, I have to stay inside the whole time?"

"Yes, and close to that room in case the soldiers return," said Maggie.

"For how long?"

"Until we figure out what to do with you."

John came in to join them. "Good morning, all," he said and headed straight for the coffee on the side buffet.

"Can't I just work for you and Uncle Gabe?" begged Wyatt, "I am good with numbers and buying things."

"We don't deal in whores," replied Maggie, sarcastically and slapped Duncan on the back because he nearly choked on his food from laughing. "Besides, you are a wanted man, or have you forgotten?"

"Oh, yes, I did forget about that part."

Duncan waved his fork around in the air. "So, tell us about this girl, Chastity. How long have ye known her?"

Wyatt broke into a smile. "I just met her a few months ago when I went to Edinburgh for a book run. She had just started at the...place we met," he spoke carefully, watching Maggie's expression. "It was truly 'love at first sight'."

"Did she charge you?" asked Maggie.

"Well...yes?" he replied.

"Then, it wasn't love. That is what we call a 'business transaction'," she smarted.

Wyatt frowned. "Well, she has to make a living somehow."

Maggie pinched the bridge of her nose, in complete disbelief at the boy's gullibility.

John, who was behind Wyatt, leaned against the buffet, and attempted to sip his coffee, but couldn't because his entire body was trembling so badly from his bout of silent laughter that his cup sloshed and spilled all over his hands. He set the cup on the table and grabbed a towel to clean himself up. Leaning over Wyatt's shoulder, he whispered in his ear, "My dear boy, I think you and I need to sit down and have a nice long talk about women and whorehouses."

Maggie got up. "Why don't the three of you do that?" she said and left the room to be sick.

John took a seat next to Wyatt and turned his chair to face him.

"How old are you Wyatt?" he asked, leaning back.

"I am twenty-one."

"Christ!" said Duncan and shook his head, "I don't even remember being that young."

"When I was that age, I was commissioned in the army, receiving special training in Germany." John smiled with a twinkle in his eye. "A woman was the reason I joined the army, as well."

Duncan pushed his plate to the side and leaned back in his chair with his hands folded behind his head.

"By the time I was that age, my father had already been dead for four years and I was laird of our castle, caring for my mother, four younger brothers, and all of the people who were on our land."

John nodded. "My father passed when I was nineteen. My mother, three sisters, and brother needed to be provided for, and the army paid a good wage."

"Wait," said Wyatt, as he put his fork down, "both of you were taking care of your entire families by the time you were my age?"

"Aye," said Duncan. "We didn't have any choice. We did what we had to do."

"I could never do that," whispered Wyatt, dropping his gaze.

"Of course, you could," said John, "but if you want to be treated like a man, you need to start acting like one. You cannot make commitments, then run away from them just because they aren't 'fun' anymore, especially when it puts the ones you love in danger."

"Aye! Be a man of your word. If ye do not have your honor, ye do not have anything," added Duncan.

John sipped his coffee. "This girl, that you claim you want to marry...do you really love her, or do you just love how she makes you feel when you are together?"

"Well, I do like THAT!" he said with a mischievous grin.

"Yes, my dear boy, we all like THAT!" replied John, dryly. "I mean, in your heart, how does she make you feel?"

Wyatt stared at the wall, as if he were thinking hard.

Duncan shook his head. "What he means is… would ye lay down your life for hers? If a man walked into that establishment, put a pistol to her heart, and pulled the trigger, would you step in front of that shot and give your own life, without a second thought, to save hers?"

Wyatt frowned, pondering the question, then grimaced. "I don't know that I would do that," he said quietly.

Leaning across the table, Duncan looked him directly in the eye. "Then, ye do not love her enough to marry her and ye are doing her no service by binding her to a man who wouldn't give everything to protect her."

"Would you? For Aunt Maggie?" Wyatt asked, seriously.

"I would give my dying breath to save that woman, then beg God for just one more, so that I could give that one up for her as well."

John watched Duncan closely, knowing as well as he knew his own name, that the man spoke nothing but the God's honest truth and that Duncan and Maggie's love for one another was something rare, pure and nothing short of astounding. He was more than a little envious.

He looked back at Wyatt.

"Duncan is right. You do not love that girl, and you should not make promises you cannot keep." John pointed his finger at him. "For future reference, don't make ANY promises to ANY women in whorehouses. It's just not a good idea in general."

"Aye! And do not mention whorehouses to your Aunt Maggie. She takes issue with them," said Duncan.

John laughed. "Most women do!"

"Aunt Maggie didn't catch you in one, did she?" asked Wyatt. "Because she was not pleased when she found me in one."

"Nay! I have been faithful to your Aunt Maggie since the day we met. I would never dream of being with another woman."

"How did you two meet?" asked Wyatt.

Duncan grinned. "I guess we have ye to thank. If she had not come to Scotland to get ye out of that whorehouse, we never would have met. I thought she was an intruder in our home. I caught her and she ended up straddled atop me, pinning me to the floor."

Wyatt and John exchanged amused looks.

"I was also fairly sure that you shattered every bone in my elbow with your stone hard stomach muscles that night," said Maggie from the doorway; she came in to sit in his lap.

"So, it was love at first sight?"

"Not so much," said Maggie. "It took a couple of days for us to warm up to each other."

"Only a couple of DAYS?" asked John, incredulously.

"Oh, I knew," said Duncan, wrapping his arms around her, "It just took Maggie a little while to figure it out."

Maggie smacked his chest playfully. "Now look at us," she teased. "An old married couple with three children and another on the way."

They gazed adoringly into each other's eyes and Maggie touched his face.

"I would never want my life any other way. Ye are my world, my love." He pulled her into a long, tender kiss.

"And you are mine!" Maggie declared when he released her lips.

John nudged Wyatt. "When you find a girl that makes you feel THAT way, that is when you marry her as soon as you possibly can. Do not ever settle for anything less."

4 CHAPTER FOUR

Later that afternoon, as everyone was gathered in the drawing room, Wyatt fiddled around with his fingers, plucking at fabric and smoothing it over after. Finally, he worked up the nerve to stand in front of all of them.

"I have made a decision," he said, his voice confident and resolute. "I am turning myself into the army. It is the right thing to do."

Everyone became quiet, so he looked around the room.

"Is that not what a man would do?" he asked, suddenly unsure of himself because of their reactions.

"It is the manly thing to do," said Duncan.

"But you cannot do it," added Gabe.

"Why not?" he asked.

"Because your punishment will still be the same," said John, coming over to join him.

"They will still hang me," he stated.

"We will not let that happen," said Maggie, "because we take care of family around here."

"Aye," agreed Duncan, "but we are proud of the fact that ye are trying to take responsibility for your actions."

"So, what now?" he asked.

Gabe shrugged. "We cannot send you home. Every ship that goes in and out is being searched from top to bottom, and the discretion we have been afforded in the past is no longer abided. If you are found on one of our merchant ships, the entire British army will rain down upon us. Besides, everyone knows who you are and, if you turn up in London with the family, they will arrest you."

"The timing couldn't be worse," added Maggie. "This area is currently a hotbed and a focal point of the war."

"Can't I just stay here?" he asked.

"Ye are too close to the army ye ran away from," said Quinn. "They will eventually catch ye if ye remain on the estate. I expect they will be back every few days just to look for ye."

Maggie stared into the fire, racking her brain for a solution.

"So, is there nowhere safe for me?" Wyatt asked, hopelessly.

"There may be one place," said Maggie softly and closed her eyes, a headache starting to come on.

"Where would that be?" inquired Gabe, folding his arms.

Maggie blew out a long breath. "He can't stay here, and he can't go home, but we may be able to send him somewhere where there is less action for the remainder of the war."

"All of the British army will be on the lookout for him, no matter where he goes." John sat down.

"The British, yes...but if he switches sides...and joins up with Washington's men..."

"No, Aunt Maggie!" protested Wyatt. "I will not be a traitor to the Crown."

"My dear boy, you already are," said John and took a sip of his whisky.

"She cannot be serious about this!" Wyatt looked to Gabe.

"It is not ideal," his uncle replied, "but it would be an option."

"I won't do it!" Wyatt shouted angrily.

Gabe placed a hand on his shoulder. "You came to us asking for help; this is how we keep you alive. Wyatt, you did not leave yourself many options, and truthfully, this might be your best chance."

Wyatt's face flushed red. "I will not agree to it!" he said and brushed Gabe's hand off. "I will not betray my country."

"Then you are welcome to get yourself out of this mess," offered Maggie. "But for the record, there are no 'good' options. There are the ones that keep you alive, and the ones that get you killed."

Wyatt became enraged and looked around at all of them, then stormed out of the house.

"Stop him before he leaves the estate," ordered an aggravated Maggie.

Gabe and Quinn went after him.

Duncan stood and leaned down to kiss her. "I will go with them. Maybe I can talk some sense into him."

As soon as Duncan was gone, John looked over at Maggie. "What are you not saying aloud?" he asked and joined her on the sofa.

"I know where, or rather who, we can send him to, where he will be protected, but no one here is going to like it."

John frowned, waiting for her to continue.

"Ben would watch over him," she whispered.

John looked down at his glass. "Major Tallmadge? You are right, no one here is going to take kindly to that idea."

Maggie rubbed her forehead. "The majority of the rest of the fighting will be here...but there, it will only be small skirmishes. If Ben takes Wyatt under his wing, he can keep an eye on him, and Ben is one of the very few people I trust enough to do exactly that. When the war is over, and he is sitting clearly on the victor's side, he will be able to go wherever he wants, in America, at least. That boy sealed his own fate with England when he deserted the army. I am just trying to figure out how to make the best out of this situation that he created of his own accord. I am open to any other suggestions."

"You are right, he did muck this up, and he has no idea what kind of trouble he has brought down upon himself."

"Yes, but Wyatt has to be fully committed to the idea. I will not send him to Ben if there is any chance he will betray him or the Patriot side. That is a risk I am not willing to take with the lives of my friends." Maggie leaned back against the sofa.

"Fair enough." He took a good look at Maggie. "Are you feeling unwell?" he asked, suddenly concerned; he touched her arm.

"I haven't been sleeping," she replied. "I have just had too much on my mind lately."

"You should not be worrying so much in your condition. It is not good for you or the baby."

"Unfortunately, stress is a part of everyday life around here. Wyatt's appearance only added to it."

John sipped his drink. "He is rather impetuous, isn't he?"

"Wyatt is a child, one that hasn't grown up. He has never had anyone who depended on him for anything, and his family has always been there to save him from any trouble that he gets into—with no consequences to suffer whatsoever," said a very weary Maggie.

"You sound a little envious," said John, softly.

"I am," said Maggie, wistfully. "Who wouldn't be?"

She curled on her side toward John. "How are you doing?" she asked. "You have had a great deal to process the past few weeks."

John grinned. "I am slowly getting used to things. Gabe and Quinn have been very good about filling me in on the details of life here."

"How about the tribe? Have you been doing your part to help them 'grow?' You now know extending the

MacGregor line is especially important, and Duncan and I cannot do it all by ourselves."

John laughed softly. "As much as I have been putting in my best effort, I do not think it will be enough."

She lifted her head. "What do you mean?"

He looked down, lost in thought. "You know how I am, Maggie. I am fairly certain that if I were able to have children, it would have happened by now."

Maggie sat up. "You think you are sterile?"

"Think about it," he said, "I have been with many women over the years and never once has any of those unions produced a child...as much as I do enjoy trying." He winked.

Maggie laid her hand over on his. "I can help you with that, you know."

"I am not sure Duncan would be too thrilled," he teased.

She shook her head and laughed. "Not like THAT! But I do have the ability to grant fertility."

John looked at her oddly.

"I am fairly sure it will work for men just like it does for women. One touch and a little intent are all that are needed."

"You think it would be so simple?"

Maggie smiled and squeezed his hand. "I do."

John nodded slowly, smiling. "That is something I will keep in mind."

Hettie stepped inside the drawing room.

"Maggie! David Percy brought some folks from town to see you."

Maggie turned around. "Who?"

"A Mr. and Mrs. Barnes?"

"Nooo! It can't be!" said Maggie aloud, but a woman's laugh from the hall that she instantly recognized, confirmed it.

"Oh, for fuck's sake!" grumbled Maggie and she dropped her face into her hands out of frustration.

"Who is it?" asked an uneasy John.

"You'll find out soon enough," she muttered.

David Percy appeared around the corner. "Oh, there you are Maggie. There were some people on the road looking for you, but this extremely dense fog that has set in seems to have gotten them turned around, so I had them follow me in."

"Thank you, David. That was truly kind of you." Maggie forced a smile.

Maggie stood and made her way into the hall, with John following close behind, to find Georgie and Martin Barnes, standing there as big as life.

"Maggie!" said Georgie, coming over to wrap her arms around her.

"Georgie...what a surprise!" Maggie turned and hugged Martin. "Martin, how good to see you!"

"Hello, Maggie!" he said and kissed her cheek.

"Allow me to introduce my husband's cousin, John MacGregor. John, this is Gabe's mother, Georgie, and his stepfather, Martin Barnes."

"Oh!" exclaimed John, trying to hide the surprise on his face. "It is indeed a pleasure to meet you both." He kissed Georgie's hand before he turned to shake Martin's.

"What on Earth are you doing here?" asked Maggie.

"Well, we can discuss that in a bit," replied Georgie. "It has been a long trip here."

"Of course!" said Maggie and turned around to speak to Hettie. "Can you please bring some refreshments?" She leaned in. "And alcohol for Gabe," she mouthed before she turned back to face her guests.

Hettie nodded in acknowledgment. "Yes, ma'am."

Maggie and John escorted them into the drawing room and offered them seats, as Hettie brought in refreshments, and served them, handing Maggie her special tea.

"It is so wonderful to see both of you," said Maggie. "Gabe didn't mention that you were coming for a visit."

"I am afraid he did not know; it was last minute," replied Martin. "Please, forgive our intrusion."

"You are always welcome here." Maggie smiled. "Although, I am rather surprised to see you."

Georgie looked at Martin. "We have a family matter that needs attention. Is Gabe close by?"

"He is attending to some things on the estate. He should be back shortly."

Maggie sent Duncan a silent message.

Get Gabe up here. His mother is at the house.

His mother? We are on our way.

"Did you just arrive?" she asked.

"Yes," answered Martin. "We hired a carriage to bring us out here, but the driver seemed to be lost. Thankfully, we ran into Mr. Percy on the road and he was kind enough to assist us by escorting us in."

"Mr. Percy says that he is in your employ," said Georgie.

Maggie nodded. "Yes, he is the personal attorney for the estate...and Cora's husband."

"That's right!" recalled Martin. "When Gabe wrote to us about your babies, he told us that. I am glad that Cora found someone."

"Yes, and they are very happy together." Maggie heard the front door open. "I bet that is Gabe now. Excuse me for a moment."

She stepped into the foyer and met Gabe halfway across the floor.

"Your mother is here," she whispered.

"Why in the hell is she here?" he whined.

Maggie shrugged. "She wouldn't tell me. It some sort of family matter."

Gabe hung his head and groaned as Duncan and Quinn came in behind him.

"Where is Wyatt?" she asked Gabe.

"He is at our house, and I have threatened his life if he steps foot out of it."

She tugged on Gabe's arm. "Come on. Let's get this over with."

Gabe stopped at the door and mumbled a prayer, "Dear God, give me strength." He took a moment to mentally prepare himself, sucked in a deep breath, and stepped inside.

"Mother! Martin!" he exclaimed and plastered a pleasant expression on his face, moving to kiss the older woman on the cheek.

"Gabe, darling! It so good to see you."

Martin smiled warmly and held out his hand to shake. "Hello, Gabe!"

"Martin!" said Gabe, taking his hand, genuinely pleased to see his stepfather.

Maggie brought Duncan and Quinn in, and made formal introductions. After everyone was acquainted, Gabe took a seat.

"Mother, what in the world are you doing here?"

"We have come about Wyatt," she said bothered and set down her cup. "He left us a note. It seems he joined the army and was sent here to Virginia. We are here to see to his welfare."

Gabe sighed and John handed him a large drink. "We know, Mother."

His mother's face lit up. "Oh good! So, you have seen him?"

Martin noticed the grave look that Gabe and Maggie exchanged. "What did he do now?"

"He deserted the army," replied Gabe.

Martin wiped his mouth with his hand. "Please, tell me you are joking."

"I wish we could," said Maggie. "He showed up here about fifteen minutes before the group of soldiers looking for him did. We managed to conceal him, but we cannot do that for very long."

"He led them here, to your home, with all of these children?" asked an astonished and horrified Martin.

Maggie nodded.

"I am so sorry, Maggie. I do not know what gets into that head of his sometimes. He just doesn't think things through."

She waved off the notion. "Martin, this isn't your fault. Wyatt is his own man and his choices are his own."

Georgie looked back and forth between them. "Well, this is good news. We will just take him back to England with us and that will be the end of it."

"No, Georgie, it won't," said Martin and took her hand. "He deserted the army and that makes him a traitor to the Crown. If they catch him, they will execute him immediately."

"Furthermore, we cannot get him out of the country anyway," added Gabe. "Any and all cargos are being searched, and he will endanger the crew of any ship he is found on."

"Well, can't we just talk to them? He is only a boy after all," argued Georgie.

"He is twenty-one," corrected John. "He is a man in the eyes of the army and the law and responsible for the obligations that he makes."

"So, what can we do? We cannot let them have him," said Georgie, flustered.

"We were trying to figure that out before you arrived," replied Maggie, suddenly feeling ill. "Excuse me." She stepped out of the room into the hall where everyone heard the distinct sound of her getting sick.

Martin got up to go check on her, but Gabe held up his hand to stop him.

"There is nothing you can do. Maggie has an extremely severe case of pregnancy sickness."

"Maggie is pregnant...again?" asked Georgie in disbelief.

"Congratulations!" said Martin, narrowing his eyes at Georgie, silently warning her to behave. "That is wonderful news!"

"Thank ye. We are very blessed," said Duncan and stepped out to check on her. "Pardon me."

"Where is Wyatt now?" asked Martin.

"Locked in my house until further notice."

Georgie turned to Gabe. "Where is my granddaughter?"

"She is upstairs in the nursery, napping. She will be awake soon."

"Well, why don't we take our things to your house and get settled in? We will have a chance to see Wyatt, and then we can come back to get Kat from her nap."

"You want to stay with me? At my house?" asked Gabe and the blood drained from his face.

"Yes, dear, of course. Where else would we stay?" asked Georgie.

Gabe downed his glass; John stepped over and immediately refilled it.

"I have a better idea," suggested Maggie, leaning against the doorway. "Gabe's house is rather small, and he does not keep a full staff there, so why don't you two stay here in Quinn's room while he and his son, stay with Gabe and Kat. You will be much more comfortable."

"Aye," Quinn readily agreed, "that is a wonderful idea."

"We don't want to put anyone out," said Martin.

"It is no trouble at all. I don't mind staying at Gabe's house, if it is alright with him?" Quinn nodded at Gabe coaxingly.

Gabe downed his second glass. "Of course, it is. It is a much better arrangement. Quinn and Alastair are always welcome since we are all like family here."

"Kat will be up in the next few minutes anyway. I will have Quinn's room made ready for you while you are in the nursery," said Maggie.

"Are you sure?" asked Martin.

"I insist," replied Maggie.

Gabe led them upstairs; Maggie went into the kitchen and leaned against one of the tables, her fingers splayed on the surface.

"Hettie, Georgie and Martin are staying here for a bit. We will give them the bedroom that is the furthest away from everyone."

"How long are they staying?" she asked.

"Too long? We must be overly cautious around them. Warn everyone who comes anywhere near the house, and if anyone outside of this estate asks, Wyatt does not exist."

"I will take care of it, Maggie."

Maggie winced. "By the way, Hettie, don't let Georgie get under your skin. She can be a bit much to handle sometimes."

Hettie shook the wooden spoon in her hand. "Don't you worry about me, Maggie. I have dealt with a few tough old birds in my day. I'm sure she is no different."

Maggie touched Hettie on the back as she started out of the kitchen. "Want to bet?"

Maggie joined them upstairs. Duncan, Quinn, and Martin each had a baby while Georgie was sitting in a chair with Kat.

"I cannot believe how much she has grown," she said.

"Oh, my goodness, look at these little ones!" Martin grinned and he raised Alanna up in the air as she kicked her feet.

"We have our hands full around here," said Duncan and kissed Morgan.

"And about to again, it seems," remarked Georgie haughtily and nodded to Duncan. "You could have let your poor wife have a break you know? She did just give you three."

Duncan scowled back at her.

"Georgie!" scolded Martin, through gritted teeth. "Mind your manners! We are guests in Maggie and Duncan's home."

Alastair appeared from around the corner of the door.

Quinn waved him over. "Ah! I would like ye to meet my son, Alastair. Son, this is Mr. and Mrs. Barnes, Gabe's mother and stepfather."

Alastair's face lit up. "Ye are my grandparents?"

Quinn and Gabe both started to loudly cough, and Alastair's eyes went wide as Georgie's mouth dropped open.

Maggie came over and took the boy by the shoulders. "Alastair calls Gabe, 'Uncle Gabe', because we are just one big family around here. Gabe has become like a brother to all of the MacGregors."

Martin nodded. "Of course! The more family a child has around, the better and blood does not necessarily matter in that case. You know that, Georgie."

"Where is his mother?" she asked.

"My mother passed away," said Alastair.

"Oh, my dear, I am so sorry," she replied and gave him a consolatory nod.

Maggie pointed towards the hall. "I believe your room is ready whenever you would like to get settled in. I am sure you would like to rest before supper."

"That sounds lovely," said Martin. "Thank you so much, Maggie!"

"Come, I will show you where it is."

A short time later, the five of them locked themselves in the drawing room. Gabe had taken out a full bottle of whisky and began to chug it. "This is bad!" He sat down, rocking forward as if in physical pain.

"I take it your mother doesn't know about your lifestyle?" asked John.

"God no! She would fall dead on the floor and then come back to life just to take Kat away from me, before murdering me with her bare hands."

Quinn took the bottle from Gabe and took a swig for himself. "What are we going to do about them?"

"We are going to be very careful of what we say and do," answered Maggie, "and we are going to figure out what to do about Wyatt. The sooner he is sorted out, the sooner your mother goes home. They do not need to be here with everything that is coming. They will not be safe." Maggie walked over to Gabe and rubbed his back. "Let's just hope we get this taken care of before we run out of whisky."

Duncan and Quinn went to bring Wyatt back to the house. He was still upset, but they had managed to talk to him, and calm him down before he came inside. He went to Maggie as soon as he returned.

"I am sorry, Aunt Maggie. I know you are just trying to help me."

Maggie sighed and hugged him. "Wyatt, we all love you, and we want what is best for you. But you need to understand, this is not just another bill you have run up that you cannot pay. This is a great deal more serious.

Your life is on the line and we must tread very carefully. You NEED to listen to us for your own sake."

"Your Aunt Maggie is right," said Gabe. "You are not a child anymore, and it is time for you to grow up."

"I understand," he replied and hung his head, contrite.

"In addition to that," said Gabe, "You now have your grandmother to deal with."

"What the hell are you talking about?" The color drained from his face, and a sense of panic seemed to overtake him.

"Mother and Martin are here," said Gabe. "They came to check on you. Thanks for that, by the way."

"Oh God!" he exclaimed and slowly sat down.

"My sentiments exactly," replied Gabe, sitting down next to him. "Why don't you run up and say 'hello' to them?"

Wyatt started to rise slowly.

Gabe held out his arm to stop him and handed him the glass of whisky he had been nursing. "Wait! Drink this first. It might help."

The young man nodded and downed the entire glass, then gradually made his way out of the room, his shoulders slumped down.

As soon as he was out of earshot, John turned to look at the rest of them. "I know we don't have many options for the boy, but the more I am around him, the less convinced I am that he will make it in either army, help or no help."

Gabe rubbed his eye with the palm of his hand. "I am afraid I have to agree with John on this point."

Duncan folded his arms, watching Maggie. "They are right. He is not cut out for that type of life; it is just not in him."

Maggie leaned back and closed her eyes. "I know." She sighed. "So, what ARE we going to do with him?"

The room went completely silent.

They all gathered in the dining room at supper time. Maggie pushed her plate away.

"You are not eating?" asked Georgie.

"No, I cannot keep anything down except the tea that Quinn makes for me."

"Were you this ill the first time around?" asked Martin.

"I am afraid so."

"The doctor in Philadelphia said it was one of the worst cases he had ever seen," said Duncan, rubbing Maggie's leg.

"I have to say, that I was rather surprised when Gabe wrote to us that you had married so quickly after leaving London," said Georgie.

"Oh, you know how it is when you find the right one, Georgie," replied Maggie and kissed Duncan on the cheek.

"Yes, I do." She smiled at Martin.

Georgie turned to John. "You do not sound like a Scot. Where are you from?"

John swallowed his bite of food, before washing it down. "I grew up all over. My parents traveled quite a bit."

"Do you have family in London?"

John looked around the room. "No. My cousins here are all I have left, but I am tremendously grateful for them."

Maggie smiled at John. "We could not be any happier that he found his way safely to us."

"So, you stay here at the house, as well?" Georgie asked John.

"Yes," Maggie blurted out. "He is a great help to us here on the estate."

John used his napkin to wipe his mouth and conceal his surprise at her answer.

Georgie tilted her head. "I am not entirely certain where you put all of these people."

"We are making do. We are actually planning an expansion to the house in the spring," she replied.

"Well, your home is lovely," complimented Martin.

"Thank you...we have grown quite fond of it."

"How long are ye planning on staying?" fished Quinn.

"Well, our main goal was to see to Wyatt, but other than that, we are in no hurry to return," replied Georgie. "I want to spend as much time with Gabe and Kat as we can."

Gabe and Wyatt groaned and then each drained their glasses.

"Did you say something dear?" asked Georgie.

"No, Mother, just clearing my throat," Gabe replied with a forced smile.

Maggie cast a sympathetic look in Gabe's direction. "I am afraid you may find it rather boring here compared to London, Georgie. The social scene is rather lackluster since the beginning of the war and it is only going to get worse. We mainly remain here on the estate."

"Oh, don't worry, Maggie, I am sure we can find some way to entertain ourselves around here."

After everyone had gone to bed that night, Maggie found John sitting alone in the drawing room.

"Couldn't sleep?" she asked.

"Gabe's mother and stepfather were keeping me awake," he said and smirked behind his glass.

"Oh no!" Maggie plopped down beside him. "I'm sorry for that and for trapping you here in the house. I may have panicked slightly."

"Nonsense," he said. "It wasn't like you were expecting them to show up."

"No, not by a long shot."

"What are you doing up?" he asked.

"I couldn't sleep, so I came down to make tea, but I saw you in here first."

"Come on," he said, helping her up and leading her into the kitchen. "I will make it for you."

Maggie took a seat at one of the tables. "Hettie just leaves a pot of water boiling for me in the evening." She pointed to the fire.

John grabbed a towel and a cup with the herbs already in it and poured it for her.

"Thank you," she said and took a sip.

"What's in that anyway?" he asked.

"I have no idea, nor do I care. I just know it helps. Want a taste?" She held out her cup for him.

John made an unappetizing face. "I think I will pass."

"Don't knock Quinn's concoctions. He has some good ones, as you well know."

"He is a wonder with those, isn't he?"

"I am surrounded by men who are wonders," she said and smiled.

John pulled up a chair. "Gabe seems very upset by his mother's arrival."

"I don't think 'upset' is the right word," she said. "Gabe has just never been able to be himself around Georgie and she can be a bit much for most people. She loves her children dearly and wants what she perceives is best for them. She actually threw a party to find him a wife when we had only been in London for a few days."

"Really? How did Gabe feel about that?"

"He wasn't too excited, especially since he didn't know about it."

"Ah, it was a surprise!" John laughed.

"On many levels, and Georgie is full of those. When I first met her, she was in bed with Martin; it was right after Gabe walked in on them. I think he has yet to recover from seeing his mother being thoroughly pleasured while straddling a man half her age."

John's eyebrows shot up and he burst into laughter. "They are a peculiar couple, aren't they? What IS the age difference?"

Maggie counted in her head. "Thirty-seven years? They do seem quite happy though, and Martin is a wonderful soul."

"He is very likable," said John. He sipped his drink and watched Maggie.

"Yes, he is." Maggie smiled at John. "I have missed this; our time just sitting and talking. We don't get to do it enough."

"As have I," he said. "My life was always lacking something whenever you were not around, and I am extremely happy that we were able to find a way for me to remain here. Life in Europe would have been miserably boring without you."

"As opposed to crazy and insane, as it is now?"

"I'll take it any day!" He grinned behind his glass.

Duncan appeared around the corner, wiping the sleep from his eyes.

"There ye are," he said, coming over and kissing her. "Trying to steal my wife again, John?"

"Always!" he teased. "You should keep a closer eye on her—or I may just take her away from you."

Maggie snuggled against Duncan's chest and he wrapped his arm around her.

"Tired, my love?" he asked.

"It has been a very long and stressful day."

"Let's get ye to bed," he said and helped her to her feet.

Just as he slipped his arm around her waist, Maggie suddenly doubled over, and cried out in excruciating pain, while clutching her stomach.

"Oh, God!" she exclaimed.

"Maggie?"

She tried to straighten up, but folded over again, almost collapsing to her knees.

Duncan gathered her up, carried her upstairs and laid her on their bed.

"Get Martin!" he shouted to John.

Maggie curled on her side as a troubled Duncan stroked her face and they waited for Martin to come in.

"What happened?" he demanded as he came through the door.

"I am having cramps," cried Maggie through the pain. She looked to Duncan with tears in her eyes. "It feels like before....when..."

"Nay, my love!" Duncan gripped her hand tightly assuredly. "Do not even think that."

Martin's physician side took over and he gave her a complete examination.

"Am I losing the baby?" she half-sobbed.

"I don't believe so," he said, after a few minutes, covering her back up, and patting her arm. "I think you are just dehydrated from the sickness, and you have had too much upset coming into the house between our unexpected visit and Wyatt's escapades. So, to be on the safe side, you need to stay in bed, resting, avoiding all distress, and holding down as many liquids as possible for the foreseeable future."

"She will!" replied a very worried Duncan. "Whatever it takes."

"I will go make you some more tea," said John from the doorway, and he and Georgie went downstairs together.

"Are you sure the baby is alright?" she asked anxiously.

"You are not bleeding, and it is obvious that you are not keeping anything down, so I am fairly certain, but that can change at any time, which is why you need to be off your feet until you are out of any danger."

Maggie squeezed his hand. "Thank you, Martin. You always seem to be right by my side when I need you the most."

"Must be fate," he whispered.

Georgie and John returned a short time later with a cup and handed it to Martin.

"Try to get all of this down," he said.

Maggie sipped it slowly.

"Don't you worry about anything," said Georgie. "I am here, and I will take care of the household while you are confined to your bed. It seems our timing was fortuitous."

Uh oh!

After Martin shooed everyone out of the room, Maggie curled against Duncan and he embraced her tightly. He rocked her gently and whispered soothing words into her ear. "Everything is alright, my love."

"I thought…" she choked.

"I know, my love," he said, and kissed her head. "But ye and our bairn are going to be fine, even if it means you and I spend the next nine months right here in this bed together."

5 CHAPTER FIVE

The next morning, Gabe knocked softly on the bedroom door and cracked it open a bit.

"Mags?" he called out. "Up for a visit?"

"Yes, come in."

Gabe went to her side and sat on the bed next to her, looking worried as he took her hand.

"Duncan told us what happened. How are you feeling?"

She blew out a long breath.

"Last night, I was terrified, but the pain is gone this morning. It seems that I will need to stay in bed for a while."

He gently kissed her forehead. "We will handle everything around here. You just worry about yourself and the baby."

Maggie pointed to the table next to the bed and he handed her a cup.

"Your mother has decided to take charge of the household."

"I thought Martin said 'no stress'," he said, dryly.

"Speaking of that," she replied, "has anyone had any ideas on what to do about Wyatt?"

Gabe placed his hands on her shoulders. "Stop it! Do not worry about Wyatt!"

He lightly touched her stomach. "You worry about this little one right here."

"But Gabe…"

"But nothing! I mean it! I will not allow you to endanger your child by upsetting yourself over his childish misadventures. Wyatt has caused enough uproar in this house."

Maggie frowned. "Have you seen the babies this morning?"

"Yes, they are fine. Do not worry about them either, because Alastair is keeping a watchful eye over everyone."

"I love that little boy so much," said Maggie, shifting herself around. "He is the greatest." She reached up and touched Gabe's face, noticing the tiredness and the redness in his eyes. "How much did you drink last night?"

"Not enough," he quipped. "My mother showing up here was the last thing I ever expected or needed."

Maggie rubbed his leg. "You will be happy to know that they are still acting like newlyweds. They kept John up last night," she said with a chuckle.

Gabe groaned and made a face. "I could have gone the rest of my life without knowing that."

"The sad part is that your mother and stepfather are the only ones getting any action under this roof," she said and rolled her eyes.

"Stop!"

Hettie announced herself and came into the room carrying a tray. "How are you feeling this morning, Maggie?"

"Better, thank you."

Hettie handed her a cup of broth. "Dr. Barnes said that you need to try and get this down."

Maggie turned her head and made a face when the smell hit her. "I don't think I can."

"You need to try," said Gabe and he urged it towards her.

She took a small sip, then handed it back. "Maybe later." Maggie turned to Hettie. "How are you making out with Georgie?"

Hettie folded her arms and frowned.

"That good, huh?" asked Gabe.

The housekeeper shook her head. "I don't know how in the world you ever came from that woman," she said to him.

Gabe dropped his forehead into his hand. "I'll stash a few liquor bottles in the kitchen for you, if you think it will help."

Hettie laughed, and patted him on the back. "I see why you left England."

"I am sorry, Hettie," he apologized. "I will try to reel her in. Mother is happiest when she is needed somewhere and becoming a doctor's wife...well, let's just say that she is in her element."

"It's alright," she replied. "I can handle her as long as Maggie is taken care of and Dr. Barnes...well, he is a real nice fellow. I really like him."

"Martin is the best," said Maggie. "Georgie is lucky to have him. Actually, we all are."

Gabe held the cup up to Maggie.

She took another sip before she pointed to Hettie to hand her a bowl—and threw it all back up.

Hettie brought Maggie a cold rag and she laid back down on the bed.

"I am sorry, sweetheart," said Gabe.

"I think I am going to try to sleep a little more," she said and closed her eyes. "Some tea would be nice later."

"It will be waiting when you wake up." He kissed her head.

Gabe pulled the covers over her before he and Hettie went back downstairs to the dining room where everyone was gathered.

"Did she get it down?" asked Martin as soon as he saw them.

"She did," said Hettie and looked down at the bowl she was carrying, "right before it all came back up."

"She is resting now," added Gabe.

Martin shook his head. "I do not believe I have ever seen a woman this ill from pregnancy before."

"Quinn's tea is the only thing that comes close to staying down."

"That is very interesting," said Martin to Quinn. "What is in it?"

"A mixture of herbs from an old family recipe," replied Quinn. "I will be happy to show ye when I mix it up."

"Please! I am always looking for ways to expand my knowledge, especially with herbal cures."

"Quinn has several remedies that work very well," said Gabe, proudly.

Georgie appeared in the doorway. "Oh Hettie, there you are. We need to discuss the dinner menu for the next few days."

Hettie put her hands on her hips. "What do you want to know?"

"Well, we need to plan what we will be having at meals."

"Mother!" interrupted Gabe. "Hettie handles all of that. Maggie has given her free reign to prepare whatever she likes."

Georgie looked back at them both in disbelief. "The help decides what you are eating each day?"

"Yes, Mother, and Hettie does a magnificent job."

Martin cleared his throat. "I have to say, Hettie," he gave Georgie a disapproving look, "I have enjoyed everything that you have cooked. The food has been absolutely delicious."

"Thank you, Dr. Barnes," said Hettie.

Georgie made a face. "All right then, when will the house servants be here? I wish to speak to them as a group."

It was Duncan's turn to clear his throat. "Hettie handles all of that, as well."

Georgie looked at Hettie, who was attempting—and failing—to conceal a look of satisfaction.

"Does Maggie attend to any of this personally?"

"No," replied Duncan. "Hettie supervises everything that concerns taking care of the house and she is in charge of who comes and goes in those duties."

"What does Maggie do?"

"Well, Mother, she and I run a profitable shipping company, in addition to having the business of the estate that needs attending, along with a large number of other ventures, not to mention providing for a great many people who live here and depend on her for all things during this war, and oh yes, three babies and pregnancy sickness on top of it all," said an exasperated Gabe. "We all thank God every day that Hettie is here to take care of the household duties."

Georgie opened her mouth to say something, but Martin cut her off.

"Georgie! We are guests here. This is Maggie's household, and she can run it any way she sees fit. This is not London, and I am sure there are a great many things done very differently here than they are there. I know you love Maggie and you wish to help, but perhaps it would be of more service if you just let things move along the way they normally do and just offer your assistance as the need arises."

Gabe agreed. "Mother, just enjoy yourself and spend some time with the children while you are here. The estate is equipped to run very efficiently on its own since we are away so often."

"Very well!" said Georgie, obviously annoyed. She turned to go into the kitchen, and just as she disappeared, they all heard her let out a blood-curdling scream. Another scream from someone else in the kitchen reciprocated. Everyone rose at once and rushed to see what the matter was.

"There is a savage in the kitchen!" shouted Georgie and pointed dramatically towards the back wall.

Duncan moved past her to see a familiar—but very frightened—face. He moved to the boy and placed his hand on his shoulder.

The boy pointed back at Georgie. "There is a strange woman in Hettie's kitchen!"

"He is no savage," said Duncan. "This is Kitchi. He is part of the Indian tribe that lives nearby."

"Who's that?" asked Kitchi, his finger still pointed at Georgie.

"This is my mother," replied Gabe.

"Your mother?" repeated Kitchi confused. "The one who birthed you?"

"Yes, I do actually have one," said Gabe dryly. "I wasn't born from a cabbage patch. She lives far away, across the ocean, but she is here for a visit."

Martin put his arm around Georgie. "Things are different here, my dear. Calm yourself. You have terrified that poor boy."

"Do people just come and go like this all the time in the house?" asked Georgie.

"Yes, they do," said John, moving past her to get to Kitchi.

"What are you doing here, Kitchi?" he whispered when he reached him. "Is anything wrong?"

He shook his head. "We were worried about you. Mingan sent me to check on you when you did not return yesterday."

John smiled, took him by the arm, and pulled him to the side. "I will be staying here for a while. There are matters that need attending and Maggie is terribly ill."

Kitchi looked worried. "Is she going to get better?"

"Yes, she will be fine. Just let Mingan know I may not be around as much for a while."

The boy nodded.

Kitchi worked his way back to Gabe's side, eyeing Georgie warily. "We will go hunting soon?"

"Yes, we will, but only if you have been practicing." Gabe winked.

"My aim is good; you should look less like a deer," Kitchi teased.

"I will try to keep that in mind." Gabe laughed and he touched his shoulder.

"What does he mean by that?" asked Georgie.

"Oh! We had a little hunting accident a while back, but I am fine."

Hettie maneuvered around them to get to Kitchi. "Do you want something to eat while you are here?" she asked and put her arm around him.

He grinned and nodded.

"Come on," she said and led him away.

Georgie still looked a little pale and unnerved, so they all moved back to the dining room for her to sit down.

"Are none of you concerned about the fact that strangers just stroll in and out of your home all the time?" asked Georgie, fanning herself.

"They are not strangers!" replied a perturbed Duncan. "They are our friends and they are always welcome in our home. Now, if ye will excuse me, I am going to check on my wife."

When Maggie woke up, Duncan lay beside her, propped up on his elbow.

"Hello, my love," he said with a dreamy smile on his face.

"Surely you have better things to do than to watch me sleep," she yawned.

"Nay, not one thing I can think of."

"Liar," she said, "but I do appreciate the effort."

"How are ye feeling?" he asked.

"Better."

Duncan touched her face. Maggie closed her eyes and relaxed.

"Ye are my world, do ye know that?"

"No, you are mine," she said and covered his hand with hers. "I do not even remember my life before you came into it. I don't think it even began until the day I met you."

He kissed her sweetly. "I never imagined I would find a woman who would hold my heart and soul in her hands the way that ye do."

Maggie snuggled against him and he wrapped his arms around her tightly, so they were as close as they could be.

"I will be glad when I feel well enough for us to be 'together'. I feel so out of sorts when we go too long without being with each other."

"I know," he said with a sigh, "but it is to keep ye and our baby safe. The time will pass quickly, and it will all be worth it in the end."

Maggie groaned when they heard a soft knock at the door. "Come in," she called out.

It was Wyatt. "I brought up some tea for you." He held out the cup.

Maggie pushed herself up. "That was very sweet of you. Thank you."

Wyatt handed it to her, and she took a sip. "I'm sorry, Aunt Maggie," he said, looking miserable. "I feel like you are unwell because of me."

Maggie took his hand. "No! Do not blame yourself for this. I had plenty of things going on before you came along. It is always something around here."

"But I did not help things. I will do whatever you think is best and if you think I should join up with Washington...then I will."

Maggie looked at Duncan who had propped himself up against the headboard and crossed his feet.

"Nay, ye will not," said Duncan. "I think we have all figured out that ye are no soldier. We will come up with another plan."

"But you are all in danger while I am here."

"So, you stay close to the drawing room and hide if anyone shows up," replied Maggie. "At least for the time being. Just, don't do anything rash and listen to what we say."

"I will! You have my word."

Duncan smiled at him. "Ye have grown up quite a bit the past few days. We are proud of ye."

"Thank you, Uncle Duncan...I can call you 'uncle', right?"

"Aye, I would like that very much."

"Get some rest, Aunt Maggie." Wyatt smiled and left.

"That kid makes me crazy, but I can't help but love him," said Maggie.

"He is a good boy, just a little misguided at times," agreed Duncan. "He is learning."

"I think you are being a good influence on him. Fatherhood is bringing out the best in you."

Maggie made a sour face and rubbed her stomach. "And motherhood is bringing out, or rather 'up', the worst in me."

She set her tea on the table by the bed. "I feel like I am neglecting the babies."

"They are fine. We have a houseful of people with idle hands that need filling."

"Georgie?" she asked with a wince.

Duncan rolled his eyes. "She has already had a run in with Hettie, scared Kitchi half to death, and threatened to take over the house because apparently, ye are neglecting your 'wifely duties'. Thankfully, Martin knows how to handle her. Poor Gabe! He is at his wit's end."

"She does that to him...rattles him, unlike anyone I have ever seen. There is a reason he left London for the Colonies...and it wasn't the army."

"So, I am beginning to understand."

"Speaking of the army, any idea on what we are going to do with Wyatt?"

"I know what ye are NOT going to do!" he said as he gave her a disapproving look.

She wrinkled her nose at him. "You sound like Gabe."

"Good, then we are all in agreement. Ye let us worry about young Wyatt and ye worry about taking care of yourself and our child."

"I have not been in bed for a full day and I am already bored out of my mind." She smiled wickedly and tugged at his shirt. "Are you sure you don't want to…just have a little fun?"

He kissed her and groaned. "Do not tempt me, my love."

Another knock at the door interrupted them and they both dropped their heads in defeat. Duncan chuckled. "Come in."

It was Martin. "Wyatt said you were awake. I wanted to check on you."

"Please, Martin...and thank ye," said Duncan.

"Any pain today?"

"No! It is all gone."

"Have you gotten anything down?" he asked and came to stand next to her.

Maggie looked back at the side table. "A little bit of tea, but that is about it."

"Well, that is something at least. Quinn showed me everything he puts in it and it is actually incredibly good for you."

"He has been a lifesaver."

"He and Gabe are very close, aren't they?"

Maggie smiled. "Yes, they are."

Martin frowned and scratched his forehead as he looked towards Duncan. "Allow me to apologize for Georgie. She can be a little overwhelming to people who do not know her. She really does mean well, but her methods could use a little polishing."

"We are grateful for all both of you are doing," said Maggie.

"I am not sure Gabe is," he muttered and cringed.

"The liquor cabinet is stocked," she whispered back. "He will be fine."

"I have to say, I spent some time this morning with Wyatt and he seems...different. I think being here has been good for him. I daresay he has grown up a bit. In London, after you and Gabe left, he did very well for a while, but eventually, he started getting into trouble again. Robert and I did our best to keep it from his mother and grandmother, but I think our help did more harm than good."

"Ye cannot become a man until ye are held accountable for your actions," said Duncan. "I think he is learning that the hard way, unfortunately."

"You said you had some ideas on what to do with him?" he asked.

"We had considered having him defect to Washington's side and sending him to some friends away from the worst of the fighting to keep him safe, but we have all agreed that he is not cut out to be a soldier."

"We will come up with something," assured Duncan.

Martin nodded. "When he left a note that he had joined the army, I thought perhaps he had finally found his way. I have no idea what got into him."

"We do," scoffed Maggie. "He wanted to marry a girl from the whorehouse in Edinburgh and he thought this was the way to prove his love."

Martin's jaw dropped. "Oh, dear God in Heaven!"

Duncan chuckled. "Chastity is her name, in case ye were wondering."

"Of course, it is," said Martin and shook his head. "What else would it be? That boy!"

"Duncan and John sat him down and had a long talk. Hopefully, they got through to him, and after an afternoon with the triplets, I am quite sure he is no longer in a hurry to have children with her."

"He wanted to have babies?" asked a completely dumbfounded Martin.

"It's a terrifying thought, isn't it?"

"I think he is rethinking a great many things now," said Duncan.

"Well, at any rate, thank you for trying to put him on the straight and narrow. He needs all the help he can get." Martin patted Maggie's arm. "Get some rest."

6 CHAPTER SIX

After a long week in bed, Martin felt comfortable enough to let Duncan bring Maggie down to the sofa for short periods of time. Maggie was sitting in front of the fireplace with Duncan by her side and sipping tea one afternoon when Gabe came into the room.

"Look who escaped," he remarked with a smile, came over, and kissed her on the cheek.

"Thank goodness. I was losing my mind up there. Where is everyone?"

Gabe took the chair across from her. "Mother is resting, Martin and Quinn are in the 'regular' library discussing herbal remedies, and Wyatt is upstairs in the nursery, helping Cora and Cecile with the babies."

Maggie lowered her cup and turned her head as if she had heard wrong. "Wyatt is taking care of OUR babies -- the triplets?"

"Yes, believe it or not. He has stepped up and has really been pitching in," replied Gabe.

"He has even let Cecile and Cora teach him a few things about changing them," added Duncan.

"I am truly impressed," she said, "and greatly disturbed and concerned at the same time."

"He is not so bad," said Duncan. "The boy just needs a little pointing in the right direction. I daresay no one has ever given him a chance to be responsible for something that really matters."

"I think you have been a good influence on him," she said as she leaned over and kissed him.

Georgie entered the room with her nose buried in a book.

"I thought you were resting in your room, Mother," said Gabe, as she came over to join them.

"Oh, no dear. I decided to make myself useful." She looked up. "Maggie, you should be in bed resting."

"I have been in bed plenty!" She sighed. "I just need to actually sit up for a while."

"What are you reading, Mother?" asked Gabe.

"Hmm?" she said, looking back at the pages. "Oh, I am just going over the books for the shipping company that Mr. Percy brought over for you."

Gabe, Duncan, and Maggie exchanged horrific looks.

Gabe sprung from his chair and snatched the book from Georgie. "I'll take that," he said and snapped it closed.

"Well, that was very rude of you, son," she scolded. "What on Earth?"

"Mother, you have no business going through our company books."

Georgie folded her arms. "I am just trying to help, and it's a good thing I did." She tapped on the front of the book. "There is something very odd about that record-keeping. You know, I kept the accounts for the law office for your father and I can spot discrepancies from far away; those numbers are most definitely off there."

Maggie squeaked slightly and looked to Duncan as she sent him a message.

David must have brought both sets of books, the ones for the British and the actual ones. Georgie will have us in all sorts of trouble.

Duncan rubbed her leg.

Calm yourself, my love. Think of the bairn.

"Nothing is off, everything is fine, Mother. Furthermore, you had no right to even open those books," fussed Gabe.

"I have every right to look after my son's welfare!" Georgie shouted, as she threw her hands up in the air and looked to Maggie. "This is what happens when you let the help take care of matters you should be attending to yourself. Why, that Mr. Percy is probably robbing you blind as we speak."

"No one is doing any such thing," said a very vexed Duncan, raising his voice and standing. "There is not one soul on this estate that we do not have complete faith and trust in."

"That is the problem around here. You need to have a firmer hand in running this place," argued Georgie.

"Ye need to…" yelled Duncan loudly before stopping himself. He took in a deep breath, closed his eyes and attempted to control his temper, not wanting to upset Maggie. He clenched his fist, shook it at his side and lowered his voice. "...let us worry about how things are done here, in OUR home. We manage very nicely with the way things are."

Maggie dropped her forehead into her palm and groaned slightly.

Hettie came into the room while wiping her hands on her apron. "What in the world is going on in here?" she called out with absolute authority. "I can hear y'all clean on the other side of the house."

"We are just discussing household matters," replied Georgie, curtly. "Nothing to concern YOURSELF with."

"Now you had better listen here, woman!" Hettie put both hands on her hips and narrowed her eyes at Georgie. "I reckon I had better be concerned if you are discussing something like that, since I am the one who runs this household," she barked back with a determined, annoyed look on her face. She and Georgie locked gazes and glared at each other.

A wave of nausea hit Maggie and she looked around for something to be sick into.

Duncan sensed her urgency, quickly grabbed a bowl from the table, and held it for her as she vomited.

"What's all this shouting about?" demanded Quinn, as he and Martin came into the room. "Are ye trying to raise the dead?"

"Mother is apparently trying to take over the shipping business," complained Gabe.

"Georgie!" chided Martin when he caught sight of Maggie, who was clearly in distress. He quickly moved to her side. "Are you alright, Maggie?"

She just shook her head in response.

"Take her back to bed, Duncan," he ordered.

"Aye!" Duncan set the bowl on the table, gathered her up and carried her upstairs.

Once they were gone, Martin turned to Georgie. "What is this all about?"

She took a seat in one of the chairs and plucked a nonexistent piece of lint off her dress. "I was trying to figure out how to be useful, so when Mr. Percy brought the books by for the shipping business, I thought I would go over them and save Maggie and Gabe the trouble."

Martin sighed. "Georgie, I am sure that Gabe is more than capable of handling the books while Maggie is indisposed, and if he needs assistance, he has Duncan, Quinn, and John. Surely, between the four of them, they can figure it out."

"But the books are off…" she started to say.

Martin held up his index finger to silence her. "Not your concern and none of your business! We are visitors here, and we will leave them to their own affairs. Is that clear?"

Georgie started to protest but Martin warned her with a look.

"Very well," she said and sighed loudly as she dropped her hands into her lap.

Martin turned. "Hettie, I am sure that Maggie could use some tea to settle her stomach. Would you please be kind enough to make some and have it sent up to her?"

"I would be happy to, Dr. Barnes," she replied sweetly, and gave Georgie a hateful look before she went to the kitchen.

"Quinn and I will help," said Gabe and scrambled to follow her out. He caught up to her, took her by the arm and whispered, "Please tell me there is whisky in the kitchen!"

"I have about half a bottle left from what you gave me to deal with your mother, but I am happy to share," she said in a low voice. "The good Lord knows you need it more than I do."

"Hettie, you have no idea."

Martin moved to Georgie once the room was cleared. He knelt, took her by the hand, and kissed it. "Sweetheart, I know you are trying to help, but you really need to leave the people here to their own matters. How would you feel if Gabe decided to come back to London and all of a sudden started telling us how to run our household or his brothers, the law business?"

"Martin," she said and touched his face. "I just want my family to have the best life possible and Maggie is as much family to me as Gabe is."

"What makes you so sure they don't have the best life?" he asked, lovingly.

"Well, it looks as if that attorney of theirs is playing with the books, for one. He could wipe them all out financially before they even realize it and then where will they be?"

Martin waved his hand. "Look around you. Maggie did not build this place up all by herself to let someone just snatch it from underneath her. I am sure you just misunderstood what you read, and Gabe is no slouch when it comes to business. I am sure everything is well in hand."

She cut her eyes towards the door with a look of contempt. "What about these servants? They do as they please."

Her husband smiled. "Look how well everything runs. And if I know one thing for certain, it is that Hettie loves Maggie like she is her own daughter. She looks after her and this household better than a lioness over her cubs." His mouth formed a straight line. "What's really bothering you, Georgie?"

She cupped his face and looked desperately into his eyes. "My son goes to bed each night...alone. He has no one to take care of him, to help him raise Kat, or to love him the way I love you. All my other boys have wives to care for them, but he does not. I just want to see him settled before I leave this world, and I am not getting any younger. Is that so wrong? To want to see him happy?"

Martin pulled her up from the chair, took the seat, and sat back down before pulling her onto his lap. "No, it is not, but Georgie, that is Gabe's decision, not yours. You cannot force him into marrying someone he does not love just because you want to see him with a wife. He is fresh out of the army, he has Kat to keep him busy, and with a war going on, the timing may not be ideal to find a suitable partner. Give him some time and some space. Wouldn't you rather he waits and find someone he loves and who loves him the way I love you instead of the first person who comes along?"

"I suppose you are right." Georgie kissed him and leaned her head on his shoulder.

"In the meantime," he said sternly, "you have to stop upsetting the routine around here. Maggie cannot take all of this. I know you love her and are only trying to help, but why don't you try pitching in with the children. I think your time is best spent with them."

Maggie was in bed when Gabe and Quinn brought up the tea for her.

"Thank you," she said and accepted it gratefully.

"How are ye feeling?" inquired Quinn.

"I will live, I think," she said and half-smiled. She looked over at Gabe. "Did you clean out all of Hettie's kitchen whisky stash?"

He pulled up a chair and nodded. "She took pity on me and gave me what she had left. I'll make another order to restock immediately."

"I am not sure we have a ship big enough for THAT order," muttered Duncan, pacing with his arms folded.

Gabe leaned forward with his elbows on his knees and his face in his hands. "I don't know what gets into her." Quinn sat down on the arm of the chair and rubbed his back, comfortingly.

"She is accustomed to having things her own way," said Maggie and sipped her tea. "She is just trying to help."

"Well, she can have them her own way once she is back in her own home...in London," said Gabe and put his arm around Quinn's waist. "Which can't come soon enough."

Maggie spent the next few weeks being moved between the bed and the sofa in the drawing room, bored out of her mind. Finally, near the end of January, she woke up one morning and knew the tide had turned; her morning sickness was gone, replaced with a new hunger on many levels. She rolled over and snuggled up against Duncan, running her hand over his chest and nibbling on one of his nipples.

He popped open one eye cautiously and smirked. "Good morning!"

"It is a good morning," purred Maggie and moved up to kiss him.

"Are ye feeling better?" He snaked his arms around her.

"Oh, yes I am, and we have a great deal of catching up to do," she said, letting her urges take over. They spent the next hour 'catching up' before heading downstairs for breakfast. They were still laughing and kissing as they made their way in the dining room.

"Can we assume you are in the next phase?" asked Gabe, eyeing them warily.

"Uh-huh," replied Maggie, never taking her eyes off Duncan.

"Hettie," she called out. "Please, bring me food, and lots of it."

Hettie popped her head in the doorway. "Well, it's about time!"

Martin and Georgie watched with fascination and bewilderment as she downed two plates and proceeded to start on a third.

"That's quite an impressive difference," remarked an engrossed Martin.

Maggie nodded. "It really does just change overnight. It was the same way the first time."

"Where are you putting all of that food?" asked Georgie.

"I guess my body is just making up for lost time."

"It sure is good to see you eating again," said Hettie. "You ain't nothing but skin and bones."

Duncan grinned. "Ye had better start leaving out plenty at night Hettie. She and our bairn will be needing it."

"Where are John and Wyatt?" asked Maggie.

"John took some supplies to the tribe and Wyatt went along to help," replied Quinn. "They should be back shortly."

David Percy stuck his head in the doorway as they were chatting. "Here you are. Good morning all."

"Good morning, David," said Maggie and bit into a piece of bread.

"You are feeling better, I see," he commented.

"Much! Come in and join us."

"Thank you." He poured a cup of coffee and took a seat. "I thought you should all know that I was in town yesterday and the news from Richmond is not good."

"What do you mean?" asked Georgie.

"A group of British troops marched on the capitol earlier this month and it was basically undefended when they arrived. Governor Jefferson was barely able to escape with his family. Benedict Arnold demanded the city's military and tobacco stores, and when Jefferson refused, he looted the city, then burned it to the ground. The Governor sent out Colonel Matthews and his militia, who caught up with them, and were able to get in a few good licks before chasing Arnold and his men all the way back to Portsmouth. However, on their way back through, Arnold did take time to burn several of the plantations along the James River."

"Who is this Arnold?" asked Martin.

"He was one of Washington's closest men and he turned traitor," answered Maggie. "He has a bone to pick and he is taking it out on the citizens of the Colonies any way he can. I am afraid Williamsburg will be the next to suffer at his hands."

"How many men did he have?" asked Gabe.

"Around sixteen-hundred with an armada of twenty-seven ships," replied David, gravely.

"Dear God!" mumbled Duncan.

"Well, it sounds like our troops are doing very well taking on the traitors," said Georgie and everyone stopped what they were doing to stare at her.

"It is not that simple, Mother," said Gabe.

"We have friends and neighbors on both sides," explained Maggie, "and we worry, not only about them, but what this war is doing to this country."

"Of course, you do," said Martin. "There is nothing glorious about war; death and destruction are all it leaves in its wake."

"I am afraid we will be caught right in the middle," said Maggie and sighed. "David, check with our neighbors and see if anyone is in need and while you are doing that, quietly advise them to lay in some stores and to conceal them where they will not be found in case their homes are searched or looted."

"That is an excellent idea," he replied. "I will take care of that immediately."

Maggie drummed her fingers on the table. "In addition to that, I do not want anyone leaving this estate without letting one of us know first. I would rather be safe than sorry."

David stood up. "I will spread the word."

"Thank you."

Duncan rubbed Maggie's back. "Do not worry, we are well prepared here," he reminded.

Maggie propped up her elbow on the table with her cheek in one hand. "Are you going to eat that?" She pointed to Duncan's plate.

He smiled and slid his dish over. "Maybe we do NOT have enough stores laid in," he teased.

They heard John's voice from the back side of the kitchen. "I am fine, Wyatt!"

"Hold your hand above your heart to stop the bleeding," fussed Wyatt. "We need to clean it out, so it doesn't get infected."

They all got up from the table and went to the kitchen to see what the matter was. John's hand was wrapped in a cloth and blood soaked the front of his shirt.

"Oh, my goodness, what happened?" asked Maggie.

Martin quickly moved to John and started unwrapping his hand while Wyatt got a bowl of fresh water and some clean rags.

"I was cutting a rope that held some of the supplies on the wagon when the knife slipped." John had a three-inch gash across his palm.

Martin dipped one of the rags in the water and started to clean it up. Once he got a good look, he frowned. "I can't really sew it up where the cut is, but we do need to wash it out and keep it covered."

Quinn came over to take a look. "I can make a poultice that will keep the infection out." He went to gather the things he needed in the kitchen.

"Will you show me what you are using while you do it?" asked Wyatt.

"Aye, come on," said Quinn, and they moved to a side table to work.

"It's a clean cut and not too deep. The bleeding has almost stopped," said Martin.

"Wyatt knew exactly what to do," said a smiling John, a hint of pride in his voice.

"He is learning," said Martin, glancing over his shoulder at the young man.

Wyatt brought over the poultice and applied it to John's hand as Quinn instructed him. He then wrapped it up and tied it off.

"How's that?" he asked.

"I couldn't have done a better job myself," replied Martin and laid his hand on Wyatt's shoulder, pleased by what he saw.

"Aye, and you have picked up the herbal knowledge faster than anyone I have ever seen," said Quinn, wiping his hands on a towel.

"Did I miss something?" whispered Maggie to Duncan.

"Aye, young Wyatt has taken an interest in healing and he is learning a few things from Quinn and Martin."

"Huh!" said Maggie. A sudden thought occurred to her. "Quinn isn't teaching him ALL of the potions, is he?" she asked under her breath, inwardly concerned.

"Nay, only the ones that won't hurt anyone."

"Oh, good." Maggie moved closer. "So, you have developed an interest in caring for the sick?" she asked Wyatt.

He shrugged. "I like helping people. It makes me feel like I am needed."

"He is actually a very quick study," said Martin. "I hope you don't mind that we borrowed some of the medical books we found in the library off the drawing room. You have a particularly good collection in there."

"Oh no, you are welcome to them all," she said. "They mostly belonged to the previous owners, although I have added a few myself."

Maggie turned to John and rubbed his shoulder. "Want me to kiss it and make it better?"

He laughed. "You can kiss whatever you like," he teased, before he caught sight of Duncan with his arms folded and giving him a stern warning with his eyes. "As long as Duncan approves, of course."

John looked her over. "You look like you are feeling better. Over the worst of it?"

"I had three plates this morning for breakfast, so I believe so!"

"Now, the real fun begins," he said with a devilish smirk.

Maggie turned to Gabe. "We have some business to discuss. Mind if we do it now, while I am feeling up to it?"

"Certainly," he replied.

"Excuse us," she said to the others and she led him out of the kitchen. Maggie looked towards Duncan and gave him a message.

Breakaway and join us as soon as you can.

He subtly nodded.

Maggie let Gabe escort her to the drawing room, but she leaned toward him to whisper, "See if Kat can heal John's hand when no one's around."

"Good idea. It would be good to know what she can and cannot do."

They reached the desk and took seats.

"What do you want to discuss?" he asked.

"Are our hidden stores fully stocked?"

"I will speak with Joshua, but I am fairly certain they are."

Duncan came over to her side of the desk and joined her. "Aye, they are. Joshua and I have been making regular checks," he assured.

"Will it be enough?"

"I think so," said Duncan. "We will still have the spring crops, but even without that, the estate will be more than fine."

"And…we still have the scattered offices up and down the coast with their secret stores. Once the war is over, people will need them to reestablish themselves," added Gabe.

"Good," she said, "and make sure we extend credit to any merchants that buy from us who may be running short on cash. Allow them to pay when, and if, they can. Also, we need to designate a percentage to those hardest hit to hand out strictly as donations. Getting people back on their feet is as important as getting through the war, and we have been more than blessed here. After the baby is born, I plan on making some trips to the areas where the land has been scorched and giving it a little 'helping hand,' so to speak, to get their crops and gardens growing again as quickly as possible."

Maggie leaned back in her chair. "I had another thought, as well. I think we should fence some pasture in the middle of the property, to move the horses to once spring gets here. With both armies coming in, they will be a hot commodity, and we will need to safeguard them. We can move them and add an extra fog layer around them."

"That is an excellent idea," agreed Gabe.

"How is the fog holding up?" she questioned.

"So far, so good," said Duncan. "Quinn and I check it every few days and it does not seem to have dissipated in the least."

"With all of that under control, at this point, our only real concern is still Wyatt." She played with the quill on the desk. "We have pushed our luck for well over a month and we have to make some sort of decision soon."

Gabe and Duncan nodded in solemn agreement.

Maggie looked over at Duncan and bit her lip, dropping the quill and slipping her hand over his backside, shifting her head to get a better look.

"I think that is enough business for now," she muttered as she leered and rubbed his behind.

"Oh, here we go again." Gabe threw up his hands. "At least take it upstairs. My mother is here, for goodness sake."

"Yes, we know because we hear them each night!" teased Maggie, "Let's see if we can drown out Georgie and Martin's nightly escapades with our own, or at least give them a good run for their money."

Gabe sneered and shook his head. "I despise you so much right now!"

But Maggie did not hear him. She had already stood and was lost in Duncan's eyes.

Maggie came back downstairs for a snack before dinner after she and Duncan spent some time with the children, who were glad to see their mother. She came into the drawing room, chewing on a piece of bread to find John nursing a glass.

"How's the hand?" she asked.

"I will live. The whisky is dulling the pain," he replied. "How's the bread?"

"Delicious and staying down, for a change!" Maggie picked up the decanter and topped off his drink.

"As soon as the coast is clear, we will get Kat to take care of that," she whispered and used the bread in her hand to point to his hand.

"You think she can?" he asked.

"I think it is time we found out." Maggie sat down across from him. "David Percy brought news while you were gone. Arnold burned Richmond to the ground. He has been driven back to Portsmouth, destroying homes all along the James. It is time for us to do what we need to do to ensure everyone's safety. Make sure the tribe has plenty of supplies hidden just in case. Let Mingan know that they need to remain on the estate where it is safe, and if they must leave, to let one of us know first."

"I will speak with him and take an inventory of what is needed."

Maggie turned her attention to his bandage. "Wyatt did very well when you cut your hand today, didn't he?"

"He did. I was rather surprised. He remained calm and immediately moved into action. I think he actually has a knack for it."

"Did I hear my name?" asked Wyatt from the doorway.

"You did," said Maggie. "Come and sit down. I want to talk to you about something." She leaned back and motioned to him with her bread as a pointer.

"Wyatt, back when you said your father wanted you to join the law firm and that you went to work for Henry instead, did anyone ever ask you what you actually WANTED to do?"

"No! They just assumed I would take my place in the family law business." He sighed and sat down.

"Well, I am asking you now. If you could do anything for a living, what would it be?"

He thought for a moment. "Can I get paid to lay with women?" he asked, hopefully. "I mean, women get paid to lay with men, so can't it work in reverse?"

"No, you cannot!" she scolded.

John burst into laughter. "My dear boy, if that were a profession, I would have hung out a shingle a long time ago."

"Stop!" Maggie swatted at John. "Don't encourage bad behavior!"

"Careful," teased John, "your Aunt Maggie might let the whorehouse give you an unexplained rash."

Wyatt winced. "Oh, I have already had one of those, and I don't care to have another." He shifted uncomfortably at the memory.

Maggie threw her bread at him and hit him square in the chest which caused him to burst into laughter. "Ignore your Uncle John. Apparently, he and Uncle Gabe have been chatting about our last dinner party."

Maggie turned back to Wyatt. "What would you do?" she asked, seriously.

"What difference does it make? I can't go back to England and I can't show my face here…"

She held up her hand and interrupted him. "There are ways around everything, given enough time and distance."

"You were very good today when I cut my hand," said John. "You kept your wits about you, you moved quickly, and you knew exactly what to do."

"Since I have been confined inside, Quinn has been teaching me some of his healing tricks, and when I asked Martin some questions, he started telling me about some of his medical school training. I have to say, I find it interesting, and it felt good to feel like I was helping someone for a change."

"Is it something you would like to pursue as a career?" asked Maggie.

Wyatt shrugged. "I wouldn't hate it, but how would I go to school being a wanted man?"

"You do know that here, a great many skills are learned through apprenticeships? It just so happens, that since it is wartime, medicine is one of those things."

"I wouldn't have to go to school?"

"Not if you are in the right place."

"Young Nathaniel never went to medical school. He joined the army hospital at the tender age of sixteen and learned in the field," John reminded her.

"It would be nice to feel like I was accomplishing something with my life." Wyatt sounded wistful.

Maggie looked at John and chewed on her thumb, lost in thought.

"Nathaniel is up north, with Ben, where the fighting is lighter and working in the field hospital WOULD keep him off the battlefield. They need all the medical help they can get and, though it would be the hard way, he would learn a great deal there."

"What are you saying?" asked Wyatt.

She turned back to him. "It would be horrible work; I am not even going to pretend otherwise. You would be working in the worst conditions with disease and the wounded, short of supplies and medicine, but you could learn and when this war is over, you could set up a medical practice here in America, if you wanted to...but you would have to join Washington's side now."

Maggie moved over next to him. "Wyatt, I cannot tell you how I know this, but the British aren't going to win this war, and what side you are on when this is over will make all the difference in the world. You could make a life here...a good one and Gabe, myself, Duncan, Quinn, and John will all be here if you need us, so you have a family to support you. We cannot make this decision for you, but if it is something you genuinely want to do, to make a difference with your life, we can make this happen for you. We have friends that will look after you there."

Wyatt stared down at the floor, unsure of what to say.

"Why don't you think about it?" suggested John. "It is a big decision, so do not take it lightly, but do give it serious consideration."

"John's right," agreed Maggie. "Think about it for a few days and let us know. We will not pressure you either way, and if you do not wish to, we will figure something else out."

Wyatt nodded and pointed his thumb back towards the door. "I am going back to the kitchen. Quinn wanted to show me how to make a drink for pain and I will give it some thought."

Maggie smiled as she watched him go.

"That was a good idea, Maggie," said John. "A purpose in life is exactly what that boy needs."

"What he 'needs' is to be out of harm's way, and he will not be if he stays here," she whispered.

7 CHAPTER SEVEN

After being cooped up and sick for so long, Maggie decided it was time for a change of scenery—and to give the household a break from Georgie—so she rounded up the whole family, minus the children and John and Wyatt, to go into town during the calm before the storm of the war. Maggie and Georgie did some shopping while the men scattered for different errands; they agreed to meet at the Raleigh Tavern.

"The shopping choices are very slim here," said Georgie, picking through some fabric.

Maggie held up a piece of blue material for a better look. "It is because of the blockade. The British army isn't allowing many things through."

"Your estate does not seem to be suffering."

"Yes," said Maggie. "It is because we are self-sufficient there. We are a great deal more fortunate than many of our neighbors, and we try to help them whenever we can."

"Your place is very impressive, Maggie. Although, I do think you give the servants a little too much leeway in the running of your household."

Maggie turned to look at something so she could roll her eyes without being seen. "I have a wonderful staff, Georgie, and they have never let me down. I have more important matters to deal with than what I am having for dinner."

Georgie put the fabric back down in disgust. "What about when you entertain?"

"We don't. We like our privacy and we are far enough away from town to maintain it."

"You never have parties for your friends?" asked Georgie, disbelief on her face.

"No, not really. We are in the middle of a war, after all. It wouldn't be right to hold an expensive party when people are losing their homes and livelihoods and wondering where their next meal is coming from."

"Well, no wonder Gabe and Quinn can't find wives. They really need mothers for those children, you know?"

Yeah, that is exactly what they need.

"Kat and Alastair are doing just fine, Georgie. They are loved, well-cared for, surrounded by people who watch out for them, and want for nothing."

The door to the shop they were in flew open.

"Maggie! How good to see you!" called a voice from behind her.

Maggie immediately recognized the voice and cursed under her breath before she turned around.

"Charlotte, how are you?" She plastered a fake smile on her face.

"I haven't seen you since the party. I do hope you got through to those wayward gentlemen friends of yours," said Charlotte

Maggie winced. "Charlotte, allow me to introduce you to Georgie Barnes, Gabe's mother. Georgie, meet Charlotte White."

"Gabe's mother?" Charlotte was giddy at the possibility of new gossip. "What a pleasure it is to meet you."

Georgie smiled. "It is nice to meet you as well."

"Did you come to straighten out that unmanageable son of yours?"

"I beg your pardon?" asked Georgie, affronted and taken aback by her forwardness.

"I know about Gabe's little problem," she leaned in and whispered. "Are you here to help Maggie get him back on the straight and narrow, back to the path of righteousness?"

Georgie looked at her strangely. "What 'problem' would you be referring to?"

Lovely! Time to change the subject.

"Charlotte, I have not told you our good news. Duncan and I are expecting again," she said and rubbed her stomach.

Charlotte turned to face Maggie. "Again? So soon? That husband of yours must always be bothering you for...well, you know...that!"

"More like the other way around," said Maggie, with a scandalous wink. "I can't keep my hands off that man!"

Charlotte covered her mouth with her hand and feigned impropriety.

"Speaking of which, we are expected for dinner. Please pardon us, Charlotte, we must be going. Good day."

Maggie hurried Georgie out the door as fast as she could.

"What was that woman talking about? What is wrong with Gabe?"

"Nothing, Georgie," she said, leaning closer and trying to come up with an explanation—fast. "Poor Charlotte....is a bit touched in the head. The whole town feels so sorry for her that we all just play along. She becomes terribly upset if you try to correct her, so it is best to just smile and agree with whatever she says."

"Oh! I see!" she said. "That is very sad."

"Yes, it is," said Maggie and they turned to go inside the Raleigh Tavern.

Maggie waved to Gracie as they went to find a table.

"Maggie!" Gracie came over and hugged her. "How are you?"

"I am well! Gracie, meet Gabe's mother, Georgie Barnes...Georgie, this is Gracie."

"Well, it is nice to meet you. The Colonel is one of my favorite customers."

"Oh, my son seems to be quite popular," said Georgie.

"The rest of the family will be joining us shortly," Maggie said to Gracie.

"Oh good! Take the large table over there and I will be right with you."

When they took a seat, Maggie noticed a group of British soldiers off to the side and as she and Georgie chatted, one of them, who was very intoxicated, got up and stumbled over to their table.

"Well boys, it looks like we have two lovely ladies over here who are in need of some company," he called back to his friends. He pulled out a chair and helped himself to a seat.

"Thank you, but we are waiting for others to join us," said Maggie and tried to ignore him.

"I will keep you occupied until then," he said and moved his chair closer.

Maggie wrinkled her nose when she caught the smell of sour alcohol and putrid body odor that rolled off him.

"I think we are good." She covered her nose with the back of her hand.

He slammed his hand down on the table. "I don't recall asking," he sneered and grabbed Maggie by the arm.

Before Maggie could lay her hand on the dagger in her boot that she always carried, the disgusting man was already on his back on the floor. Maggie turned to see what had happened and realized that a British officer, who had appeared from just behind them, had pulled the man out of the chair and shoved him backwards. His friends had sprung to their feet when they saw what was happening.

The officer crouched down and grabbed the man by his shirt. "We are here to protect the citizens of this town, not harass them, and your behavior towards these fine ladies is inexcusable. Apologize, and then report back to your commanding officer to await your punishment, that I will personally see to."

The face of the soldier on the floor went from enraged to terror when he realized to whom he was speaking. He rolled over until he was on his hands and knees with his head bent down. "Please forgive me, ladies. I seem to have had too much to drink. I beg that you accept my sincerest apologies."

He scrambled away from the officer towards the door, refused to look the man in the eye, and never stood upright until he was outside. The other men hastily exited the tavern, trying to go unnoticed.

The officer turned to Maggie and Georgie.

"Ma'am are you injured?" he asked, a great deal of concern in his voice.

"No, I am perfectly fine, thank you," she replied.

The man's jaw tightened when he looked out the window. "Ladies, please allow me to offer my personal apology for this man. On my honor, he will be severely punished for his actions here today, I give you my word."

"Thank you, sir," said Georgie. "It is nice to know there are a few gentlemen left."

"Allow me to introduce myself. I am Major Jackson Pennington, at your service," he said and bowed.

"Thank you, Major. I am Mistress Maggie MacGregor, and this is Mrs. Georgie Barnes."

The Major slowly took her hand and kissed it. "It is a pleasure to meet you both."

"Your timing was impeccable," said Georgie. "I was not aware that men behave so rudely in the Colonies."

"It upsets me as well, ma'am, but I will do my best to put a stop to it. I take it from your statement, you are not from here?" he asked.

"No. My husband and I are here visiting my son from London."

The Major turned to Maggie. "Are you visiting as well?"

"No," she replied. "This is my home." Maggie cocked her head to one side. "Forgive me, Major, but I am unfamiliar with your name, and I know just about all of the officers in our fair town. Are you new here?"

"I am," he confirmed and smiled warmly. "I arrived two weeks ago and will be staying on for a bit. Although, if all the ladies of Williamsburg are as lovely as the two in front of me, I may need to make a more permanent move."

"Where are you from?" inquired an interested Georgie.

"Liverpool originally, but I have been all over, and I go where I am needed for the army."

"Williamsburg is a sleepy little town, Major. I am sure you will be begging for a transfer out of sheer boredom before too long."

He looked Maggie directly in the eye, "I doubt that. So far, I am impressed by what I have seen."

The door of the tavern opened as Duncan, Quinn, Gabe, and Martin made their way inside. The Major was still staring at Maggie when they approached the table.

"There you are," admonished Georgie. "It is about time you got here."

"Everything alright, Mother?" asked Gabe.

"You mean other than the fact that we were accosted?"

"What?" asked Duncan.

"By whom?" demanded Gabe.

"This horrible drunk soldier that grabbed Maggie by the arm," replied Georgie.

"Are you alright?" asked Duncan, looking Maggie over.

"I am fine," she said. "It was nothing, really. One of the men just had a little too much to drink and overstepped."

"What man?" he pressed, searching the tavern with his eyes.

Maggie grabbed his hand in an attempt to quell the fury rising in him. "It really doesn't matter, Duncan. There was no harm done."

"Thanks to Major Pennington," said Georgie. "He was gracious enough to come to our assistance."

The Major looked around. "I simply escorted the drunkard out, and I will see to it that he is disciplined appropriately for his behavior. We cannot allow our men to behave so improperly."

"Thank you," said Martin and held out his hand.

Major Pennington shook his proffered hand. "It was my pleasure, sir."

Georgie made formal introductions.

"Gabe Asheton. You wouldn't be Colonel Gabe Asheton, by any chance?" asked the Major.

"Former Colonel Asheton...I am retired."

"Of course!" the Major said, "I have heard others speak of your work, always favorably, I might add. Your service to the army is greatly missed."

The Major looked around. "If you will excuse me, my services seem to be no longer needed. I will leave you all to your meal."

"Thank ye for helping my wife," said Duncan.

The Major nodded. "You should keep a closer eye on her. If she were my wife, I would never let her out of my sight."

His gaze lingered on Maggie a bit longer than Duncan considered proper.

"Believe me, Major," replied Duncan when he took notice, "it will not happen again."

Duncan placed his hand protectively on Maggie's shoulder and she leaned back against him.

The Major smiled. "Good day to you all," he said before he moved to a small table in the back.

"Are ye sure ye are alright, my love?" asked Duncan, turning his attention back to Maggie.

"Yes!" she assured him. "Right now, all I am is hungry. Your wife and child are starving. Can we please just sit down and eat?"

Duncan leaned down and kissed her. "As ye wish, but I want full details later."

"I will give you anything you like when we are alone," she said so only he could hear.

Major Pennington sipped his drink, watching the interaction at the table he just left. When Gracie brought him another, he stopped her. "What do you know about that woman?"

Gracie followed his gaze. "That is Maggie MacGregor."

"Tell me about her," he said, lighting a pipe.

"She is one of the wealthiest women in the Colonies. She has a large estate several miles out of town. Maggie and Colonel Asheton own a shipping company together here in town. She is well-known and well-liked by everyone here."

"What is her relationship with Colonel Asheton?"

"Oh, they are just friends; they have been for a very long time."

Gracie looked towards the table with a look of envy on her face. "She and her husband are very much in love with each other. I have to admit, I am a little jealous of what the two of them have."

After Gracie left, Pennington leaned back in his chair and watched the group intently, but mainly regarded Maggie, while smoking his pipe.

When they were done eating, Maggie sighed and ran her hand over her belly bump.

"Feel better?" asked Duncan, slipping his hand over on her thigh.

"Much!" she replied with a satisfied look on her face.

"Do we need to get Gracie to pack food for the trip home?" teased Gabe.

"No!" she answered in her best-annoyed voice. She turned to Quinn. "You did pick up candy at the apothecary, didn't you?"

He laughed. "Aye, I did, and I even got some for the children, as well."

Georgie looked up and noticed Charlotte White pass by the window.

"Oh, there goes that poor woman," she said to Maggie.

"What woman?" asked Gabe, turning to follow her gaze.

"Charlotte White. Maggie introduced us today."

Gabe rapidly turned back around and cut his eyes over at Maggie. "Oh really?"

"Yes, she asked if I had come to help with your little 'problem'." said Georgie.

"Oh, dear God," muttered Gabe, under his breath.

Duncan snorted and used his napkin to cover his amusement.

Gabe paled and downed his drink in one shot, waving to Gracie for another.

"I explained to your mother," said Maggie to Gabe, "that Charlotte's mind was unwell and how we all humor her while taking what she says with a grain of salt."

"It is so heartbreaking to see someone that way," said Georgie.

"Yes, it is," replied Gabe. "You wouldn't believe the things that come out of that woman's mouth."

"Indeed," mumbled Quinn and rolled his eyes. "I know I was shocked the last time I was in a room with her."

Duncan chuckled to himself, laid down his napkin and stood. "I will take care of the bill so we can go."

As they went to leave, Gracie came over to hug Maggie. "Take care, Maggie, and don't wait so long to come back. We haven't seen you in months."

"That is because I have been too ill to eat," she said and rubbed her stomach.

"Again?" asked Gracie, with a huge grin on her face. "Congratulations!" She leaned close and glanced in Duncan's direction. "Of course, if my husband looked like that, I would be pregnant all the time too."

Maggie laughed and waved goodbye.

After they left, Pennington got up to leave and noticed something on the floor, beneath the chair where Maggie had been sitting. He stopped to pick it up. It was the lovely silver bracelet that she had been wearing earlier. He looked closer and noticed that it was engraved. He read the verse to himself.

'The course of true love never did run smooth.'

"Shakespeare," he whispered to himself, pleasantly surprised.

He looked around to make sure that no one was watching and slipped it into his coat pocket for safe keeping. He would be sure to return it personally.

When they arrived back at the house, Maggie excused herself to go upstairs to take a nap. She undressed, climbed into bed and propped herself up on a fluffed pillow. She sent Duncan a silent message.

I need your assistance.

He was at their door within minutes. "What do ye need, my love?" he asked, as he opened the door.

He closed the door when he caught sight of her. "Ah, I see what ye need," he said and came over to the bed.

"What can I say?" She shrugged seductively. "I sleep better when I am relaxed."

She watched him as he undressed and climbed into bed next to her.

He kissed her slowly, taking the time to tease her. She moaned when he moved his attention down to her breasts, biting, kneading, and tasting one before moving over to the other.

"That drives me crazy," she whispered, threading her fingers through his hair.

"I know." He slid down, kissed her small baby bump, and took a moment to lay his head there. "I love ye so much, Maggie."

He kissed his way down and felt her buckle when he touched her with his tongue. He pushed her knees up and wrapped his arms around her hips, holding her in place with his mouth until she cried out his name and let go. After she shuddered the first time, he continued to hold her there, locked in place and worked her up until she did once more.

"I need to feel you," she pleaded.

Moving up her body, he kissed her mouth hard and entered her, slowly at first, then with a certain urgency until they climaxed together.

"I don't think I will ever get enough of you," she said, pushing the damp hair back from his face.

She curled into him and he wrapped his arms around her. She was asleep before he knew it. He did not have the heart to move, so he laid there and held her until she woke, and they made love again.

After they dressed, Maggie searched all around on the floor and then in the bed.

"Lose something?" asked Duncan.

"My bracelet is gone; the one that John gave me. I just noticed it missing," she said and rubbed her wrist.

"Let me help ye look."

They searched the entire bedroom to no avail.

"Where could it be?" she asked, her hands on her hips, frustrated.

"I am sure it is here in the house somewhere. It will turn up. I will let Hettie know and she can be on the lookout for it."

"I hope we find it soon," she said. "I love that bracelet and I feel lost without it."

Before they went into the dining room for supper that night, Duncan pulled John off to the side. "I need a word with ye in private."

They stepped away from the others so they would not be heard.

"What is on your mind?" asked John.

"Have ye ever heard of a Major Jackson Pennington?"

John thought for a moment. "The name seems vaguely familiar, but I don't recall from where. Why do you ask?"

Duncan frowned. "He assisted Maggie and Georgie at the tavern today and I just like to know who is around my wife."

"Did something happen?" he asked, concerned.

"Before we arrived, a soldier who'd had too much to drink got out of line with them. This man stepped in before things escalated."

"It sounds like it was a good thing this man was there. Some of the men do not know how to behave properly, especially when they have been drinking at the taverns."

John noticed Duncan's pensive look. "What is bothering you about it, other than the fact that it happened in the first place?"

"I don't know. Something about that man did not sit well with me, but I am not exactly sure why."

John nodded in acknowledgment, as he folded his arms. "Hmmm...I know what the problem is."

Duncan tilted his head, inquisitively.

"Don't take this the wrong way, Duncan, but you aren't fond of ANY man that gets too close to Maggie, not that I blame you."

Duncan nodded slowly in agreement when he realized that there was some possible truth in the words he had spoken. "Maybe I AM overreacting."

Getting ready for bed that night, there was a soft knock at Maggie and Duncan's bedroom door. Duncan opened it to find Wyatt and John standing on the other side.

"I'm sorry, I know it is late, but Wyatt wishes to speak with the two of you alone," said John.

"Of course!" Duncan opened the door wider and held out his hand towards the chairs by the fireplace. "Please, come in."

Maggie pulled her robe tighter and came over to join them. "What's this all about?"

"I think I want to take you up on your offer to become a doctor," said Wyatt. "I have been giving it some thought, and John and I talked about it a great deal today while you were gone. I cannot continue to put all of you in danger."

"Are you sure?" asked Maggie. "This will not be easy, and it will be far from pleasant; in fact, it will be down-right gruesome."

"I know," he replied, "but, it's time I got myself together, and started acting more like a grown man."

"I sat him down today and explained the harsh reality of war," said John. "He understands and he knows what he is in store for."

"I wouldn't have to fight, and I would be helping people on both sides in the hospital," agreed Wyatt. "I want to do something good for a change and medicine is something I think I would like."

Maggie and Duncan exchanged approving looks.

"That is a very responsible thing to do," said Duncan, placing his hand on Wyatt's shoulder. "I want ye to know how proud we are of ye."

Maggie hugged him. "Duncan is right. The war will not last much longer, and afterwards, you can come back here to build a life, if that is what you want."

"I think I would like that, Aunt Maggie!"

"We will make the arrangements in the morning. Now, go enjoy your comfortable bed and Hettie's cooking while you can."

"I miss her food already," he groaned, rubbed his stomach and headed for the door.

"Goodnight," he said.

"Goodnight, Wyatt."

After he left, Maggie took John in an embrace and kissed him on the cheek.

"What was that for?" he asked.

"For talking to him and giving him some good advice."

John shrugged. "What can I say...young Wyatt grew on me. He reminds me of myself at that age in many ways," he said with a smile. "Goodnight you two."

After John left, Duncan took Maggie in his arms. "Our boy is growing up!"

"So, he is," she said and kissed him. "Now, take me to bed, my love."

The next day, when Maggie saw Gabe, she took him by the hand and whispered, "We need to talk." They slipped away from the others and up to Maggie and Duncan's room so they would have some privacy.

"I made an offer to Wyatt a few days ago, and last night, he decided to take me up on it."

"What kind of offer?" He took a seat.

"To send him to Nathaniel, so he could learn how to become a physician."

Gabe's mouth opened, then closed.

"Wyatt? A doctor? You think he can do that?"

Maggie sat down next to him. "He has a knack for it, he is a fast learner, and it is something that he wants to do. He is much brighter than we give him credit for. If we send him up north, he will be away from the fighting and this way, he will not even have to be a soldier. He really wants to help people and this way he can. When the war is over, if he wants to continue with it and wants to learn more than he has learned in the field, Duncan and I will pay for him to go to an actual medical school."

Gabe blinked. "That's quite an offer, Maggie."

Maggie took his hand. "I just want him out of harm's way, and you know as well as I do, he needs to be away from here sooner, rather than later. We have enough friends up there to keep an eye on him."

"Do you think he can handle it? The boy has never been uncomfortable a day in his life and field hospitals...they are horrible places for even the most seasoned soldiers. I am not sure he will have the stomach for it."

"He has grown up quite a bit. Being around all of you has helped him a great deal and he wants to do better. In England, he always had someone to bail him out, so he never had any reason to own up to anything; but being here has shown him that he needs to make some changes in his life. He needs to be 'uncomfortable' because it is the only way he will learn anything of value."

Gabe blew out a deep breath. "I have to say, I am somewhat relieved to hear it. Our choices for him were slim at best and getting thinner by the day. How do we get him there?"

"Captain Russell's son is serving in a regiment stationed near the current encampment of the Second Continental Light Dragoons and he has been terribly worried about him. I am sure he would be thrilled to take a few men and escort Wyatt there. If they travel the backroads and use the shipping company as a cover, they should be fine. I will write Nathaniel, as well as Ben, and ask them both to keep an eye on him.

"What will we tell Mother and Martin?"

"That we got him into a medical school. They don't need to know that it is 'hand's on' training."

8 CHAPTER EIGHT

A few days later, the preparations were underway.

Captain Russell readily agreed to escort Wyatt, jumping at the chance to see his own son. He and a few men stocked one of the 'special wagons' that contained several secret compartments while Gabe and Quinn went into town to gather all the medical supplies they could find to send to Nathaniel, knowing the army was in short supply of everything. They told Georgie and Martin that Wyatt had decided to go to a teaching school, which made them both incredibly happy and proud.

John decided to spend some time with Wyatt, so he took him down to the village for the evening, which Wyatt found that he liked very much, especially with all of the young women that seemed to find him interesting as well.

Maggie sat down at her desk to work on some correspondence while Georgie was taking a nap. Duncan had taken Martin down to the stables to see the new foals; he and Martin had grown quite fond of each other. Maggie was absorbed in her work when Hettie interrupted her.

"Maggie, there is a Major Pennington here to see you."

"What is he doing here?" whispered Maggie, laying down her quill and attempting to conceal the letter to Ben she was writing. She slid the paper into the top drawer of her desk and quietly closed it, before she looked around to make sure nothing conspicuous was out. She stood, put her hand on Hettie's shoulder, and whispered, "Keep an eye out in case John and our guest come back early. If they do, warn them."

Hettie nodded.

"Show him in," she said and moved to the front of the fireplace.

He came inside the room and removed his hat.

"Major Pennington! What an unexpected and pleasant surprise. Please, come in."

"Mistress MacGregor." He bowed and took her hand. "Please, forgive my unannounced visit."

Maggie smiled and motioned him to a chair. "No need to apologize. May I offer you a drink?"

"Please and thank you."

"Any preference?" she asked.

"I am sure whatever you have is fine," he replied and looked around to admire the room. "Your house is quite lovely, by the way," he said and sat down.

Maggie handed him a glass, which he graciously accepted. "Thank you."

Maggie took the chair across from him. "What can I do for you today, Major?"

"Actually, I came out to bring you something."

Maggie looked at him questioningly, as he reached into his coat pocket and pulled out her lost bracelet. "I believe this belongs to you."

A look of delighted relief crossed her face. "My bracelet!" she said, excitedly and stood to take it from him. "I have been looking everywhere for this."

She looked back at him. "How in the world did you end up with it?"

Pennington smiled. "I found it in the tavern after you left the other day, but you were already gone. It must have come off when that despicable man grabbed you. The latch was broken, so I took the liberty of having it repaired. It was the least I could do; consider it an apology from the army for the distress you were caused."

Maggie smiled at him warmly. "That was not necessary, but I am beyond grateful that you returned it. It is very special to me."

"A gift from your husband?" he asked.

"No, not from him, but from a close friend of mine. I never take it off and I was beside myself when I realized it was gone."

"Well, I am happy I was able to return it to you." He pointed to it. "May I have the honor of putting it back where it belongs?"

"Of course, thank you." She handed it back to him and held out her wrist.

He set down his drink and fastened it before turning it around to admire it. "Shakespeare's words of love. Your friend has good taste in literature." Pennington picked his drink back up.

"I do not know how to repay your kindness," she said, and took her seat.

"I am just happy to get the opportunity to enjoy your company, even for a short time." He sipped his drink. "Although I must confess, I do have another reason for my visit. I am here to inquire about Colonel Asheton's nephew who deserted."

Maggie looked down at the floor. "As I told your Captain Jones, Wyatt is not here. You are more than welcome to search the house if you wish."

"I will take you at your word, Mistress. Although, I do find it a little strange that he would not come to his uncle for help, especially when he is so close by."

Maggie adjusted herself in her chair. "Yes, well Major, I take it you have never actually met young Wyatt. He is not the clearest of thinkers, and I would not be surprised in the least if he hastily departed Williamsburg as soon as he decided to run off."

"Why would you say that?" he asked, curiously.

She leaned forward. "Because Williamsburg, forgive my frankness, does not have the sort of entertainment that he desires and by that, I mean whorehouses. If you wish to find him, I suggest you start searching for them

in any nearby towns that may have them. I have no doubt
he is somewhere knee deep in sinful deeds and running
up a bill he cannot afford to pay."

The Major blushed slightly. "I take it he has an affinity
for them?" he asked, touching his chin and suppressing a
smile.

"Don't most men?" she asked as she got up to pick up
the decanter and refill his drink.

"Not all of us," he replied and held up his glass, the
corners of his mouth turned up, amused. "Some of us
prefer to find more meaningful companionship."

"Well, be that as it may," said Maggie, "Wyatt knows
he would garner no sympathy here. His uncle had many
years of loyal service to the Crown, before his retirement,
and Gabe has no respect for someone who would forgo
their responsibilities so easily and in that way."

Returning the decanter to its place, Maggie retook her
seat across from him.

"I understand Colonel Asheton left the army for a
woman," he said and looked down at his glass.

Maggie fixed her gaze on him. "That is true. You see,
he left the army for me."

Pennington lifted his head, perplexed. "For you? I do
not understand. You are married to another man."

"Yes! You see, I was severely injured in Philadelphia
by some stray gunfire and he took it upon himself to
retire and bring me home to Virginia to care for me.
Gabe and I are closer than family; we always have been."

"Is he the one who gave you that bracelet?"

"No," she said softly, "that was my friend Major John André."

"Major André?" he asked, somewhat surprised. "The two of you were close as well?"

Maggie nodded. "Yes, and since he has left us, you can see why I was upset when I lost it. Did you know him?"

"No. Unfortunately, he died before I had the pleasure of meeting him. I understand he was a fine soldier and quite the gentleman to boot."

Good to know that he would not recognize John.

"He was the best," she said. "Major, we have many friends in the service of the Crown, and it is not hard to determine where our loyalties lie here on this estate." Maggie leaned back in her chair and interlocked her fingers. "That IS what you are trying to determine with your subtle line of questioning, is it not?"

"You are a very keen woman, Mistress MacGregor." He smirked and pointed at her with the glass in his hand.

"If you are still unsure about our allegiances, feel free to mention my name to General Clinton. I like to think he would speak favorably on my behalf after some of our past dealings where we have proved beneficial to each other."

Pennington smiled. "I have no doubt in my mind," he said.

Maggie held out her hands. "If Wyatt shows up here— not that I expect him to—we will send word to you immediately."

"That is good to know, ma'am." He set down his glass. "Thank you for your hospitality, but I must be going."

She stood to escort him out. "I am extremely grateful to you for reuniting me with my bracelet. I will find a way to repay the favor."

"I look forward to that," he said, put on his hat and departed.

Maggie watched him leave from the window by the front door and when she was sure he was gone, she sent Duncan a message.

I need you at the house.

She was still at the window when he appeared shortly thereafter.

"What is it?"

"We need to get Wyatt out of here as soon as possible. Major Pennington just paid us a visit."

"What was he doing here?" demanded Duncan.

Maggie turned and held out her wrist. "Returning my bracelet for one, but he used it as an excuse to ask about Wyatt. We have kept him here far too long, and that man very well may be back. It is time to move him."

"They can be ready to leave in the morning." Duncan took her hand. "How did that man get your bracelet?"

"The clasp must have broken at the tavern the other day. He said he wanted to have it repaired before he brought it to me."

"Did he now? Wasn't that kind of him to do something so nice for another man's wife?" he asked, sarcastically.

Maggie's face split into a grin, a little taken aback as she stared at him. "Duncan MacGregor! If I did not know any better," she said, slipping her hand over his chest, "I'd say you were a little jealous."

He pulled her close to him roughly. "Damn right! I do not want another man anywhere near MY wife." He pulled her into a long, passionate kiss that took Maggie's breath away.

"Remind me to make you jealous more often," she purred as he slipped his hand over her backside and grabbed her. He picked her up and she wrapped her legs around him as he carried her into the drawing room, kissing her thoroughly the entirety of the trip, and sat her down on top of the desk. Duncan turned long enough to close and lock the pocket doors, before returning to her. He urgently pushed her skirts up around her waist and undid his breeches. She was more than ready for him as he pushed inside her in one rapid motion, exhaling loudly as he did. Maggie pulled at his bottom lip with her teeth and he pounded into her over and over, until they both exploded together. He leaned his head against her chest, and she clutched his head with both hands, laughing.

She kissed him, pulling up his face to gaze into his eyes. "You are the only man for me, Duncan MacGregor. I shall never need, nor want, another, in this world or the next. You are part of my very soul. Remember that!"

Just as they were about to continue, they heard Gabe and Quinn in the foyer.

"Where is everyone?" Gabe attempted to open the doors to the drawing room.

Maggie hung her head. "Give us a minute," she called out.

Duncan buttoned his breeches and helped her off the desk as she adjusted her skirts. Maggie opened the door to see Gabe standing there with his arms folded, a stern look on his face, with Quinn beside him, trying to conceal his amusement.

"Really? It is the middle of the day and my mother is visiting," he lectured.

Maggie kissed him on the cheek. "Jealous?" she whispered.

"Actually? Very!" he replied with a wink.

"Don't be. That desk isn't very comfortable," she teased.

"The desk? Oh, never mind," said Gabe, and held up his hand. "I don't want to know."

"I am glad you two are here." She changed the subject. "Major Pennington paid me a visit. Wyatt needs to leave in the morning for everyone's safety."

"Everything is almost ready," said Quinn. "I will send word to the Captain and let him know while Duncan and I finish things up."

"Where is Wyatt now?" asked Gabe.

"He and John are at the village," replied Duncan.

"I will ride down and get him."

"I will go with you, Gabe," said Maggie. "I have not been down there in a while and I could use some air."

Duncan pulled her close. "We will finish what we started later tonight," he growled and kissed her.

"Oh...I look forward to that!" she said and smacked his behind.

"Have you ever heard of this Major Pennington?" Maggie asked Gabe on the ride.

"No, but I am not in the loop anymore and the army brings in new people all the time. Why do you ask?"

"Just curious about his visit," she replied, staring blankly ahead.

"It was to search for Wyatt, wasn't it?" asked Gabe.

"No. The main reason he claimed was this," she said and held out her hand. "He said that he found my bracelet at the tavern after we left. The clasp was broken. He wanted to have it repaired and return it to me himself."

"Well, that was very nice of him."

"Yes, it was."

Gabe noticed her pensive stare. "Is there something in particular bothering you about him?"

"I just got the impression he was trying to figure out where our loyalties lie."

"That makes sense. That is always good information to have, especially when you are new to town. I always did the same thing."

"Yes, but you were in intelligence."

"True, but many commanders do it as well."

Maggie sighed. "I suppose you are right. Still, the sooner we get Wyatt on his way, the better I will feel."

Maggie was freezing by the time they reached the tribe and Gabe helped her down. "You should have stayed at the house where it was warm."

"I am fine. Besides, I have not ridden Onyx in forever," she said, rubbing the big horse's muzzle.

"I am sure you want to visit with Powaw," she said to Onyx. "Have fun, but don't get lost."

Onyx whinnied in response and trotted off.

Gabe wrapped his arm around Maggie as Mingan came out to greet them.

"Maggie! Hello! We have missed you."

"Hello, Mingan. I have missed all of you, too. We have come for Wyatt. He has to leave in the morning."

"I am sorry to hear that. He is popular here," he said and grinned.

"I am sure he is, but it is not safe for him to stay here right now."

Mingan walked with them towards John's house.

"Are things well here?" she asked.

"Yes! All the women that you blessed at the ceremony are with child now. We owe you a great thanks," he replied.

"That is wonderful news," she said and smiled. "I am glad I could help."

"We are hoping John will take a wife or two soon," he said optimistically.

Maggie laughed. "I am not sure I can help you there. John is somewhat of a free spirit."

"Yes, he is, and one we are proud to have with us. How are you?"

"The pregnancy sickness is waning, so I am feeling much better."

He bid them farewell when they reached John's house. Gabe knocked on the door.

"A moment, please," called John.

Gabe rubbed Maggie's arms while they waited.

John finally appeared, half-dressed. "Come in!" he said, as Gabe escorted Maggie to the rudimentary fireplace they had added to the longhouse.

"I hope we are not interrupting," said Maggie, rubbing her cold hands together.

"No," he replied. "My guests were just leaving."

Two giggling women appeared from John's bedroom and kissed him before they departed.

"You should be ashamed of yourself, letting those two women take you to bed at once," scolded Maggie, jokingly.

"Says the woman who took a man's virginity, and the son of a Reverend, no less," he retorted with a devilish smirk on his face.

"And the woman whose skirts were hiked on the desk in the drawing room earlier this afternoon," added Gabe.

"Maggie!" said John, feigning propriety. "How very unladylike of you!" He laughed with a twinkle in his eye. "I'm sort of impressed."

Maggie wrinkled her nose at Gabe. "I blame the hormones," she said and rubbed her belly.

Gabe leaned down to speak to her tummy. "Stop turning your mother into a degenerate."

A large kick was the response. Maggie laughed, taking each of them by the hand and placing those hands over her growing baby bump. They both grinned as another kick followed.

"That is amazing," said John and moved a chair closer to the fire for her. Once she sat down, he placed a deerskin over her lap and kissed her on the top of the head.

John made some hot tea for Maggie while Gabe poured himself and John a drink.

"What brings you down?"

Maggie sipped her tea. "Wyatt needs to leave first thing in the morning."

"Is there a reason for the urgency?" he asked.

"Major Pennington paid Maggie a visit earlier."

"I see." Concern filled John's voice.

"He will be safer on the road than he will be here," said Maggie.

John agreed. He noticed the bracelet back on Maggie's arm. "Where did you find it?" he asked.

"The Major had it," replied Gabe.

John leaned forward. "The Major? How did he come by it?"

"He found it broken on the floor at the tavern, so he had it repaired and brought it back to me."

"Interesting," said John, stroking his chin, deep in thought.

"Where is Wyatt anyway?" asked Maggie as she looked around.

"I am sure he is around here…somewhere," replied John. He turned his head and winced.

Maggie narrowed her eyes at him. "Is he with a woman?"

John sighed. "The boy is going off to war. Let him have a little fun."

"What about Chastity?" she asked mockingly.

"He has written to tell her that he will not be returning for her, so I daresay their affair has concluded."

"Oh, I do hope he let her down gently," said Gabe, dryly.

"He did indeed…with my help, of course. I told him what to write, so it was very 'star crossed lovers that can never be together'. It will be a letter she will hold dear until her dying day."

"I'm sure!" Maggie rolled her eyes. "Can you round him up by suppertime and let him know the plan?"

"Of course."

9 CHAPTER NINE

John and Wyatt arrived just in time for supper, the family enjoying one last meal before the young man's departure. The next morning, they all said their 'goodbyes' as Wyatt, Captain Russell, and a few other men left on the wagon. It was decided that Wyatt would use the name MacGregor for the time being, just as an added layer of protection for him and the family.

The next few days passed uneventfully, until a messenger came to the door with a note for Maggie.

"Oh, for crying out loud!" she exclaimed.

"What is it now?" asked Duncan.

"The shipping company office in town has been broken into. The army is looking into it, but they are asking for me and Gabe to come into town today to assess the damage and answer some questions."

"Quinn and I can handle it," offered Gabe.

Maggie held up the letter. "They are asking for us both by name—or ordering, I should say."

Duncan looked none too pleased. "I will have Harm prepare the carriage, so the ride will be a little bit easier on ye."

Quinn decided to remain behind with the children, so Maggie, Duncan, and Gabe went alone. They were met at the office by Captain Jones.

"I am sorry to have to bring you into town for this," he said, "but we are unsure of what is missing, and your manager is unaccounted for."

"Captain Russell is out of town on a personal matter," said Maggie. "I am not sure when he will return."

"May I ask what sort of matter?"

"He is visiting his son," answered Gabe.

They made their way inside the office. There was broken glass all over the floor. A back window had been busted in and the backdoor lock was broken. Papers were strewn everywhere, and the desk had been ransacked.

"Take your time and make a list of what is missing," said the Captain. "I will be outside when you are done."

They picked the papers up off the floor and Maggie started looking through the desk. When she was done, she leaned back in the chair.

"This is very strange," she said. "There is absolutely nothing missing."

Gabe went through the cupboards and cabinets. "Everything seems in place here, as well."

"This makes no sense," she said.

Maggie pulled out the accounting books and ship logs that Captain Russell kept there, the ones for the benefit of anyone who was searching...the real books being kept at David Percy's home office in his secret room. She noticed that a couple of the pages were curled on the top corners, as if someone had gone through them quickly.

"It looks like the books were searched." Maggie looked up. "Why don't you two check the storage cellar to see if anything has been disturbed? The keys are still here."

"We will be right back," said Duncan, and he grabbed the keys and kissed her.

Maggie was so caught up in looking through the desk, she never heard the man come in.

"Mistress MacGregor," he said and caused her to jump. "Forgive me! I didn't mean to startle you," he said with a smile while he held up his hands reassuringly.

She clutched her hand to her breast. "Major Pennington, I did not hear you come in."

He crossed the floor to where she was sitting. "I was made aware of the break-in. I have the men trying to find the perpetrators. Have you determined what is missing?"

"So far, nothing that I can tell, which is very odd. Gabe and Duncan are checking the storage cellar as we speak."

"What of your office manager? Have you had some disagreement with him, perhaps over finances or compensation?"

"No, not at all. He is out of town and we are aware of it. His loyalty has never been in question. I trust him completely."

"I see." He looked around at the mess with his hands folded behind his back. "Mistress MacGregor, please allow me to get some of the men to clean this up. A lady such as yourself should not have to deal with it. I will be more than happy to escort you to the Raleigh Tavern for refreshments while this is taken care of."

"Thank you, Major, but I should wait for Duncan and Gabe to return from the cellar so they will not be worried about where I have gotten off to."

Maggie stood to put something back on the shelf and the unmistakable swell of her belly was revealed.

"You are...with child," he said slowly, his eyes locked on her midsection, clearly shocked by the revelation.

She smiled. "I am." She ran her hand over her baby bump. "Did I not mention it to you before?"

"No, you did not," he said quietly and quickly regained his composure. "In that case, I am afraid I must insist that you let me take you away from here."

"Pardon me?" she asked.

"The broken glass," he said, pointing to the floor, "it is not safe for you here and it is also very cold since there is no fire. I would never forgive myself if you or your unborn child were endangered under my watch. I will have a man wait here for your husband and he can tell him where we are."

"I am fine, really."

He held out his hand. "And again, I MUST insist."

Deciding it was best to not have a disagreement, Maggie sighed and accepted his offered hand.

He broke into a broad smile. "Thank you for indulging me."

They found a table near the fireplace where a roaring fire burned. He pulled out the chair and helped her to get settled.

Gracie came over to greet them. "Hello, Maggie!"

"Hello, Gracie!"

"Would you please bring Mistress MacGregor something to warm her up, perhaps some hot tea?"

Gracie looked to Maggie for clarification.

"Some hot tea would be wonderful," she said.

Gracie nodded and left.

Maggie sent Duncan a message.

Do not freak out when you cannot find me. I am at the Raleigh Tavern with Major Pennington.

Pennington sat down. "I must say, I am happy to see you again, although the circumstances could have been more pleasant."

"Do you have any idea who may have broken in?" she asked.

"There are a few unsavory characters roaming around town, but it could have been anyone." He looked over at Maggie as she blew on her hands and rubbed them together. "You are still cold," he said and stood. "Please, take my coat."

"That is not necessary," she replied, but his jacket was already around her shoulders before the words left her lips.

"That's better," he said and patted her shoulder.

"Thank you." She half-smiled for his benefit. "How do you like our little town, so far?"

"I find it quite charming," he said as he took his seat.

"Tell me about yourself, Major," she said, giving him a good once over. She took note of how particularly neat his appearance was and how much he seemed to go out of his way to project himself as a man of importance.

"Not much to tell, really. I grew up in Liverpool, joined the army, and was sent to the Colonies three months ago. I was in South Carolina before my work brought me to Williamsburg."

"What exactly is it you do for the army?"

"Whatever is needed," he said with a smile and brushed her question off. "When is your child due, if I may ask?"

"My best guess would be around the middle of July."

"Do you have other children?"

"We do! Triplets. One boy, two girls.... they turned a year old in December."

"Triplets?" he asked, pleasantly surprised. "They must be quite a handful."

"Not really. They are exceptionally good babies and we have a great deal of help."

Gracie brought her tea and a drink for the Major.

"Thank you, Gracie." She wrapped both hands around her cup to warm them and took a sip.

"Do you have a wife or children, Major?" she asked.

"Unfortunately, no. I have never married...unless you count the army," he said and grinned sheepishly.

"The army can be a fickle mistress," quipped Maggie. "She takes far more than she gives back in return."

He leaned back, hooked his arm over the back of the chair and nodded, amused. "Indeed, she does, but I suppose I am a glutton for punishment. Your turn," he said. "Tell me about Maggie MacGregor."

"I am afraid you would find my story rather boring, Major."

"I doubt that. I understand you are one of the wealthiest women in the Colonies, making a small fortune out of a place that no one would go anywhere near, yet you managed to single handedly turn it around by yourself."

"I wouldn't say a fortune, but we make do," she lied. "And there are too many people to name on that estate that I could not have done it without."

Maggie took another sip of her tea. "You have been checking up on me?"

"Making inquiries is part of my job. It is good to know the people around you that you can trust, especially during wartime."

"Part of 'whatever is needed', you mean?"

"Something like that. You and Colonel Asheton own the shipping company together?" he asked.

Maggie nodded. "I gave him half of the business when he retired."

"That was very generous of you."

"Gabe and I are very close, and he gave up a great deal to take care of me. It was the least I could do."

"You are quite a remarkable woman, Mistress MacGregor," he said, watching her intently.

"You give me far too much credit, Major Pennington," she said and looked down at her cup.

"I would be very pleased if you would call me by my given name...Jackson," he said, softly and leaned his arms on the table.

Before she could respond, Maggie looked up to see Gabe and an extremely displeased Duncan briskly coming inside the tavern and headed straight for their table.

"Major!" said Duncan, gruffly, in passing as he went to Maggie's side.

Pennington stood to greet them. "Mr. MacGregor, Colonel Asheton. How good to see you both."

He turned towards Duncan. "Please forgive me for bringing your wife here without telling you first. I did not want her to become injured with all the broken glass on the floor, and I thought she would be more comfortable here."

"Thank ye, Major," he managed, forcing himself to be polite, before taking Maggie's hand.

"My love, we should get ye home to rest," he said as he removed the Major's coat from around her, tossed it aside and helped her to stand.

"Major Pennington," said Gabe. "There is nothing missing from the shipping office. I am afraid we were simply victims of vandals. I will make arrangements to have the glass replaced as soon as possible."

"That very well may be, Colonel, but we will continue to investigate just to be sure."

"It was completely unnecessary to have my wife come into town in her delicate condition for this, Major," said Duncan, doing his best to restrain himself. "In the future, Gabe and I will be the only ones YE will need to deal with on such things...or any other, for that matter."

"Of course," he replied and bowed his head, "had I known Mistress MacGregor was with child, I would have never let anyone disturb her with this unpleasantness. My apologies. If we need anything else, I will ride out to you myself."

"Nay, ye will not!" Duncan raised his voice in response, his temper flaring before he could stop himself.

Gabe stepped between the two men to diffuse the situation. "What he means to say, Major," he said and gave Duncan a sharp look, "is that Maggie is having a difficult pregnancy and has been warned by her physician to avoid any sort of distress. You can contact me directly if you need anything at all. I am at your service."

The Major nodded. "Certainly."

Duncan placed his hand on Maggie's back and escorted her towards the door.

"Good afternoon, Major," she said. "Thank you for the tea and the company."

"The pleasure was all mine, Mistress." he bowed slightly. "Please take care of yourself."

Duncan guided her outside as Gabe bid the Major farewell.

Major Pennington watched them leave, then moved to a small table in the back corner with his drink. He put his coat back on and caught a faint whiff of the subtle perfume that she wore lingering on his collar. He closed his eyes, inhaled the scent...and smiled.

"I do not like that man!" grumbled Duncan as he brooded in the carriage the entire way home. "There is something about him that unsettles me."

Maggie took his hand. "Duncan, you are overreacting."

"I do not believe I am!" he retorted sourly.

"You must control yourself around him, Duncan," warned Gabe. "We don't know anything about him, and we cannot afford any enemies with what is to come, especially none who are part of the British army."

Maggie leaned against Duncan, and he wrapped his arm around her.

"Gabe is right. There is no need to borrow trouble. Besides, he has given us no reason to distrust him," she said and snuggled in closer.

"I cannot help it. I still have a bad feeling when it comes to him."

"You are worrying too much," she said and drifted off to sleep.

Duncan was still in a foul mood when they got ready for bed that night and he forcefully yanked back the covers.

Maggie came up behind him, touched his back, feeling the tension in his shoulder muscles. She took him by the arm and turned him around. "Why are you so upset?"

She watched him chew on his inner cheek.

"Say it!" she demanded.

"The Major...he is fond of ye."

Maggie cocked her head. "What do you mean?"

"The way he acts toward ye," he said, raking his hand through his hair, "having your bracelet repaired, escorting ye from the shipping office for your own safety, his coat around your body. He is taking liberties with ye, and I do not like it one bit!" he said, angrily.

Maggie sighed, and placed her hands on her hips. "Duncan MacGregor! You ARE jealous! Do you think for one second that I would ever be unfaithful to you?"

"Never!" he immediately answered.

"Then, what are you worried about?" She placed her hands on each side of his face. "I love you, and only you. You are my husband, the father of my children, the love of my life, and if all of the men in the British army fell to their knees, proclaiming their undying love for me, it wouldn't matter one bit. I will never want anyone but you, by my side, for the rest of my life."

Duncan slipped his arms around her waist and pulled her into a tight embrace. "I am not concerned about ye being unfaithful; I would never think that," he whispered. "It is the actions of other men who desire ye that worry me."

Maggie kissed him. "I am not worried. I have you to protect me, and I know you will always keep me safe."

"I would lay down my life for yours," he said sincerely.

"Please don't," she said. "I would never be able to live without you."

He pushed her hair back from her face, cupped her cheek and tenderly kissed her before she took him to bed and showed him how much he meant to her.

10 CHAPTER TEN

The following Saturday, Maggie was at her desk attempting to work on some letters when Quinn came in and closed the pocket doors behind him.

"I need to speak with ye," he said.

Maggie laid her quill down and watched him pour himself a large glass of whisky. He drained it in one gulp, then refilled it before he plopped down in a chair and sprawled out.

"Something bothering you?" she asked and took a seat across from him.

"Aye! My mother-in-law!" he grumbled.

Maggie scrunched up her face and scratched her nose. "Oh God! What has Georgie done now?" she asked.

He pulled at a loose thread on the arm of the chair. "She is literally making Gabe insane. I have never seen him act like this before."

"Yeah, she does that to him."

Quinn leaned forward. "He is a nervous wreck, unsure of himself or anything that he does. He is not the Gabe I know and love." He took another swig. "We have not even slept in the same bed...or done anything else for that matter, since her arrival because he is afraid she may drop by at any time. After we put the children to bed, he drinks himself into a stupor each night. Maggie, I am worried about him, and I do not know what to do."

"Have you tried talking to him?"

"Aye, but I am not getting through to him, not the way ye can. Will ye talk to him?"

"Yes, I will speak to him," she said, "if you will talk to Duncan for me."

"What's going on with my brother?" he asked.

"Green is not his color. He seems to think that Major Pennington has developed a fondness for me, and I am afraid he is making himself a little crazy with jealousy."

"Has the Major made advances towards ye?"

"No!" she replied. "He has been a perfect gentleman, but Duncan has it in his head that the man desires me. If he loses his temper with him, we very well may have the entire army upon us, and we cannot afford that right now."

Quinn nodded. "In his defense, he has never been very clear-headed when it comes to ye. I will try to settle him down."

"And I will work on Gabe for you."

Quinn left to go find Duncan and Maggie went back to her desk and the letter she had been working on. She managed to write three whole words before Gabe came into the room.

"Hello, Maggie," he said, came over and kissed her on the cheek before he poured himself a drink and sat down on the sofa.

Maggie laid her quill back down and frowned.

This damn letter is never getting finished.

"Hitting the whisky a little hard and early, aren't you?" she asked.

"It's been a long morning," he muttered.

"What have you been up to?" she asked and stood to close the doors.

"I just returned from town. The new windows were installed at the office today and things have been put back in order, good as new."

"Any news on who might have done it?" she asked and sat down next to him.

"No! I saw Major Pennington today and he said there were no new leads. He sends his regards, by the way."

"What is your initial impression of him?" she asked.

Gabe shrugged. "Well, he is definitely in intelligence," he said and took a sip. "He was doing his best to pick me for information using the techniques that I taught to other intelligence officers. You would think they would pick up a few new tricks along the way."

"What was he fishing for?" she asked.

"He was trying to find out about the estate...and you and Duncan, for some odd reason."

"Us? Why us?"

"That is a good question," he replied. "He seems to have taken quite an interest in the both of you."

She pulled her feet up underneath her and leaned closer in to face him.

"Speaking of good questions...why are you letting your mother get under your skin?"

He slammed his head back on the sofa. "You know how she is, Mags," he groaned.

"I also know that she is taking a toll on your marriage."

He looked down somberly. "Did Quinn say something to you?" he asked, softly.

"He is worried about you and, truthfully, so am I. As much as I love Georgie and Martin, it is time for you to speak to them about going home to England and not just because of what it is doing to you. The armies will be moving into the area soon and they will be much safer back in London."

"You are absolutely right," he said. "I will bring it up."

"You should bring something ELSE up too," she wiggled her finger. "Your husband desperately needs some attention, the kind that only you can give."

"Right again," he agreed with an exaggerated sigh. "I have been neglecting our relationship. I will make it a point to rectify that as soon as possible."

"I am glad to hear it!"

They all gathered for dinner in the dining room later that afternoon.

Gabe pushed his food around with his fork for several minutes before he finally worked up his nerve and looked over at his mother. He cleared his throat and said, "So Mother, now that you know that Wyatt is alright, have you and Martin given any thought as to when you will be returning home? I am sure you are anxious to get back to your social activities in London."

"Oh, we are not going home, at least not until I have found you a suitable wife," she said matter-of-factly and put a fork full of food in her mouth.

Gabe's own fork made a rather loud 'clunk' as he dropped it onto his plate.

Maggie and Quinn exchanged wide-eyed, nervous glances as they waited for his response.

"What did you say?" Gabe was taken completely off guard.

"Well, yes dear. It is well beyond time that you married again. You are not getting any younger, and Kat needs a mother to raise her. All of your brothers have settled down and I will not be satisfied until I know that you have as well."

Maggie looked down at her lap and rested on elbow on the table, rubbing her temple. "Here we go again," she whispered to Duncan. "The same old song and dance."

"Georgie!" exclaimed Martin and wiped his mouth with his napkin. "I thought we agreed you were going to leave

Gabe alone about this matter. He is a grown man who does not need his mother dictating his personal life."

"I know," she said, "but I am not getting any younger, and I will see all my boys happily married before I die."

"What makes you think a wife would do that?" smarted John under his breath.

Gabe pushed his plate away. "Mother, I have told you before that I am not the least bit interested in taking a wife." He glanced at Quinn. "I am delighted with the way my life is right now and I would not change one single thing about it."

Quinn smiled discreetly and squeezed his leg underneath the table.

"Men don't necessarily need to take wives to make them happy," offered John with a smirk. "I can attest to that. I have never been married, and I am ecstatic."

"But dear," said Georgie, waving her hand across the table. "Look at how blissful Maggie and Duncan are. Don't you want what they have? If you will not do it for yourself, at least do it for Kat. You have a daughter in your life to consider now and her welfare comes first and foremost. Who is going to teach her all the things a mother does?"

"Mother! Kat is loved and well-cared for; she has Maggie, whom she loves very much and for anything I cannot handle myself, not to mention a whole estate full of women who adore her and would do anything for her."

"It is not the same," shouted Georgie.

Martin laid his hand on her arm in an attempt to rein her in and settle her down.

"So, I should just bring a strange woman into our home that she has never met and knows absolutely nothing about and tell her that she now has a new mother. What kind of sense does that make? Kat is thriving in a stable environment and she does not need to have her routine upset in that way."

"Gabe! Little girls need mothers to raise them and to teach them the things that a woman of her standing will need to know."

Maggie started to feel very strange as their argument continued. Soon, their voices became louder and the room started to spin and darken as her eyes involuntarily closed and she felt herself falling to one side. She saw a panicked expression on Duncan's face and heard him call out her name just before everything went completely black.

She woke up a short time later in their bed, Duncan beside her, stroking her face while a worried Martin hovered over her. Everyone else was in the room as well.

"What happened?" she asked.

"Ye fainted," whispered Duncan and kissed the back of her hand.

"How are you feeling now?" asked Martin.

"I am extremely tired, and I have a horrible headache." Martin checked her eyes.

"What caused this? Are she and the bairn alright?" asked Duncan, anxiously.

"My best guess? The distress from the rather inappropriate dinner conversation this afternoon is the reason," replied Martin, scolding Georgie with his eyes, before turning back to Maggie. "I want you to remain in this bed until further notice. Complete rest and allow absolutely nothing else to upset you, and I mean nothing!"

Maggie nodded and Duncan kissed her forehead.

Martin looked around the room. "I want everyone in this room, except Maggie and Duncan, in the drawing room…THIS INSTANT!"

They all looked around at each other as if they were children being sent to the principal's office for being naughty, slumping their shoulders as they filed out of the room.

Martin turned to Maggie. "Maggie, I cannot tell you how sorry I am for this. I know most of your trouble is coming from Georgie and Wyatt being here and I promise you, this will end tonight. I have had entirely enough, and I am stepping in. Please, get some rest and I will check in on you later. In the meantime, I need to set a few people straight!"

"Thank you, Martin," said Maggie.

"Aye, thank ye." Duncan echoed.

He nodded and determinedly left the room.

Duncan stretched out beside Maggie and wrapped her up in his arms. "Martin is right. Our home is a place to feel safe, peaceful and comfortable, but as of late, it has turned into nothing but chaos, and that is unacceptable."

"I am not worried anymore." Maggie snuggled against his chest. "I think Martin is about to kick some ass and take some names."

"He is about to do what?" he asked, confused by her words, but Maggie had already fallen asleep.

Martin heard Georgie and Gabe arguing before he even made it down the stairs. He stopped outside of the room, steeled himself, and dramatically stormed inside. He slammed the pocket doors together and turned to face them.

"ENOUGH!" he shouted and silenced them all instantly. Everyone in the room fell silent and turned to gawk at the normally mild-mannered man. Martin marched over and stood in front of Georgie and Gabe, his arms folded with a stern expression on his face, much like a father about to lecture his disobedient children.

"Let me make something painfully clear to each of you; Maggie and that baby are in an extreme amount of distress because of the sheer volume of chaos in this house. If she does not get some peace, quiet, and rest, she WILL lose that child and I refuse to let that happen. I need everyone in this room to understand exactly how serious this situation is."

Martin turned to Gabe. "Your mother loves you very much and she wants the best for you even if she does not always know how to show it. Please remember that above all, she means well, even if her methods could stand a great deal of improvement."

He looked to Georgie. "I know you think you are doing what you perceive as best for Gabe, but he is a grown man that can make his own decisions. If he says he does not need nor want a wife, then you need to accept him at his word, and move on."

"But Martin..." she began to protest.

Martin held up his hand to silence her. "But nothing! Georgie, I love you, I truly do, but sometimes you try me. Dear Lord woman, some days I think Job himself would not have enough patience to deal with you. Gabe has seen carnage on the battlefield that has done less damage then Georgie Asheton Barnes when she is on a mission to do what she perceives is best for one of her children. Why do you think he chose to stay here and not return to London? For God's sake, the man is forty-eight years old and he deserves to live his life on his own terms without interference from his mother, of all people." Martin sat down and took her hand. "Your best intentions have landed Maggie, a woman whom you care for deeply, in a bed on the verge of losing her unborn child," he said softly. "Shouldn't that tell you something?"

Georgie closed her eyes for a moment and sighed before turning to Gabe. "Is that true? Am I the reason you didn't return to London to stay?"

Gabe moved to his mother and knelt in front of her. "I chose to remain here because my life is here now, and I am happy with the way things are. I love you, Mother, and I do miss you, but here, I feel no pressure to please anyone. I am accepted for who I am, the way I am, without question."

"I see," she said curtly.

"No, you don't," said Martin. "You forget, he is a man, not your little boy anymore. Children are meant to grow up and lead their own lives, not the ones their parents think they should live."

Martin cupped her cheek tenderly. "If I had chosen to do what my mother and father wanted me to do, I would not be married to the love of my life right now." He smiled.

Georgie's anger faded and a few tears slipped down her cheeks when he kissed her. Martin took out his handkerchief and wiped her face as she smiled sweetly back at him.

Georgie turned back to face Gabe. "I may have stepped out of line and for that, I AM sorry. I will make it a point to leave you to your own decisions from now on, but I will not apologize for wanting the best for you."

Gabe took her hand and kissed it. "Mother, I have a wonderful life, and you do not need to worry about me in the least."

Georgie touched his face. "My dear, I will always worry about you. That is my prerogative as your mother."

"Fair enough," he said.

Quinn moved next to John, lightly touched his shoulder and pointed to the door.

"Let's give them some privacy," he whispered.

John nodded an acknowledgment. Quinn laid his hand on Gabe's shoulder as he passed, giving it a little squeeze as Gabe smiled up at him. John and Quinn quietly slid open the doors, stepped into the foyer, and closed them again. They met Duncan, who was half-way down the stairs.

"How is Maggie?" asked John.

"She is resting now."

Duncan looked towards the drawing room. "What did I miss?" he asked.

John chuckled. "Martin putting his foot down hard right between Georgie and Gabe."

"Is it doing any good?" he asked.

"I hope so," said Quinn, looking back towards the door. "I desperately need the man I married back."

Quinn turned his gaze upstairs. "Is there anything we can do for Maggie?"

"Aye! We can keep the house peaceful and her away from any sort of distress. I will not allow anyone or anything to upset her from now on, no matter who I have to tell to 'piss off'."

"Tell us what you need, and we will do it," said John.

Maggie spent the next few days in bed, mostly sleeping and eating. The entire household made it a point to not disturb her with any issues regarding the business or the estate. Late one evening, after Gabe and Quinn had returned home for the day, Martin came to the conclusion that the best thing for Maggie and the baby's health was to take Georgie back to London and remove a big part of the tension. He had already made up his mind, but wished to discuss it with Gabe, so he slipped out, borrowed a horse and rode in the direction of his stepson's home. By the time he reached the house, it was already starting to get dark and a rising full moon shone down on the path to the house. The windows were illuminated by the candlelight shining from within. Just as he was about to knock on the door, he noticed some movement in the window to his right. He stepped to the side to wave, when he saw them...Gabe and Quinn, half-dressed, locked in a lover's embrace, their lips upon each other. Gabe caught sight of Martin just as he stepped back, startled, and tripped over an unlit lantern that was on the porch, knocking it over and shattering it. He was half-way down the steps when the door was flung open.

"Martin...wait!" begged Gabe, holding his hand up, a horrified look on his face. "Please!"

"I...am...forgive me..." stuttered Martin, moving away.

Gabe rushed down the steps, putting on his shirt as he moved. He made it to Martin just as he reached the horse.

"Martin! Please! Let me explain!" pleaded Gabe.

"I do not think any explanation is necessary," said Martin. "I should leave."

Gabe frantically grabbed for the reins. "I am begging you, come inside so we may speak. PLEASE!"

Martin looked down, still breathing hard. He closed his eyes, for what seemed like an eternity, before he looked back at Gabe. He nodded, then slowly turned towards the house.

"Thank you!" whispered an only slightly relieved Gabe.

Quinn was nervously pacing the floor when they came inside.

Gabe looked to him, sheer terror in his eyes, before he quietly closed the door behind them.

"Martin, please sit down," he said, and wiped the sweat from his forehead with his palm before he turned to Quinn.

"Drinks may be in order," he said to Quinn, who moved quickly to bring a bottle and three glasses.

Martin sat down; his face buried in his hand. He looked up when Quinn handed him a glass.

Gabe took a chair across from him, and apprehensively leaned forward while Quinn sat on the arm of the chair beside him.

"So, this explains why you have not taken a wife," whispered Martin.

Gabe nodded slowly as he looked down into the glass Quinn had given him. "I have no desire for women. I never really have."

"But you were married!" declared Martin, confused.

"I was—because it was what was expected of me. I cared for Penny a great deal and I would have been a good and faithful husband to her had she lived, but I was, and would never have been, content; not the way I am now with Quinn." Gabe took Quinn's hand and smiled up at him.

"So, the two of you live here together...with the children?"

"Aye," replied Quinn. "They consider themselves brother and sister. They are well-cared for and happy. Gabe and I love them more than anything in this world and they know it."

"They do not ask questions?"

"They are children not yet jaded by society," answered Gabe. "They only know that they have two parents that love them dearly and would do anything to keep them safe, no matter what the cost."

"I don't know what to say," said Martin, and downed his drink.

Gabe hung his head. "I know you must think me abhorrent," he whispered, as Quinn rubbed his back and tried to calm and soothe him.

Martin stared at the two of them and paid close attention to their physical interaction with each other for a moment before he cleared his throat and finally spoke. "I had a best friend in medical school; his name was Tommy and we were closer than blood could have ever been. Tommy was always pulling me into some sort of crazy scheme, playing practical jokes, dragging me to taverns and having me drink with him until we could not remember our own names. He was always up for an adventure and boy, did we have some over the years. He, like you, was good at concealing who he really was."

Gabe and Quinn looked at each other, perplexed, as Martin continued, lost in his own memories.

"He would flirt with the ladies, knew exactly how to turn on the charm, much like you do. I had no idea that he preferred to be with men, until I accidentally stumbled into the wrong room at a tavern we were staying at late one night. I was astonished; never had even an inkling as to his inclinations. I did not know what to think. He followed me out when I ran, would not leave me alone until I agreed to hear him out. We went somewhere we could speak freely without being overheard and he told me that he had always been that way, but he was terrified of anyone ever discovering it for fear of what would happen to him or the disgrace he would bring upon his family. We talked for hours, and I came to realize something...that his being that way didn't bother me nearly as much as the thought of losing him as my best friend, so I promised to keep his secret and we never spoke of it again. Our friendship only deepened after that."

Martin's mood suddenly turned melancholy and he looked down into his empty glass.

"Where is he now?" Quinn stood to refill his glass.

"He is dead," he said sadly and took a sip to swallow the lump in his throat. "He was in the wrong place at the wrong time and was caught in bed with another man. A drunken mob formed, dragged them both outside, still naked and hanged them on the spot, leaving their bodies swinging in the tree to rot. All because they were different."

Martin wiped his nose with his sleeve.

Gabe leaned forward. "I am so sorry, Martin."

"Me too," he said quietly. "Tommy was a bright light in this world and that flame was put out far too soon." Martin looked up at Gabe. "I was shocked when I saw you and Quinn through the window, but please do not mistake my surprise for abomination. I simply was not expecting it and was caught off guard. I understand that some people are born differently, and I do not feel they should suffer for it." He let out a deep breath. "Does anyone else know?"

Gabe nodded. "Maggie, of course, Duncan, John, and Quinn's mother and brother. That's all."

A sudden realization came over Martin. "Of course! Maggie has been protecting you all this time, hasn't she?"

"Maggie is very understanding, not to mention cautious and loyal to a fault to the ones that she loves. She has done a great many things over the years to keep me safe, some of them at great peril to herself."

"I now understand why your mother gets to you so badly; it is because you are afraid she will find out about how you live...which is why I am taking her home."

"You are leaving because of this?" asked Gabe.

"No! I had already made the decision, which is why I came here this evening. I think Maggie and the baby will be better off if things can get back to a normal routine, and I wanted to let you know before anyone else."

"What about Maggie? She needs you."

"I will speak to the physician in town and the midwife, advising them of her condition. I expect once we leave, and now that Wyatt is gone, things will settle down around her and she will be just fine."

Gabe and Quinn exchanged uneasy looks.

"Will you tell Mother?" asked Gabe tensely.

"No, I will not. Your mother is a remarkable woman, but I am not sure she would understand. I give you my word, you have nothing to fear from me. I will never reveal your secret." Martin smiled at Gabe. "The two of you seem very happy together and for that, I am glad."

"Thank you," whispered a grateful Gabe.

"Yes! Thank ye," added Quinn and squeezed Gabe's shoulder as Gabe composed himself.

"Martin, you are good for my mother and you have become family, not only to me, but to my brothers, to Maggie and everyone here. I am proud to call you my stepfather...even if I am older than you."

Martin nearly spat out his drink, laughing. "I suppose that is still a little strange, isn't it?"

"Strange is a relative term around here!" muttered Quinn.

"Indeed!" said Gabe and he looked to Martin. "Can I ask you something?"

"Ask away," replied Martin.

"What did you ever see in my mother? I mean, what made you pursue her to begin with?"

Martin grinned. "That is a fair question. Your mother is something special. I swear, I think I fell in love with her the day we met, at one of those God-awful garden parties that she is so fond of throwing. I heard her laugh, and knew I had to meet her. She was the most charming creature I had ever encountered, and we spent hours just talking that day, about anything and everything. I made excuses to see her every chance I could. Then, she became ill with that fever. I did not think she was going to survive and the thought of losing her was more than I could bear. I stayed with her around the clock until she was completely well. By then, I knew I was in way over my head. The difference in age never even occurred to me. Even now, when I look at her, all I see is the beautiful woman I fell in love with. I am a lucky man. I have her as my wife and the family that came along with her is a bonus."

Gabe smiled warmly. "I guess, I sometimes forget that my mother is indeed, every bit a woman." He sighed. "Does it bother you that you will never have any children of your own with her?"

Martin shrugged. "Not really. If not having children is the price I pay for being with your mother, I will gladly pay it." The doctor smirked. "Besides, I have four wonderful sons now, and a whole slew of grandchildren I adore, plus Maggie and everyone here who is as much as part of our family as you are. Our cups overfloweth and we will never lack for anything."

"Martin, you are a blessing to all of us and we love you. I hope you know that."

"And I love all of you as well."

11 CHAPTER ELEVEN

The following morning, while Quinn took Georgie, Martin, and the children to the stables to see the colts, Gabe decided to peek in on Maggie. He heard them from the hall.

"Duncan, please!" Gabe heard her beg.

"Ye are supposed to be resting and that is not resting."

"It can be, depending on how you do it."

He hesitated before he knocked on the bedroom door softly.

"Come in, please!" said Duncan.

"Up for some company?" He peered around the door.

"Yes," said an exasperated Maggie, who was sitting up in bed.

Gabe came over to her and kissed her on the cheek. "You look much better."

"I feel fine, but I could feel amazing if my husband wasn't so damn stubborn."

Gabe crossed his arms and looked back and forth between them quizzically, as Duncan shook his head.

"Maggie is being a difficult patient," Duncan explained.

"I really am feeling well, and there is no reason I cannot go downstairs, especially since I have no reason to stay up here."

Duncan folded his arms and came to stand beside Gabe.

"Nay! I think ye should stay right where ye are." He turned to Gabe. "What do ye think?"

Gabe nodded to him. "I agree with Duncan." He turned back to her. "Really Mags, I don't know why you would even want to leave this room. You have everything you need right here. A comfy, warm bed, all the food you can eat, and your loving husband by your side. Just relax and enjoy it while you can! You will be back to chasing babies soon enough."

"I would enjoy being in bed more if my husband would...indulge me," she said, annoyed. "Duncan is holding out on me."

"Ah!" said Gabe and suppressed a smile, finally understanding the issue.

"Maybe later, if ye are a good girl and do what ye are told," suggested Duncan with a wink.

Maggie wrinkled her nose at him, annoyed.

"Speaking of husbands," said Maggie to Gabe, "are you still neglecting yours?"

Gabe sat down on the side of the bed and sighed. "No! I am happy to report that has been remedied." He smiled and took her hand. "Quinn and I are just fine in that department."

"Oh good," said Maggie, sarcastically, "so Duncan is officially the only one in this house not performing his 'husbandly duties'."

"Ye are very cranky today," teased Duncan, amused.

"I know how you can put me in a better mood," she quipped. "Besides, wasn't there something in our vows about keeping your wife satisfied in that capacity?"

"Nay, I don't think there was," he said with a grin and turned to Gabe. "Ye were at our wedding, do ye remember anything about that?"

"No," he replied and played along, "I don't recall anything about that either."

"Well, there should have been," she said waving her hands in disgust. "Right now, lack of THAT is the only thing that is causing me distress."

"Well, I have some good news for you. Martin told me he is taking my mother home."

"Really?"

"Yes! He feels like the sooner things get back to normal around here, the better off you will be."

"I have to admit, I would feel more comfortable if Martin were here for the birth," she said.

"I know, but he is making arrangements with another doctor and the midwife to make sure you are well taken care of."

"How are things between you and your mother?" she asked.

"We had a nice long talk after Martin reigned her in and we are in a better place now; in fact, better than we have ever been before."

"I am so glad to hear that," she said. "He knows exactly how to handle her..." Maggie cut her eyes over at Duncan, "in EVERY way judging by the sounds that come from their room."

Gabe stood and turned to Duncan.

"I think it is best if I leave you two alone to work this out."

"I will check on you later," he said to Maggie.

"God be with you," he whispered to Duncan on his way out.

After they returned from the stables, Martin went up to check on Maggie.

"How is our expectant mother today?" he asked.

"Extremely unreasonable," replied Duncan.

Maggie scowled at him.

"Oh?" said Martin. "What's the problem?"

"Martin, I am feeling perfectly fine. Do I have to stay in bed?"

Martin looked her over intently. "I don't see why you can't move around—as long as you get plenty of rest and are avoiding any upset."

"See!" exclaimed Maggie to Duncan. "There is nothing to stop us."

"That is NOT what he said! It is a far cry from moving around a little bit to doing... THAT!" fussed Duncan.

"What am I missing here?" asked Martin.

"Well, let's just ask him, shall we?" said Maggie and turned to face him. "Is it safe for us to resume our regular activities...in the bedroom?"

Martin looked down and raised his hand to his mouth, attempting to conceal his amusement. "I don't see why not," he replied, "as long as you are not having any pain or generally feeling unwell."

Maggie let out a deep breath. "Thank goodness! Thank you, Martin."

"My pleasure ...and things will be a great deal easier when Georgie and I have departed."

She took him by the hand. "Gabe told us. We are really going to miss having you around here."

"I am going to miss all of you as well," he said and squeezed her hand. He let out a deep sigh. "I want to personally thank you both for protecting Gabe all of these years. I know he is not my son by birth, but I love him just the same."

Maggie and Duncan looked at him, puzzled.

"I know about Gabe and Quinn's relationship and I also know that the two of you look out for them."

Maggie and Duncan exchanged uneasy looks.

"Their secret is safe with me and I will never tell a soul, not even Georgie, on my word. I just want Gabe to be happy and he seems to be with Quinn."

Closing her eyes, Maggie smiled. "Yes, he is, and we will do whatever it takes to keep them that way."

"When did Gabe tell ye?" asked Duncan.

"I found out last night, purely by accident. I went to speak to Gabe at his house and saw them together through the window. He explained everything."

"Oh!" said Maggie. "That must have been quite a shock for you."

"It was a surprise, but they are not the first I have known to live that lifestyle. I understand that you cannot help who you fall in love with and no one should be afraid for simply loving another. Those two seem very much in love."

"They are," assured Maggie. "I have no doubt they were meant to be together."

"Just make sure they stay safe," said Martin, "and maybe have Cecile make them some curtains for their front windows." He laughed.

"That's an excellent idea. I will get her right on that!"

Under Duncan's watchful eye, Maggie made it down for dinner that afternoon, which was relatively calm and quiet. Maggie and Duncan spent some time with the babies before he ordered her back to bed, afraid that she would overdo it. As soon as they were alone, Maggie started to remove her clothes; Duncan leaned against the wall, with his arms crossed, watching her, thoroughly entertained.

"What are ye doing?" he asked.

"What do you think I am doing?' she asked, playfully tossing a piece of her clothing in his direction.

"Getting ready to take a nap?"

"I will take a nap," she said and bit her lip seductively…. afterwards."

He shook his head, moving to her and taking her in his arms.

Maggie pulled him into a kiss. "You heard the doctor," she purred.

"We may need a second opinion," he teased.

She started undoing his breeches with her lips still pressed to his. "Martin is the best doctor I know. I trust him completely."

Duncan groaned as she freed him, his erection already firm.

"Don't tell me you are not interested," she goaded. "I know better."

"Nay, I never said that!" He growled and kissed her neck.

"Good!" she said, pulling his shirt off. "Then, you should get busy satisfying your wife. Doctor's orders."

"Well, if ye insist."

A few nights before Georgie and Martin were due to depart, Gabe and Quinn laid next to each other after their lovemaking and listened to the rain beating down on the roof.

"She is leaving soon. Don't ye think it is time ye talked to her?" asked Quinn, lightly stroking Gabe's chest.

"I talk to her every day."

"That's not what I mean, and ye know it," said Quinn, pushing up on his elbow to look into his husband's eyes. "Gabe, this may be the last time ye get to see your mother, and I would hate for ye to feel guilty for the rest of your life because the two of ye did not part on the best of terms. I know ye made a lot of progress the other night after Martin intervened, but there is still some tension there. I feel it every time I touch ye."

Gabe turned on his side to face Quinn. "I am not sure that will ever completely resolve. My mother is just so…"

"…so concerned for the ones she loves? So determined to see them protected at all costs? So wanting of what's best for them?" finished Quinn and lovingly pushed the hair back from Gabe's face. "I know someone else that has a few of those traits, and they aren't so bad," he said before kissing him.

"Easy for you to say," replied Gabe, interlacing his fingers in Quinn's and brushing them to his lips. "Your mother is a joy to be around."

"Obviously, ye have only seen her in her later years." Quinn chuckled. "Ye know nothing of the woman from when we were younger, whose patience we tried to no end, especially after our father passed and she had to be both parents to the five of us. It is a wonder she didn't drown us all in the loch just to have a moment's peace for herself." Quinn squeezed his hand tightly. "The point is, while their methods may leave a great deal to be desired, a mother's love for her children is unmistakable. Ye just need to remember that when ye are dealing with Georgie."

Gabe sighed and gazed into Quinn's eyes. "I suppose you are right."

"Of course, I am! Ye were fortunate enough to marry a very smart man."

Laughing, Gabe rolled over to kiss Quinn. "Yes, I was. How did I get so damn lucky?"

The following day, Gabe found Georgie in the drawing room with Martin and John.

"Oh, Gabe dear, come and join us!" Georgie waved him over. "We were just chatting."

"I was actually hoping to spend some time with you, Mother," he said.

Martin looked up at Gabe and smiled approvingly. "I think that is a wonderful idea." He stood. "I think I will go look in on Maggie," he said and looked to John.

"And I think I will go with you," said John, taking the hint and getting up from his seat.

Martin kissed Georgie on the cheek and nodded to Gabe before he and John exited the room.

Gabe sat down next to his mother on the sofa, crossed his legs and took her hand in his.

"What's on your mind, son?" she asked and patted his hand.

"I just wanted to have some time alone with you before you and Martin went home, because we haven't had much of that since you got here."

"Yes, well, it is a little chaotic around here," she said. "I'm not sure how anyone can even hear themselves think with all the comings and goings in this house."

Gabe looked around the room. "I don't know, after the army life, I find this place rather serene. It is home. I have so many good memories of this house and the people in it from over the years, and I look forward to making many more."

For the first time since he was a little boy, Georgie actually took a good look at her son and she saw something in Gabe's eyes and demeanor, unlike anything she had ever seen before; a true expression of peace and contentment. She touched his face. "You truly are happy here, aren't you?"

He closed his eyes and smiled, brushing his cheek against her palm. "I am, Mother." He opened his eyes. "I need you to understand that above all else, that for the first time in my life, I am living on my own terms and I am good. I don't want you to spend one moment of your time worrying about me." He kissed her hand. "I want you to worry about yourself and Martin, because I don't know if you have noticed or not, but that man is desperately in love with you."

"Nowhere near as much as I am with him," she said bashfully. "I never thought I would fall in love again after your father, but when Martin came along, he changed my entire world." She looked down. "I just want the same for you," she whispered sadly.

Gabe thought back on Quinn's words and it made him realize that his mother's peace of mind, especially in her later years, was just as important as his own.

"Mother, I have a confession to make."

Georgie straightened up. "What is it, dear?"

Gabe closed his eyes. "First of all, let me make this perfectly clear. You are to ask me no questions or for any further information other than what I am about to give you. I need your word."

His mother looked at him oddly. "What do you mean?"

"I mean, you will take what I am offering and be content with it. This also must remain strictly between us; no running off to tell the rest of the family. Give me your promise."

She sat there, dumbfounded. "I don't understand."

"Your word, Mother, or you get nothing!"

"Alright!" she said, annoyed by his strict demand.

Gabe wiped his mouth with his hand and sighed, working up his nerve. "I am in love with someone, and this particular person makes me happier that I have ever been."

Georgie's face immediately lit up, her hand flying to cover her mouth. "Who is it? Tell me everything!"

"I said no questions, Mother!"

"Gabe," she scolded, "you cannot do that to me!"

He held up his index finger. "Part of the deal. You gave your word."

"Why the secrecy?" she asked, her eyes narrowed in suspicion.

Gabe chose his words carefully. "The situation is complicated and, for the time being, it must remain discreet, for the sake of everyone's safety, but I want you to know that I have found the person that I intend to spend the rest of my life with. I could not be more delighted with this individual, and the way my life is right now."

Tears spilled down Georgie's face and she broke into a wide grin before pulling him into a tight embrace. "That's all I have ever wanted for you, Gabe!" She kissed his cheek. "This makes me so happy, although I would like to meet this person."

Gabe hugged her back. "I'm glad, so no more worrying about me and no, I am not introducing you."

"Alright," she conceded with a grimace. "I love you, son!"

"I love you too, Mother!"

12 CHAPTER TWELVE

The first week of March, after many hugs and tears, and a much stronger formed bond between mother and son, Georgie and Martin boarded a ship back to London. Everyone breathed a collective sigh of relief when the boat pulled away from the shoreline.

The second week of March, Captain Russell returned from escorting Wyatt to Nathaniel, who was thrilled to have an apprentice in the field hospital. He brought back correspondence from Nathaniel and Ben, each reassuring her that they would look after the boy while doing their best to keep him safe and out of the line of fire. Everything seemed to be moving along smoothly until the third week of March...when all hell broke loose.

Maggie was sitting on the floor of the drawing room playing with the babies, Kat, and Alastair. Duncan, Gabe, Quinn, and John were out riding the property trying to determine what crops needed to be laid in for the spring and where.

Hettie stepped into the doorway. "You have a visitor," she said. "Major Pennington."

Maggie sighed. "Show him in and ask Cecile and Cora to come take the babies, please."

Hettie left, then reappeared with the Major.

"Major Pennington, how good to see you." She smiled up from the floor.

"Mistress MacGregor!" He bowed and looked at all the children on the floor around her. "You seem to have your hands full today," he said as he smiled and knelt to greet the babies.

"That is every day around here."

"Your children are beautiful," he said.

Cecile and Cora appeared, taking Morgan and Alanna. Alastair picked up Kendric and they filed out with Kat right on their heels. The room cleared, leaving Maggie still sitting on the floor and with the Major now standing. Maggie attempted to get up but was having some difficulty, her belly having become quite large.

"Allow me," he offered as he took her hands and helped her up.

"Thank you," she said. "I am afraid I am not as nimble as I normally am."

"You are radiant. Motherhood agrees with you," he said as he escorted her to a chair.

Hettie brought in refreshments and served them before leaving them alone.

"What brings you out?" asked Maggie.

"I am afraid I must inconvenience you. I will need use of your home for a little while."

Maggie thought she had misheard him. "I beg your pardon?"

"In a few days' time, General Benedict Arnold will arrive with fifteen hundred troops and shortly thereafter, General Phillips will be arriving with an additional two thousand," he explained. "They will only be here for a few days, but we will be in need of every available home in town, including the one I am currently staying at. Seeing as your estate is quiet and out of the way, I thought this would be the perfect place for me to work and reside temporarily."

Maggie smiled for his benefit, but inwardly wanted to scream. "Surely, Major, we are too far away from where you would need to be."

"Quite the opposite. My work does not require me to be with the troops, even though I do have a handful of men that report to me."

"We are already bursting at the seams here, as you can see," she said, rubbing her belly for emphasis.

"I understand, Mistress, but I would be the only one staying inside the house and my men would camp outside on the lawn. It would only be until the troops in town depart, which should not be exceedingly long at all. You would hardly know we were here." He leaned back in his chair. "I would actually be doing you a service. If I do not move in, with an estate this size, one of the generals would want to move their troops here, and they may not be as 'respectful' of your household as I will be."

Maggie groaned inwardly. She was stuck between a rock and a hard place. It was either let a man, that Duncan had no fondness for, move in, or take the chance of General Arnold staying there, which would be a little too close for comfort with John nearby. There was no doubt Arnold would recognize him if he saw him and there was a good chance Arnold might blame her personally for setting him up with John to begin with. She did not have much of a choice.

"Of course," she said and plastered on a smile. "I do however have a few boundaries I would respectfully ask and insist that you and your men would adhere to."

He nodded indulgingly and waited for her to continue.

"The people who work on my estate are terribly busy with their assigned tasks that I depend on them to do. I would need your men to leave them unmolested and undisturbed at all times to do what is needed of them, without interference."

"That is agreeable," he said.

"In addition to that, there is an Indian tribe on the edge of our property. We have worked extremely hard to establish a good relationship with them to keep the peace. I must ask that your men leave them alone, as well. I cannot afford trouble here."

"You are a very kind-hearted soul to allow them to remain."

Maggie looked down. "It is their home, Major, and I could not sleep at night if I forced someone from the only place they have ever lived."

"Anything else?" he asked.

"Your men will need to camp at the front of the house. The estate gets rather foggy, and they may become lost if they venture any further back."

"Surely, my men are skilled enough to find their way through a little bit of fog," he said with a chuckle.

"I wouldn't be so sure about that. This fog is unlike any you have ever seen or experienced before. This estate has a rather checkered history and the mist that surrounds it is, well, not of this world. I can assure you of that from personal experience."

"Are you saying this place is haunted by ghosts? Surely, you don't believe in such nonsense!"

"I am saying there are other forces at play here, and it is not wise to upset them," she said gravely.

"You do not seem afraid," he pointed out.

"I am a part of this place, and it is a part of me, so no, it does not bother ME. I have made peace with my demons and we have learned to coexist quite nicely."

"Well, Mistress MacGregor, I am not afraid of a child's fairy tale."

"Maybe you should be," she warned.

He light-heartedly tapped his fingers on the arm of the chair. "At any rate, I will be happy to abide by all of your requests," he said.

"In that case, Major, I will have a room made up for you, and you can use the library in the next room for your office. It will be quieter and more suitable. Come, I will show you."

Maggie took her time getting up and he quickly rose from his chair to assist her.

"How are you?" he asked, sincerely. "The Colonel said you were having some difficulty the last time we spoke."

Maggie pointed him in the direction of the library as they walked. "The doctor has advised me to avoid anything that may cause me distress."

He looked extremely concerned. "I see. I will do my best to make sure that my men and I are not a disruption to you."

"I appreciate that," she said, opening the door to the library.

He stepped in and looked around. "This will be perfect," he said. "I will return tomorrow morning with my things and the men will move their camp here the following day."

Maggie escorted him to the front door. He bowed and kissed her hand.

"Until tomorrow!" He smiled before he opened the door and departed.

She closed the door behind him.

"Well fuck!" she exclaimed.

Maggie sent Duncan a message.

I need everyone here now.

What is wrong?

A lot.

Maggie was sitting in a chair in front of the fireplace when they arrived.

"Maggie, are ye and the bairn alright?" Duncan rushed in, eyes wide, his gaze dropping to her belly and their awaited child.

"Yes, we are fine," she replied.

"What's going on?" demanded Gabe taking off his gloves. "What's the emergency?"

"It seems we will be having some unexpected guests starting tomorrow; Major Pennington and his men."

"Like hell, we are!" snapped Duncan, angrily.

Maggie rubbed her forehead. She had known that was coming.

"I will not have that man under my roof, Maggie."

"Brother, calm down," said Quinn. "Give Maggie a chance to explain before ye lose your temper."

Maggie sighed. "There are thirty-five hundred troops moving into town for a few days and it was either take him and a dozen of his men, or Benedict Arnold and his FIFTEEN HUNDRED men."

"Arnold?" asked John, stunned. "Here in Williamsburg?"

She frowned. "I couldn't take the chance of ending up with Arnold in our home. He would recognize you in a heartbeat if he saw you. Pennington doesn't know you, so if he happens to see you, it will be a great deal less dangerous."

"Why didn't ye just tell him 'no'?'" demanded a seething Duncan.

"Because if she had, he would have taken it anyway and probably marked us all traitors," answered Gabe. "You made the right decision, Maggie."

"I have asked them to stay confined to the front lawn and to not disturb anyone here. Just the same, we should move our personal horses and the children's. I will have Onyx guard them. We should also add a layer of fog along the front of the house to keep the men contained to that one area." Maggie shifted in her chair. "Advise everyone on the estate that the plan is in play."

"What plan?" asked John.

"The one I set up years ago in case someone shows up unexpectedly to make it appear we run this place with slaves instead of paid workers. If the main bell is rung, everyone moves into a job that makes it look like it is run like all the other estates in town, so as to not raise any suspicions."

"We have a great deal to do; we need to get to work," said Quinn.

Duncan did not move, only stood in front of the fireplace with his arms folded, staring into the flames.

"Duncan," said John, concerned by his demeanor, "are you coming?"

"I will be along," he mumbled.

John looked to Maggie for reassurance that it was safe for them to leave.

Maggie waved them off. After they left, she stood, moved behind him, and slipped her arms around his waist.

"Please don't be upset with me," she whispered. "I only did what I thought was best."

"I do not want that man anywhere near ye or our children."

Maggie pressed her forehead against his back. "I know, but it is only for a few days and he will be on his way. Besides," she said, kissing the middle of his back, "I have a very handsome Scot who will keep me safe."

Duncan turned and embraced her. "I am worried about the trouble that man may cause us," he whispered.

"Is there something you are not telling me?" she asked. "Why are you so concerned about him in particular?"

Duncan shook his head. "I have no explanation, just a bad feeling that man is going to tear our family apart."

Maggie took his face in her hands, looking him straight in the eye. "I will NEVER let that happen," she promised.

Major Pennington arrived early the following morning while Maggie was still asleep. They had been up late, making preparations on the estate, and Duncan intentionally kept her up until almost dawn making love to her so he, alone, would be the one to greet the Major.

He waited in the drawing room and instructed Hettie to bring him there as soon as he arrived.

"Good morning, Mr. MacGregor," the Major said as he came in.

"Major," said Duncan. "I wish to have a word with ye in private."

"Certainly," he said.

Duncan motioned for him to sit. "Hettie will show you to your room and the library is all set up for you."

"Thank you," said the Major. "I will try not to bother your household any more than I must."

Duncan fixed his gaze on the man sitting across from him. "Major, let me make something very clear. My wife, as ye know, is with child and having a difficult go of it. I will not allow anything or anyone to put her life or our child's life in danger by causing her undue distress."

"I would never do anything to intentionally harm Mistress MacGregor. I am quite fond of her and would never wish to see her troubled," assured the Major.

"I am well aware of your 'fondness' for my wife," scoffed Duncan. "I will thank ye to remember that she is MY wife and conduct yourself accordingly while ye are under my roof and for her sake, I will assume that ye will only be here as long as needed and not one moment longer."

"Of course," he replied with the tilt of his head. "On my word as a gentleman."

"I am glad we understand each other," said Duncan and stood to leave. "Hettie will assist ye with whatever ye need. If ye will excuse me, I have some estate matters and my wife to attend to."

Duncan left the room.

The Major looked down and smiled smugly, inwardly pleased that he had managed to get under MacGregor's skin so easily.

It was near noon when Maggie finally woke up. Duncan sat in a chair by the fireplace in their bedroom and was reading when she opened her eyes.

"Good afternoon," he said, closing his book, and came over to the bed.

"Afternoon?"

"Aye!" He nodded and kissed her.

Maggie sat up. "I didn't mean to sleep so late. The Major! I was supposed to meet him when he arrived."

Duncan sat down on the edge of the bed and touched her face with the back of his hand. "Ye were up late, so I let ye sleep in. The Major is already settled in, so ye have nothing to do but let your husband take care of ye."

She relaxed and laid back sporting a glorious smile, a blanket the only thing that covered her from the waist down. "Last night was wonderful!"

He smiled back, moving his hand down to one of her exposed breasts, before taking over with his tongue and sending a wave of ecstasy throughout her body.

"I am happy to give ye a repeat performance," he said and slipped his hand under the blanket, and back up the inside of her thigh.

"But the Major..." she trailed off.

Duncan moved up, kissed her deeply, and cleared her mind completely as only he could. "The Major can take care of himself."

He continued his work until all he heard from her for the next hour were her cries of pleasure and her calling out his name.

Before dinner that afternoon, Maggie stuck her head into the library. "Hello, Major."

He stood and his face split into a broad smile. "Mistress MacGregor, good afternoon. I am pleased to see you are well."

Maggie stepped into the room. "Please, forgive me for not being here to greet you. I did not get much rest last night, and I slept in this morning."

The Major held out his hand and helped Maggie to one of the chairs. "No apologies necessary. Your husband was here to greet me, although I must admit..." he hesitated slightly as he watched for her reaction, "...your absence did give me cause to be concerned for your safety."

Maggie looked at him oddly. "My safety? I am afraid I do not understand what you mean by that."

"My reception was rather 'cool' this morning," he explained. "When you were not here, given his obvious displeasure with my presence, I was concerned your husband may have been upset with you when you told him of my imminent arrival, and that he may have taken it out on you in some way. I get the distinct impression that he has a quick temper. However, Hettie assured me you were perfectly fine."

Maggie was completely taken aback. "I swear to you, Major, Duncan has never been unkind to me in the least. In fact, he is quite the opposite and he would never raise a hand to me if that is what you are implying. I do apologize that he was not friendlier to you this morning, but I am afraid my delicate condition has made him more than a little overprotective. I will have a word with him."

He folded his hands behind his back. "Please, do not allow my words to cause any undo strife in your marriage. The fact that you are safe is all that concerns me." The Major smiled. "I suppose, if you were my wife, I would feel the same way. I cannot fault the man in the least for wanting to protect you."

Maggie looked around. "I trust you have found everything to your satisfaction?" she said to change the subject.

"Indeed! The bedroom you have provided is more than adequate, as is this room for my office. Thank you."

Smiling, Maggie went to stand; he took her hand and helped her up.

"Dinner will be ready shortly and I think you will find Hettie's cooking quite a treat compared to your usual fare."

"Thank you, but I think I will take my dinner here at my desk today. I have a great deal to accomplish. I hope you will forgive my lack of formality."

"Major, I completely understand. Feel free to do whatever is best for you while you are here."

"Thank you, ma'am, I will," he said, and she left the room.

Maggie found Duncan in the drawing room with Gabe and Quinn. She closed the pocket doors behind her and walked over to him. She took his face in both hands and pulled his forehead to hers. "I love you more than life itself and I know that you are just trying to keep me safe, but you are going to get us all killed."

"What's going on?" asked Gabe.

Maggie dropped her hands and pointed to Duncan.

"Ask him!" Maggie took a seat and rubbed her temples. "What exactly did you say to him anyway?"

"I don't know what ye mean," replied Duncan, innocently.

"I know you better than that," said Maggie as she leaned back and eyed him suspiciously. "You need to tell me what you said to him so that I can do some damage control."

Duncan rolled his eyes. "I simply reminded him that ye were my wife and asked him to remember his place while he is an unwelcome guest in our home."

"Brother, please tell me ye didn't," said Quinn, linking his fingers behind his head.

"Oh, he most certainly did!" grumbled Maggie. "And now, Pennington has the distinct impression that my husband beats his wife."

"I gave him no such reason to believe anything of the sort," scoffed Duncan. "That man is playing you!"

"Duncan, we all know how you feel about Maggie," said Gabe, "but antagonizing an officer in the British army is not wise, especially at a time when thirty-five hundred of their troops are about to descend on Williamsburg."

Duncan raised his voice. "I will offer no apologies for protecting what is mine!"

"Exactly what are you protecting me from?" demanded Maggie, becoming upset. "That man has never even remotely stepped out of line with me. He has given you no cause for this, and even if he did, do you think I would do anything except put him right back in his place? How little do you think of me?"

"It is not your actions I am worried about!" he growled.

A sudden thought occurred to Maggie. "Did you keep me up all night just so you would be able to catch him alone this morning?"

Duncan rocked on his heels, with his arms folded, and his eyes cast downward.

"Oh my God, you did! I cannot BELIEVE you did that to me!" Maggie stood, shook her head in disbelief, and started out of the room.

Duncan gently took her by the arm. "Maggie," he said, softly.

She jerked her arm free and pointed her finger in his face. "DON'T!" she shouted and stormed out.

He went to go after her, but Quinn placed his hand on his chest and stopped him.

"She is right. You are going to get us all killed if ye do not learn to control yourself."

"I need to go after her," he said and went to move past him.

"You had better let me go," said Gabe, holding up his hand. "She is pretty upset. Let me talk to her first and see if I can get her to calm down."

Maggie found herself outside. She stomped over to the frozen flower garden, and took a seat on one of the benches, so angry that she did not even notice how cold it was.

Duncan was being completely unreasonable and that hot-headed Scot that she loved more than anything was going to get them into something they could not get out of. She huffed and kicked at the ground.

"Hettie said she saw you head this way," she heard Gabe say.

He came around the corner carrying a blanket. He moved in front of her and wrapped it around her tightly, before taking a seat next to her.

"Thanks," she whispered.

He put his arm around her, and she leaned against him.

"Duncan loves you and, as misguided as he is, he thinks that he is doing what is best for you."

"But he is doing the exact opposite." She sighed. "I don't know where all of this is coming from, Gabe. It is not like him."

"Jealousy will do that," he said, rubbing her arms, trying to warm her up. "It clouds your mind, causing you to lose all rationale and it especially makes men do crazy things."

"No," said Maggie. "It's more than that. Duncan is afraid of something and he is lashing out."

"What do you think it is?" he asked.

"I don't know. He only said he had a bad feeling about the Major, but I can't help but think there is more to it than what he is saying."

Gabe insisted that Maggie go back inside, out of the cold, for the sake of the baby. She reluctantly agreed and he escorted her back to the drawing room and planted her in a chair in front of the fireplace. Duncan was at the doorway before he had her settled.

"I will leave you two to talk," Gabe said when he saw him.

Gabe leaned down and kissed Maggie on the cheek. "Go easy on him," he whispered before he left and pulled the doors closed behind him.

Duncan crossed the floor, dropping to his knees in front of her. He laid his head in her lap and she leaned down and kissed the top of his head.

"I love ye, Maggie, more than life itself," he whispered.

"I love you too, Duncan." She placed both hands on his head, then raised his face up to look him in the eye. "Promise me you will not cause any more tension with the Major while he is here...for my sake and the sake of our children."

Duncan looked into her eyes, feeling an enormous surge of guilt for the amount of distress he was causing her. He closed his eyes and nodded before he bent his head down and kissed her belly.

"For ye and our children," he vowed.

"Thank you," she said before she lifted his head back up and kissed him.

The rest of the day passed uneventfully. The Major did not join them for dinner or supper, so their mealtimes were quiet. Duncan had barely slept the night before, so they turned in early. Maggie woke up around midnight, ravenous with her stomach growling loudly, so she slipped out of bed carefully, as not to wake him, put on her robe and went into the hall. She peeked on the babies who were sound asleep, before going downstairs. She noticed candlelight coming from the kitchen as she got closer. She found Major Pennington sitting at one of the tables, eating when she came in. He went to stand, but she waved him off.

"Don't get up on my account," she said. "We are rather informal around here."

"I hope I did not wake you," he mumbled and covered his mouth. "I was so caught up in my work earlier that I forgot to eat supper."

"No," replied Maggie, rubbing her stomach. "I am afraid my unborn child woke me because he, she, or they are very hungry."

The Major stood. "Please, allow me." He came around the table and motioned for her to sit. "Hettie left out a great deal of food for some reason."

Maggie took a seat and he started to cut off a few pieces of bread for her. "She does that for me. I am afraid I wake up most nights starving," she said and laughed. "You should have seen how much food I went through with the triplets."

He took down a plate from a shelf, placed the bread on it, then started to slice some cheese. He looked over at her curiously. "Forgive me for being so forward and I know it is none of my business, but I feel the need to ask...is everything alright between you and your husband?"

"Yes! Why wouldn't it be?" she asked.

He placed the plate over in front of her and took a towel to wipe his hands as he watched her intently. "I heard some loud voices coming from your drawing room earlier. I could not hear what was being said, but the tone was unmistakable."

Maggie smiled. "I am afraid Duncan becomes cross with me when he thinks I am overdoing it, especially when I am with child. He really does mean well."

"I see. I was worried that my presence might be causing some issues between the two of you."

She bit into the bread. "Do not concern yourself about that. Our marriage is unshakable."

He came back around the table and took his seat across from her.

"Is everything to your satisfaction here?" asked Maggie, brushing the crumbs from her mouth.

"Yes! Your home is nothing short of magnificent. I am not used to such creature comforts in my line of work. You have done an outstanding job here."

"I am afraid I cannot take the credit. It was mostly this way when I bought it. The previous owner had expensive tastes." She looked around. "We had a fire here a while back, when Duncan and I returned from Scotland a married couple, and we did a little updating then, but mostly out of necessity."

"Have you lived in Williamsburg all of your life?" he asked.

"No, I came here in '65 and bought this place for next to nothing."

He looked surprised. "THIS place?"

Maggie nodded and took another bite of food.

"The previous owners were murdered in the side yard and that tends to drive the price down quite a bit. No one would come near it. I purchased it on the steps of the Raleigh Tavern without even laying eyes on it."

"This was before you and your husband were wed?"

"Long before."

"Then, how did you purchase it as an unmarried woman?" he asked.

Maggie realized that she had just slipped up and quickly moved to cover.

"I was widowed and completely alone, with a little money in my pocket. I needed a new start, so I made one here," she partially lied.

"I'm sorry. I did not realize you had been previously married."

Maggie looked down. "I try not to dwell on the past, and I don't like to talk about it. I have managed just fine for myself."

"Indeed, you have. You are a rather impressive woman," he said, gazing upon her, his chin in his hand with his elbow propped up on the table.

She shook her head. "Not really. I just did what I had to do to survive, like a great many people these days." Maggie got up and went over to a table in the corner. "How do you feel about pie, Major?" She brought a whole one back over to where they were sitting.

"I am actually quite fond of it," he replied.

Grabbing a knife and two forks, Maggie sliced into it. "I am firmly convinced that Hettie is the best cook in the

Colonies," she said, putting a slice on his plate, then a large one on her own.

The Major seemed amused. "Well, if what I have had today is any indication, I have no doubt you are correct," he said and took a bite. "I will not be able to fit in my uniform if I continue to eat like this on a daily basis."

Maggie closed her eyes and moaned as she tasted the first fork full. "I don't know what I would do without her. She has been a God-send to me since the day I first stepped foot in this place." She opened her eyes and pointed her fork at Pennington.

"What's your story?" she asked. "I know you are from Liverpool, have never been married, and have no children. Surely there is more to tell. What of your family?"

He licked his fork. "My parents are both long-deceased. I had a sister that died at the age of three from a fever. I also have one half-brother from when my father remarried shortly after my mother's death; we try to stay in touch when we can, but mostly the army has become my family."

"I'm sorry," said Maggie. "Being alone can be quite difficult. I know I miss my parents every day, even more so since I have become a mother."

"How did you and your husband meet?" he asked.

Maggie thought for a moment. She needed to be incredibly careful about what she said to this man. "We met while I was attending to some business in Scotland."

"You travel there a great deal?"

"No," said Maggie, spreading another piece of the pie. "Gabe and I were visiting his family in London, and I decided to make the most of our trip."

"Where else do you travel to for your company?" he asked and eyed her closely.

Maggie thought the question a little odd, so she answered it as vaguely as the other ones. "Mainly up and down the coast, between here and New York, when it is needed. Why do you ask?"

"I was just wondering how you came to know Major André," he inquired innocently.

Maggie looked down at her plate. "Gabe and I met John when he was a captain in Philadelphia. We all became good friends, stayed in contact, and visited whenever possible." Maggie laid her fork down on her plate. "Why are you interested in John, if I may ask?"

"No reason," he smiled. "He was such a well-respected officer. I guess I am simply curious about him since I never had the honor of meeting him in person. Everyone speaks so highly of him and the work that he did, I can only hope to be as fine a soldier as he was."

"John was an amazing man," she said. "We had a very special friendship."

"You must miss him very much," he stated softly, sympathetically. "Did you get the chance to visit with him before his execution? To say 'goodbye'?"

Maggie pushed her plate away. "Forgive me, Major. I am suddenly not feeling very well. I think I may have overdone it."

"I'm sorry! Is there anything I can do?" he asked, suddenly genuinely concerned.

"No, thank you. I think I am just going to turn in…if you will excuse me."

He stood as she did. "Do you need assistance upstairs?"

"I think I can manage. Goodnight, Major."

He nodded. "Goodnight…and please, I would prefer if you called me Jackson."

"Goodnight, Jackson."

He watched her go before sinking slowly back into his seat. He had not expected her to come into the kitchen that late at night, but her visit had been a welcome surprise and just as he was trying to figure out how to get her alone. Maggie MacGregor was unlike any woman he had ever met; as smart and keen as she was beautiful, and one whom he found himself wanting to know a great deal more about. He picked up the candlestick and quietly climbed the stairs on the way to his room to retire for the night. When he reached the spot outside her bedroom, he stopped. He could hear her moving around inside; the sounds of her settling into bed. He closed his eyes and laid his hand flat on the door, leaving it there for a moment, before sighing, and moving on to his appointed quarters.

Maggie got back into bed, but she was not in the least bit sleepy. Her mind was now working in overdrive. She tossed and turned a few times before Duncan's arms found their way around her; he had not awakened, just instinctively did it in his sleep. She snuggled against his chest, as her thoughts continued to be unsettled; Duncan may have been more right about that man than she had given him credit for.

13 CHAPTER THIRTEEN

Major Pennington's men arrived the next day. True to his word, he had them make camp on the front lawn and instructed them to not disturb anyone working on the estate. Duncan and Quinn were keeping a guarded eye on them from the front porch while Maggie watched from the drawing-room window. Gabe came inside to join her.

"How is it going out there?" she asked.

"Nothing unexpected," he replied. "Everything seems very routine and in order."

"What about in town?"

"General Arnold's men are there already. General Phillips and his men should be arriving tomorrow. According to what I have heard, they should not be here for more than a couple of days."

"Good," she said and walked to the front of the fireplace.

Gabe watched her closely for a moment. "What's eating at you?" he asked.

"I don't know what you mean," she replied, never breaking her gaze into the flames.

He came up behind her and wrapped his arms around her. "I know you too well, Mags. What's bothering you?" he demanded.

Maggie leaned back against him. "Promise to keep it between us?" she whispered.

"Of course," he said and led her over to a chair, then pulled up another one close to her.

"I came downstairs last night, and Major Pennington was in the kitchen. We pleasantly chatted for a bit, but then he started asking some unusual questions. I got the impression he was digging for information...on John and me."

Gabe tilted his head, quizzically. "What kind of questions?"

Maggie frowned. "How we met, when I last saw him…" She shook her head. "He said he was just curious because he had never met John, but that seems very strange, doesn't it?"

"It does seem a little odd!" he agreed. "I am assuming you have not told Duncan."

"No! I am afraid his temper will get the better of him." Maggie pushed the hair out of her face. "Maybe I am being paranoid and overreacting."

Gabe took her hand. "Mags, you have the absolute best instincts of anyone I have ever known. If you think there is something to this, there probably is, and it definitely bears watching."

"I think I am going to butter him up a little bit and see if he will let his guard down around me," she said.

"That is a dangerous game of cat and mouse, Maggie."

"What choice do I have?"

They tabled their conversation when Duncan and Quinn came into the room. Judging by the look on his face, and the amount of angry Gaelic words that spewed from his mouth, the laird of the estate was not in the least bit pleased.

"It's going to be a long day," whispered Maggie to Gabe.

Duncan stomped over to the liquor table and poured himself an unusually large drink.

"What's wrong now?" called Maggie, as if she didn't already know.

"Ye have to ask?" replied Duncan, outraged.

Maggie stood up and went over to him. "You need to calm down," she said. "It will only be a couple of days and they will move on."

Duncan's nostrils flared and he downed half of the glass in one gulp.

Turning her head toward Gabe and Quinn, she signaled with her eyes for them to leave.

"Yes, Quinn and I ...have something…that...needs taking care of," stuttered Gabe, motioning to Quinn.

Quinn nodded his head. "And... right this minute. We should…go...do that...thing...that needs taking care of."

They left and closed the doors behind them as Duncan finished his glass off.

Maggie took his glass and set it down before she led him over to the sofa. "I know you are frustrated, but it will be over soon. In the meantime, why don't you let me take your mind off things." She ran her hand over his backside.

"How are ye going to do that?" he asked, touching her face, a slight bit of the tension in his voice beginning to wane.

"I'm sure I can think of something." She smirked and pulled him into a kiss.

"I bet ye can," he growled.

The Major did not join them for dinner that day, so Maggie had Hettie make up a plate while Duncan was seeing to some things on the estate. Thinking it was as good a time as any to work on him, she knocked on the door of the library.

"Come in!" he called out.

"Good afternoon ...Major...I mean, Jackson," she corrected.

He smiled and immediately stood.

"You missed dinner again," she said, "so, I brought you a plate. I thought you might be hungry."

He came around the desk. "That is very kind of you." He took the dish and set it aside. "Thank you."

"Are you feeling better today?" he asked and folded his hands in front of him, attentively.

"I am."

He pulled out a chair for her. "Please! Sit! I am actually glad you stopped in. I was going to look for you later, but I did not want to disturb you if you were resting."

He went back around and sat down across from her. "Oh?"

"Yes. I wanted to apologize to you for last night. I feel as if my questions about Major André may have upset you enough to cause you to become unwell. That certainly was not my intention, and I hope you will forgive me for being so inconsiderate, especially given your delicate condition. I should have been better company."

"Thank you. John's death is still a little raw and sometimes it catches me off guard when I least expect it," she lied.

"At any rate, it was thoughtless of me to bring it up. Please, forgive me."

"There is nothing to forgive." Maggie pointed to his plate. "You should eat before your food gets cold."

"Won't you join me?" he asked.

"Well, I have already eaten, but that may not stop me from picking off of your plate." She laughed.

"I am happy to share!"

"Are your men settling in well?"

"Yes! Everything has gone very smoothly, as I am sure your husband can attest to from his watchfulness," he said with a smirk.

Maggie winced. "My turn to apologize...again."

"Do not give it a second thought. I know you have no control over your husband's actions," he said, picking up the fork Maggie brought in with the plate and taking a bite of his food. "You are right, by the way, Hettie very well may be the best cook in the Colonies."

As he chewed, the smile disappeared from his face. "I am afraid that we will need some supplies from your estate. Things in town are depleted, especially with it still being winter."

Maggie bit the inside of her cheek, grateful that she had the supplies and the main horses hidden to take care of her own. She had no doubt that the army would decimate whatever stores they could find on the estate, which would not be a great deal. "I am sure we can help you out with that."

"I assume you have no issue with us taking things from here?" he asked.

"As long as you leave enough for us to get by...why would I? It is part of our duty to the Crown, is it not?"

The Major wiped his mouth with his napkin. "I am afraid some of your neighbors do not feel the same way."

"Oh?"

He watched her carefully for a moment. "It seems that your loyalty to the Crown puts you in the minority. Williamsburg is full of those whose sympathies lie with the traitors."

Maggie smiled. "You would know more than I. We tend to stay to ourselves out here and only go into town on rare occasions -- usually for dinner and business."

He looked down at his plate, pushing his food around with his fork. "You never visit with your neighbors?

Hear them talking on the street, in passing or at parties, about the war?"

So, that was his game. He was rooting out Patriots.

Maggie chuckled softly, as she rubbed her belly. "I have been confined to bed for most of this pregnancy because of my inability to keep anything down, in addition to the three babies upstairs. I barely have time to get dressed in the morning, much less go into Williamsburg to listen to idle gossip. I prefer to leave this war business to the professionals."

"Does your husband spend much time there?" he asked and attempted to pass off his question as casual conversation.

"Even less than I do," she replied. "I am afraid I am a very needy wife, and I am always demanding his attention, in more ways than one."

He leaned back in his chair, his gaze fixed on her, a sly grin on his face. "We should all be so lucky," he remarked.

Maggie smiled. "I should leave you to your work."

She stood and, as she reached the doorway, he stood and came up behind her. "I do have one more question for you."

Maggie froze.

Shit!

"Yes?"

"May I call you 'Maggie'?" he asked softly.

She turned to see his face. "Of course," she replied and put on a pleasant expression.

He seemed incredibly pleased as he bowed to her. "Until later...Maggie."

She nodded and as she left the room, a cold chill ran down the length of her spine.

Pennington went back to his desk, sat down, and finished his dinner. When he was done, he poured himself a drink from the decanter to his right before taking the well-worn letter out of his coat pocket and reading the pages again as he sipped from the glass. Sighing, he tossed the sheets down on the desk, shaking his head. He had no idea why his brother named Maggie MacGregor a traitor, but he was convinced that Gerald had somehow made a terrible mistake. The letter was dated a little less than two years ago, but he had not had the chance to investigate until recently because of his army duties in England before being sent to South Carolina. He had received no further correspondence from him, but that was not surprising given the fact that he moved around so much and that his post had to be constantly forwarded. He had written to Gerald to let him know that he was now in the Colonies but had received no response in return. The search of the shipping office and its books had shown nothing that was not above board, and he had even gone so far as to break the windows at the business to lure her into town so he could question her, but nothing that came from her lips gave any indication that she was anything but a loyal citizen.

In fact, Maggie had gone above and beyond to be helpful to him and his men. There was also mention of Major John André in the letter, but given the man was dead, it would be rather hard to ask him any questions.

Pennington stroked his chin and looked towards the hall. Her husband, on the other hand, might be a different story altogether. What he really needed to do was locate Gerald and have a long conversation with him about what had led him to make the accusations to begin with. He folded the letter and put it back in his coat and finished off his drink.

Maggie went up to the nursery to play with the babies after her sit-down with Major Pennington, still a little unnerved by the encounter. It was bad enough that he planned to strip the estate of supplies, but he wanted her to rat out her neighbors, as well—a thought that did not sit well on her conscience.

She sat on the floor, watching the children, laughing at their shenanigans. They were getting bigger and more active by the day, still happy and carefree as ever. Kat was doing her best to have a tea party with them, but they were having none of it.

Alastair came into the room and took a seat next to Maggie.

"What have you been up to today?" she asked.

"I had my lessons this morning and I have been inside playing with Kat the rest of the day. My fathers do not want me out of the house without them as long as the soldiers are here."

"That sounds wise," she replied. "Even though I know you hate being cooped up inside."

He grinned. "It's alright. It is easier to keep an eye on everyone when they are all inside."

Maggie looked at him thoughtfully. "You know, you don't have to watch out for everyone so much. You are allowed to go have some fun and enjoy your childhood."

"Nay, Aunt Maggie. I must protect my sister and cousins...and all of you."

"Why do you think that?"

"Because I am meant to. I knew the day I met all of ye that it was what I was born to do."

Maggie ruffled his hair. "I just want you to be a boy and have some fun. You will be an adult soon enough."

He grimaced. "Och! That doesn't sound like fun."

"It's not, so, don't be in such a hurry."

"Alright!" He giggled, and she hugged him.

Gabe came around the corner. "Here you all are."

"Tea party?" asked Kat.

"I thought you would never ask," he replied with great enthusiasm, and took his place on the floor with the rest of them.

Maggie called Kat over. "Why don't you and your brother go to the kitchen and bring up some real tea, and a big chunk of that cake from dinner for your Aunt Maggie?"

She nodded before she and Alastair headed off together to find Hettie.

As soon as they were out of earshot, Maggie turned to Gabe. "The Major is here to locate the town traitors. He was asking about our neighbors."

"The army, on occasion, does send someone like that out, but it is usually for the bigger fish. Who is he after?"

Maggie shook her head. "No idea. I get the impression he was just looking for whomever he could find."

"That would be odd. There are sympathizers in every town. What would bring him here specifically, and what does that have to do with John?"

"That's what I'd like to know." Maggie leaned over to kiss Kendric who had come to sit in front of her. "You need to speak to Quinn about helping me rein in Duncan. They plan to take supplies from the estate, and he is going to be livid."

"You have been planning for this inevitability for years. Even if they take everything in sight, we will be fine, and Duncan knows that."

"I know, but the fact that Major Pennington's men will be taking them will be a whole other matter in Duncan's eyes."

The next day, Maggie was in the drawing room with the babies when she heard a soft knock at the pocket door. It was Major Pennington.

"Am I disturbing you?" he asked.

"Not at all. Come in if you don't mind the children."

"I do not mind at all," he smiled and joined them. "I love them."

He knelt and greeted them as Morgan toddled over to him. "How in the world will you manage with these three and another?"

Maggie bobbed her head around. "We'll make do."

Pennington grinned as Alanna came over to investigate him, alongside her sister.

"You seem to be quite popular with the ladies," teased Maggie.

"As lovely as these two ladies are, I prefer my women a tad bit older," he said and laughed.

He glanced over at Maggie for a long moment. "I have good news for you. The soldiers in town are pulling out tomorrow, and my men and I will be able to relocate back to Williamsburg. I am sure you will be glad to get things back in a normal routine here."

"Thank you for being so considerate," said Maggie.

"I hope we have not been too intolerable," he said, softly.

"Not at all," she replied. "I appreciate that you and your men have conducted yourselves as gentlemen during your stay."

He pulled a folded piece of paper out of his coat and handed it to Maggie. "I hope you feel the same after this," he said sheepishly.

Maggie took it from him and read it.

"It is a list of the provisions we will be needing from here."

Maggie flinched as she looked it over. "It is a great deal," she folded it and handed it back to him, "however, if you are in need, I take no issue with it."

"You are very gracious." He nodded and looked down. "I will make sure your estate is duly compensated."

"I am sure you will."

Morgan reached for her mother and Maggie went to take her, leaning a little too far over and almost tumbling against him. Pennington caught her and placed his arm around her waist to steady her. He slowly removed his arm and hands once she was righted.

"I'm so sorry," she said, apologetically and extremely embarrassed. "I really am off balance as of late."

"Not at all." He smiled. "I am just glad I was here when you needed me."

Pennington allowed his gaze to linger upon her. God, she was beautiful and being heavy with child made her even more radiant and desirable. She must have just bathed, because the scent of lavender clung to her and the smell was intoxicating. There was something about this woman that made him not want to let her go. It was bad enough that she haunted his dreams, his desire for her waking him on several occasions since they first met, but to be able to touch her was another matter altogether. One day...

Two days later, Major Pennington thanked them for their hospitality before he and his men rode off with two wagons loaded down with supplies.

"A small price to pay to have that man out of our house and on his way," fumed Duncan.

Maggie turned to Duncan and fiddled with the collar of his shirt. "Our house is still standing, everyone is safe, and no one here will go hungry. It is a good day all around, so be grateful."

Duncan slipped his arms around her. "Aye, ye are right."

"Of course, I am. I am always right," she said with a wink.

Her husband laughed and kissed her. "We need to move the horses back to the stables," he said.

Maggie looked towards the entrance of the house. "Perhaps we should start enclosing the rest of the property with the fog. Waiting until summer may not be prudent."

"Aye, that is a good idea. We will get to work on it as soon as Pennington's men have cleared out."

"I think I am going to visit John and let him know the coast is clear, while I check on the tribe," she said.

Duncan frowned. "Ye should not be riding in your condition."

"I am fine, and Onyx will be gentle."

"Where is he anyway? I haven't seen him around."

"I had him stay with the other horses while we had guests," replied Maggie. "He was being a good father, looking out for his children."

Duncan groaned. "Speaking of which, we will be having more additions to the stables very soon, courtesy of that wretched beast."

Maggie grimaced. "Well, he IS providing protectors for our children, so do not complain."

"I will send him up to the house as soon as I see him," Duncan grumbled.

"No need," said Maggie. "He knows when I need him."

Sure enough, Onyx came around the corner at that very instant.

"See!" she pointed.

Duncan shook his head, before kissing her. "Enjoy your visit with John, but don't overdo it." He turned to Onyx, who was already saddled for some odd reason, and wagged his finger between his eyes. "Be gentle, beast. Make sure my wife and bairn are not injured."

Onyx extended his neck out and tried to bite his finger.

"Ye have a foul temper, do ye know that?" scolded Duncan.

The big black steed huffed in response and shook his head back and forth.

"Someone should teach ye some manners."

Onyx merely snickered and neighed at him.

Maggie stepped between them. "Are you arguing with my horse again?" she goaded and grinned.

"Aye, and I am afraid I am losing, again."

As they reached the main road, one of the men rode up next to the Major.

"Did you find anything?" asked Pennington.

"No sir," he replied. "We searched and we saw nothing to indicate that those people were sympathetic to the Patriots; however, Mr. MacGregor was more than a little upset that we took their supplies."

"Thank you," said Pennington, lost in his own thoughts, and the man dropped back into formation.

Askuwheteau met Maggie when she rode into the middle of the village and helped her down.

"You will not be able to ride much longer," he pointed out.

"I still have a long way to go," she groaned. "How are Wawetseka and the baby?"

"They are all well and Wawetseka is with child again," he announced.

"Congratulations! I am so happy for you."

"We are truly blessed by Spirit!" His face beamed with pride. "What brings you out?"

"I need to see John."

"Is it safe for him to come out?"

"I think so, much to his chagrin, I'm sure."

Askuwheteau escorted her to John's house, talking about the children as they strolled.

"I will see you soon," he said and bid her farewell.

John appeared at the entryway when she knocked on the side of the house.

"Maggie!" he said, kissing her cheek. "Come in!"

"I come bringing good news. The Major and his men have departed and from what I understand, so has Arnold."

"That is good news indeed," he said as he placed his hand on her back and guided her to a chair. "But you did not have to ride out for that. You could have sent word."

Maggie took off her cloak, then took a seat as he made tea for her. "Actually, I wanted to speak to you alone. Duncan is being a little unreasonable, and I didn't want to upset him any more than he already is."

John looked at her puzzled. "What's the matter?"

She explained to him about Pennington's unusual questions and his purpose for being in town.

John brought her a cup of tea, then sat in the chair next to her.

"Are you sure you don't know him, John? From somewhere?"

"The name, yes; the person, no!" he said and scratched his head, seemingly concerned. "I remember seeing the name mentioned in some of General Clinton's correspondence, but I do not recall the nature of it. If he is intelligence, as Gabe believes, he very well may have been sent from England after my untimely 'demise' to help fill the void."

"He did say he was sent to South Carolina three months ago, but he was specifically interested in OUR relationship; how we met and the last time we saw each other before your 'execution'. I can't for the life of me figure out why."

"That makes no sense. You and I do not know him personally, and he has no reason to be concerned about any relationship we may or may not have had. What does Duncan think?"

Maggie sipped her tea. "I haven't told Duncan any of this."

John looked surprised. "You haven't? Maggie! You don't think he needs to know?"

"John, he cannot control his temper when it comes to the Major. I have never seen him like this. He is convinced this man will destroy our family and he is not thinking clearly."

"Did he give you a reason why he believes that?"

Maggie shook her head. "He only says that he has a feeling."

John eyed her warily. "He is from a magical family. It would not surprise me if his gut feelings were right on target. I don't think you should keep things of great importance from him."

Setting the cup on the table next to her, Maggie leaned back in the chair, while blowing the hair out of her eyes. "I know. I will tell him after he settles down a little bit, I promise."

"You look exhausted," he remarked.

"I am. Between the Major's visit, the babies, and the pregnancy, I am just tired and a little weepy, if I am being completely honest."

John stood and held out his hand. "I have a nice comfortable bed in the next room. Why don't you go take a nap? No one will disturb you."

"I shouldn't," she said

"Yes, you should! You look like you are about to fall over in that chair. Come on."

Maggie thought for a moment before laying her hand in his. "Maybe for just a few minutes."

John led her into the room and spread a deerskin over her after she laid down. She was asleep before he could tuck her in. He kissed her forehead, closed the door, and left her to rest.

Three hours later, Duncan banged on the outside of John's abode. "Have ye seen Maggie? I expected her back sooner."

John waved him in. "She is in my bed."

"My wife is in your bed?"

"Oh yes, and she is completely worn out," he good-naturedly goaded. "She is taking a nap. She was exhausted, so I made her lie down for a while."

"Aye, she has been more tired with this bairn then she was with the babies. I am worried she is doing too much."

John followed Duncan to the bedroom.

Duncan stopped at the doorway and watched her sleep for a bit before moving to her side. He pushed the hair back from her face and she stirred slightly before her eyes fluttered open. "What are you doing here?" she asked.

"You missed dinner and I was worried."

"Dinner? Is it that late already?"

"Aye! Ye must have needed the rest."

Maggie sat up, wiping her eyes. "We should be getting home," she yawned.

"You are welcome to stay," offered John.

"We need to get back to the babies," she replied, and Duncan helped her up.

"We will see you later?" Duncan asked John.

"Of course."

Duncan wrapped her in her cloak before taking her outside and helping her on Gavina. He climbed up behind her in the saddle and wrapped his arms protectively around her. Maggie leaned back against him and dozed the entire way back to the house. When they arrived back, he helped her down and inside.

"Ye need to eat," he whispered in her ear, holding her upright.

"I want to sleep," she whined, with her eyes closed.

"Alright," he conceded, picked her up and carried her to their bed. "Ye can sleep before you eat, my love."

She found Duncan in the drawing room just before supper.

"Hello, my love," he said as she came to sit next to him. "Feeling better?"

"I am," she said, snuggling up to him and laying her head on his chest. "I am also hungry."

Duncan laughed softly. "Well, ye did sleep through dinner. Would ye like a snack before supper?"

"Maybe a little one. A couple of pieces of cake and maybe a slice of pie, and some cheese would be good… or maybe…."

"How about we just have an early supper, just the two of us?" he suggested and kissed the side of her head.

"That sounds heavenly."

When they were getting ready for bed that night, Maggie looked over at Duncan. She sat down on the edge of the bed and watched him. "There are some things I need to tell you, but I need your word that you will remain calm."

He looked at her suspiciously and crossed his arms.

"Do I have your word?" she asked.

He remained stone-faced and silent.

She rubbed her belly. "I AM carrying your child!" She smiled and batted her eyelashes. "You can't be mad at me when I am in this condition, right?"

He sighed. "Ye had just better spit it out."

Maggie told him everything that she knew about Pennington.

Duncan did not say a word until she was finished. "Why didn't ye tell me all of this sooner?" he whispered calmly.

"I'm sorry. I was afraid you might become a little insane if I had told you while he was still under our roof and done something that would have put us in danger." Maggie pulled him to her side. "Please don't be angry with me."

He embraced her tightly. "I am not angry with ye, though I wish ye had enlightened me sooner, but I do understand why ye did not. I am, however, glad that now ye see that this man is nothing but trouble."

"I think we need to proceed with great caution," she said. "This war is almost over, and we just need to keep our heads down while we wait it out."

He kissed her.

"I love you, Duncan."

"I love ye too, Maggie."

14 CHAPTER FOURTEEN

The next few weeks passed rather uneventfully. A messenger, loyal to Washington, paid a visit to the house delivering a package of mail that had been secured so it did not fall into British hands. There was a letter addressed to 'John MacGregor' from Nathaniel that John was incredibly pleased to receive. There was a letter for Gabe from Wyatt, and three letters for Maggie: one from Nathaniel, one from Wyatt, and the last one from Ben.

Wyatt spoke of how much he was enjoying the field hospital, much to his own surprise, and how he wanted to pursue becoming a doctor after the war. He thanked Maggie and Duncan for all their help and let them know how much they meant to him. Nathaniel's letter expressed gratitude for sending medical supplies and Wyatt to him. He was extremely impressed with Wyatt's enthusiasm and spoke of how fond he had become of the boy, promising to keep him close to his side.

Ben's letter spoke mainly of personal things like how much he enjoyed seeing Maggie in Tappan, even if it was for just a little while, and some of the adventures he and Caleb had been off on. He had visited to check on Wyatt a couple of times and he seemed to be adjusting fine. His words were proper, even including regards from General Washington, but the tone of the letter still indicated how much he cared for and missed her. She had just finished reading it when Gabe came in.

"Wyatt seems to have found his place in the world," said Gabe.

Maggie stared into the fire, unmoving until he laid his hand on her shoulder from behind and broke her concentration. She laid her hand over on his.

"I'm sorry, did you say something?"

He came around the other side. "I said that Wyatt is doing well."

"Yes!" she replied, distracted. "Nathaniel is happy with his work."

"Something on your mind?" he asked, sitting down across from her.

She looked up. "I received a letter from Ben."

"And?" he asked.

Maggie handed it to him. "See for yourself."

He read it over, then looked up at her as he folded it back up. "Although he doesn't come out and say it, it is obvious that he still cares a great deal for you."

She lowered her head. "Is it terribly conceited of me to worry that Ben may never get over me and move on with his life? I gave him up so he could live the life he was meant to, but if he cannot move past what we had, he may not live the life history says he will. That would mean that I screwed up the timeline while going out of my way to save it."

Gabe leaned forward. "I thought we were past worrying ourselves about the 'could haves', 'should haves', and 'would haves'."

"He deserves some happiness, Gabe! If anyone in this world does, it is him."

"Mags, who's to say he won't find it? You said he does not take a wife until after the war, so there is still plenty of time. Besides, it's not like there is anything we can do about it."

Maggie looked up. "Or is there?"

"What do you mean?"

Quinn came in. "Here ye are," he said, coming over to kiss Gabe. "I have been looking all over for ye."

"Well, here I am," he said with a sly grin.

"Quinn. Is there by chance a love potion in any of those books downstairs?" asked Maggie.

Quinn raised an eyebrow. "Surely ye do not need one for Duncan."

"Of course not! But is there such a thing?"

"Probably? I have never looked for one, so I do not know for sure, but knowing the Fae, I would be willing to bet there is one somewhere."

"Maggie," said Gabe, "surely you are not considering…"

"Just as an option," she replied. "You are right, there is still plenty of time, but if that time comes and he has not moved on, it is something to think about."

"I don't think meddling like that is a good idea," he cautioned.

"My dear Gabe, all is fair in love and war," she said with a smirk and a wink.

The following week, just as Maggie had started to relax a bit, Major Pennington made an unexpected appearance at the house. She was in a chair by the fireplace when he arrived, the rest of the men out of the house and working on the estate.

"I hope I am not disturbing you," he said as he came in.

"You are not, as long as you will forgive me for not getting up," she replied, her belly now extremely large.

"I trust you are doing well," he said.

"Yes, despite the fact that we may need to widen the doors soon," she complained. "What can I do for you?"

The Major became profoundly serious. "I need to ask you some questions about an incident."

"What incident?"

"It occurred during your time in Oyster Bay, New York, about two years ago."

Maggie attempted to conceal her shock and surprise. "Oyster Bay?"

"Yes. I understand you filed a formal complaint against a captain by the name of Wilson, under the advice of Major John André."

What the hell is this all about?

Maggie nodded. "I did indeed, though my complaint was basically brushed aside by the Provost Marshal at the time."

He looked down. "May I ask what that complaint was about?"

"Forgive me, Major, but I don't understand why you are dredging all of this up after so much time has passed."

"Please, just answer my question," he said firmly.

Maggie thought for a moment. "If you must know, I filed the complaint because when we stepped off my ship, this particular captain insulted me, then had my husband hauled away to jail for defending my honor, just before he destroyed my personal vessel."

The Major stared at her as if he were unsure of her truthfulness. "May I ask exactly what he said to insult you?"

Maggie glanced down at the floor. "Is that really necessary? It is not a very pleasant experience to recall."

"I am afraid it is, and I must insist," he pressed.

Maggie sucked in a deep breath and let it out as she turned her head to the side.

"If you really must know, he accused me of being one of 'Major John André's cock-sucking whores who demanded special attention from the army'."

"And were you?" he asked vehemently, the words spilling from his lips before he could stop himself.

Maggie rose from her chair. "I think you have forgotten your manners, Major Pennington!" she spat irately through clenched teeth. "How dare you come into my home and insult my honor?"

He swallowed hard and composed himself. "You are absolutely correct, ma'am. Please forgive my unacceptable insolence. I didn't mean to take my frustrations out on you."

He lowered his head and waved his hand towards her chair. "Please, sit back down...for the sake of your health and your child."

Maggie glared at him as she continued to stand defiantly. "Major, I think you owe me an explanation for barging in here and bringing up all of this unpleasantness so long after the fact."

"You are quite right," he replied. The Major pulled some papers from his coat. "I just received these in response to an inquiry I made about one Captain Wilson several weeks ago. It is a copy of the report written by Major André alleging that he was a spy for the Continental army. It also states that he was arrested, interrogated, and escaped from the gaol there."

Maggie nodded. "That is exactly how I remember it."

"Only, I know for a fact that it cannot be true," he proclaimed emphatically.

"What makes you so sure?" she demanded, her patience with the man wearing extremely thin.

"Because MY BROTHER would never work for Washington's army."

Maggie felt like she had been punched in the gut. She became lightheaded and her knees buckled as the thought of that bastard made her feel like she was going to vomit. She reached for the chair, to keep herself from falling.

Pennington caught her just before she did and eased her into the chair. He poured a glass of water from a nearby pitcher and handed it to her to drink. "Are you alright?" he asked when he noticed how pale she had become. "Do you need a physician?"

She shook her head and sipped the water, unable to speak for a moment.

"Mistress?"

"Your BROTHER?" she choked out when she could finally form words again.

"My half-brother, and according to this report, he has not been seen since. You were one of the last people to see him."

Maggie let out a deep breath. "Perhaps he has not been heard from because he is with the other army now and is ashamed for being a turn coat," she suggested.

"That's the very strange thing," he said. "I received a letter from him, dated about that time, and in it, he names another as the traitor to the Crown."

"Who might that be?" she asked.

"You!" he divulged and waited for her response.

Fuck!

"Me?" asked Maggie, incredulously.

The Major studied her carefully and was eerily quiet before finally responding. "I came here to investigate you solely based on that information." He knelt on one knee before her chair. "But after getting to know you, personally, I cannot believe for one minute that you are disloyal to the Crown."

Maggie let out the breath she had been holding.

"But I also do not believe what has been said of my brother. I need to find him so I can get to the bottom of this."

Maggie gazed into the fire behind him.

"You were one of the last people to see him. I have no idea why he spoke to you and treated you the way he did, and I wholeheartedly apologize for that behavior, but I need some answers. If you know anything about where he may be, please tell me."

Fuckity fuck!

She turned her gaze to him, propped her elbow on the chair with her hand on her forehead. "I am afraid I have no information that will help you in your search."

He nodded, rose and tucked the paperwork back into his coat. "I see. I will be leaving for New York in a few days to try and locate him. If you can think of anything that may help, please send word to town before then."

"Of course."

He turned to leave and as he reached the door, Maggie spoke. "Major, there is something you should know about your brother."

He stopped and turned back towards her.

"He was not a particularly good man. He did some things that were unfathomable, and those horrendous things will not be found in your report. Perhaps it is best if you leave him be, wherever he is." Maggie brushed away a tear from the corner of her eye.

The Major looked as if the wind had been knocked out of him, especially when he saw the anguish on her face. It was obvious that there was something more that she was not saying, and whatever it was, pained her greatly. He started to ask what she meant, but thought better of it, not wanting to upset her more than he already had in her delicate condition. Instead he simply said, "I will keep that in mind," and left.

Once he was outside, he stopped and looked back at the door. He had not seen his brother in several years, only keeping in contact through letters. He thought he knew Gerald well, but now he was starting to think that he did not know him nearly as well as he believed. Either way, he needed to find him and put these matters to bed once and for all. He would never be able to move forward until he knew the truth.

He put on his hat and departed.

Maggie sat in the chair as she felt an old, familiar feeling creeping back in. She had not had a full-blown panic attack since she and Duncan had married...not until now.

She closed her eyes.

Duncan, I need you. I am afraid and the darkness is closing in.

I am coming, my love.

Duncan bolted into the house; his shirt soaked in sweat because he had ridden so hard to get to her. He found her in the chair, her head down, her arms curled around her belly and folded into herself. He flew to her side and gathered her in his arms. Duncan rocked her, stroked her hair, and whispered softly in her ear; frantically trying anything he could to get her to respond. She did not speak or move for an exceedingly long time.

Gabe, Quinn, and John finally rushed in.

"What happened? Why did ye run off?" demanded Quinn.

Gabe caught sight of Maggie and immediately understood what was happening. "Oh God!" He moved to Maggie's other side, recognizing that she was in the middle of one of her attacks and started to rub her arm. "Quinn, can you make something to calm Maggie's mind that will not harm the baby?"

"Aye. I will be right back."

John came over to join them, gravely concerned. "What happened? What has caused this?"

"I don't know," replied Duncan. "She was like this when I got here, and she has not even acknowledged me."

"You should take her upstairs," said Gabe.

Duncan picked her up and carried her up to their bed, whispering to her the whole time. As soon as she was settled with her shoulders slightly up on the headboard, Quinn appeared with the drink he had mixed, handing it to Duncan.

He touched her face. "Maggie, ye need to drink this."

She did not respond.

He touched his lips to hers, trying to bring her around by whispering, "Maggie, ye need to take this for the sake of the baby."

Her eyes finally moved a bit in response.

Holding the cup up to her mouth, he waited until she was able to take a few sips then set the cup on the table as she started to slightly come around.

"Hettie said Pennington was here earlier," announced Quinn.

Duncan's face became enraged. "I will end that fecking bastard myself!" he vowed through clenched teeth.

"Wilson," whispered Maggie.

"What did you say?" asked Gabe.

"Wilson. He is Wilson's brother."

They all looked around at each other, dumbfounded, patiently waiting for her to continue as she was able.

"He is looking for him. Wilson wrote him and told him that we were traitors after everything that happened in Oyster Bay. WE are the big fish that he came to town to root out."

"That's a problem," said John.

Maggie shook her head and a sob escaped her. "After spending time here, he is convinced that his brother was wrong, but he is determined to locate Wilson. He is leaving for New York to find him."

"Well, he won't," said Gabe.

"And he will come right back here when that trail goes cold," she said quietly.

"We will deal with it," said Duncan, watching Maggie. "We will be ready."

Maggie's eyelids started to get heavy from the tonic and she swayed slightly.

"It's the drink, Maggie," said Quinn. "It will make ye sleepy while it settles your mind. Do not fight it, just let it do its work."

Duncan gently helped her to lay back on the bed and she was unconscious before her head hit the pillow.

Duncan, Quinn, Gabe, and John gathered in the drawing room and Duncan fumed.

"I think it is past time that man and I had a long talk!" he shouted incensed and started towards the door.

"NO! NO! NO! NO!" exclaimed Gabe, and the three men moved to physically block Duncan. "You will only make things worse. We need to tread very carefully."

"That man has upset Maggie and endangered her and our bairn for the last time!" he roared. "He will pay for this!"

"Brother! Stop!" pleaded Quinn. "Calm yourself! This is exactly what Maggie was afraid of!"

"They are right," said John. "Pennington knows nothing except that we were the last ones to see Wilson in Oyster Bay two years ago and that his brother was branded a traitor. He has no idea what transpired in Tappan. We are safe for the moment."

Gabe nodded in agreement. "We know he will not find Wilson to ask him any questions and Maggie said he believes we are loyal to the Crown. We are in no immediate danger. If he had any proof at all, he would have taken us all into custody."

"And if ye march down there starting trouble, he will either throw ye in gaol or hang ye," said Quinn. "Ye have already vexed the man. No need to go poke a rabid dog."

Folding his arms, Gabe stepped towards Duncan. "As much as you do not want to hear this, his fondness for Maggie is the one thing we have going for us right now."

John took a seat and crossed his legs. "He does not know Wilson is dead. He has no leads, nothing to link him back to us, and nowhere to go. The man is buried in my unmarked grave and even he will not look there for him. Pennington is grasping, that is all. Don't give him any reasons to suspect us and he won't."

Quinn laid his hand on his brother's shoulder. "The only concern ye need to worry about is upstairs. Maggie and the bairn will be the ones hurt the most if ye go after him, and she does not need that on her right now."

Duncan let out a deep sigh. "I know," he said softly. "I just want to keep her safe."

"We all do," agreed Gabe. "The best thing we can do for her is to keep things routine and quiet around here. We close-up ranks, keep to ourselves, before the army moves into town in June, and we ride out the rest of this war here where it is safe. That is the plan and we need to stick to it."

Maggie woke up two hours later in Duncan's arms, her mind still a little hazy. She laid there and was trying to focus when Duncan kissed the top of her head.

"Do not try to think, just rest. We are going to be fine."

"What about the Major?" she asked.

"He will do what he will do, and we will deal with it… if and when that time comes. Right now, our only focus is keeping ye and this child well."

"I thought I was over them," she said in a low voice, "the panic attacks, I mean. I have not had one like that since before we were married. Being with you has calmed me unlike anything else."

"I will always be here for ye." He smiled. "There is nowhere else I want to be."

15 CHAPTER FIFTEEN

The next several weeks passed quietly. Pennington was in New York and things settled down nicely. Maggie rested while the family made sure no one bothered her. They raised the fog around the entire perimeter of the estate, leaving only the entrance to the front house open, which they closed when the British arrived. Cornwallis moved his troops into Williamsburg towards the end of June, enacting martial law and overtaking the entire town with his men. They camped in every area that had available space, depleting the small town of supplies, including what little food stores were left.

The men also brought something else...disease in the form of smallpox. The people on the estate were kept safe from the decimation, protected by the gift of the mist, moving on with daily life as if the outside world did not exist.

Maggie neared the end of her pregnancy, now barely being able to move without assistance.

On July 4, 1781, the British army began to pull their troops out of Williamsburg.

Maggie was sitting on the sofa trying to relax that evening. She had started to feel some slight contractions but did not want to tell anyone until she knew for sure that it was time. She was reading a book when John came into the drawing room.

"There you are," he said, coming over and kissing her on the cheek, then rubbing her stomach. "How are you feeling?"

Maggie groaned and laid her book on the table. "Massive. I am quite sure I have seen smaller whales."

John came around and sat down next to her, pulling her feet up in his lap to rub them.

"Oh! I love you so much right now." She sighed loudly.

"How much longer do you think it will be?" he asked.

"I'm not sure," she replied. "But I don't think it will be too much longer." She leaned back against the arm of the sofa, closing her eyes. "How are the crops coming in for the tribe?"

"Wonderfully!" answered John. "Your touch has made all the difference. We have an abundance and Mingan is pleased."

"Good!"

John glanced over at her. "I was...um...hoping to catch you alone. There is something I wanted to talk to you about."

"Oh?" She opened her eyes and raised her head.

"I have been giving it some thought, and I think I want to take you up on your offer...to grant me the ability to father children."

Maggie was pleasantly surprised. "Really?"

He nodded. "I see you and Duncan with your children, and Gabe and Quinn with theirs...I think maybe it might be nice. Besides, Mingan has been hinting around about how much the tribe needs new blood and how I should do my part. We all know the MacGregor line needs to carry on any way."

"Is there someone special?"

John chuckled. "All women are special, Maggie, though not as special as you," he said and winked.

She smacked at his shoulder. "You know what I mean."

He shrugged. "You never know."

"I am happy to do it, but you need to understand, it is very potent and not to be trifled with. You will need to be incredibly careful, or you may have every woman in the village with child."

"I will remember that," he said.

"Okay," she said and straightened up. "Come over here and kneel down so I can actually reach you to lay hands on you."

He did as Maggie instructed and she placed both hands on his face, smiling. She willed the power within her, then leaned forward and planted a kiss on his forehead, sending the energy throughout his body. She felt the familiar jolt move inside her that let her know that it worked.

"You are all set," she said.

"That's all?"

Maggie nodded. "That's it. With great power comes great responsibility, so be careful where you put THAT," she teased and pointed downward.

He laughed heartily and leaned forward to kiss her. "Thank you, I will."

"My pleasure," she said, patting his face.

They heard a voice from behind them. "Kissing my wife again?"

"Every chance I get," replied John with a devilish smirk. "Someone has to fill in for you when you are not around, and I am happy to take the position."

"As long as that is the only position ye are taking," quipped Duncan, pointing at him.

Duncan came up behind the sofa, placed his hands on Maggie's shoulders, and massaged them tenderly as he kissed the top of her head. "How are ye, my love?"

"Look at me. How do you think I am?"

"It won't be much longer," he said, leaning over to rub her belly.

"Easy for you to say," she said sarcastically.

Finn stood at the edge of the yard. He shook his head, feeling lower than a snake's belly. He did not want to do this. He knew Maggie might never forgive him, but she needed the incentive to become what she was meant to be to save the world for her future and everyone else's.

"I'm sorry, Maggie," he said aloud. "There is no other way. I hope someday ye will understand." With the swoosh of his hand, he lowered the fog as the soldiers neared the road that led to the house. He frowned and was gone.

They heard the front door slam.

"Duncan!" yelled Quinn.

"In here," he called.

Quinn and Gabe rushed in, both looking gravely concerned.

"We have a problem!" Quinn's voice may have tremored.

"What's wrong?" Maggie attempted to turn around to see them.

"The fog line along the front of the house is rapidly dissipating," replied Gabe, out of breath.

"What?" Duncan moved to the window to see for himself.

"How is that possible?" demanded Maggie.

"I don't know," answered Quinn. "There is no reason for it, but it is happening."

Duncan turned back to look at them. "We need to raise it again and NOW! We are vulnerable as long as that opening is there."

Gabe moved to the other window.

"Correction," said Maggie, trying to get up. "I need to raise it so it will be stronger."

"Nay!" Duncan came back to her side. "The three of us can do it. Ye need to stay put."

"Damn it!" cursed Gabe. "I am afraid it is too late for that."

Quinn joined him, adding a few dirty sentiments of his own in Gaelic.

"What is it?" asked Duncan.

"Soldiers headed down the entrance!"

"FUCK!" said Maggie. "John and Quinn! You two slip out the back to the tribe. See if the fog is still around the village and if it is not, get it back up. Make sure they are safe. Duncan, go to the schoolhouse and ring the bell to let everyone know we have company while you strengthen the fog."

"I will stay with Maggie," said Gabe.

They quickly departed as someone knocked loudly on the door. Hettie appeared from the kitchen and made sure they were out of the house before she answered it. Maggie and Gabe exchanged worried looks while Hettie showed Major Pennington into the drawing room.

"Major Pennington! You have returned," she said.

"Hello, Mistress MacGregor, Colonel Asheton."

"Major!"

"Yes, I arrived back from New York yesterday."

The Major turned towards Gabe. "I need a word with Mistress MacGregor in private, if you please."

"I do not think that is a good idea, Major," he replied protectively. "Your last visit upset her a great deal, and as you can see, she is in no condition for that again."

The Major looked down, a look of shame on his face. "I cannot tell you how much I regret that, but you have my word that I will not allow it to happen again."

"It's alright, Gabe," said Maggie.

Gabe stood firm until Maggie tipped her head towards the door to indicate he should go.

He reluctantly came over to the sofa and whispered in her ear. "I will be right outside if you need me."

"I expect you to honor your promise," warned Gabe as he walked past him.

The Major came over to stand in front of Maggie. "I meant what I said. I have given our last meeting a great deal of thought and I want to sincerely apologize for it. I let my emotions about my brother get the better of me and I took it out on you. Please, forgive me."

Maggie sighed.

"Did you find what you were looking for in New York?" she asked, offering him the chair across from her, which he humbly accepted.

"I spoke with several of the other men who were involved with my brother's arrest and they all corroborated everything in Major André's report," he replied, troubled.

"I'm sorry, Major," she said sincerely. "It must have been very difficult for you to find out such disturbing information about him."

He chewed on his bottom lip as he watched her. "The most troubling part was that I found out that you were kidnapped in Oyster Bay and that the evidence pointed back to my brother being the one behind it. You failed to mention that when we last spoke."

Maggie propped her elbow on the arm of the sofa and rubbed her temples. "I told you that he was not a very good man," she whispered.

He sat quiet as he looked down. Clearing his throat, he said, "I am afraid I need to inconvenience you once more. Every place in Williamsburg is occupied until the army completes the current troop movements. My men and I will need to stay here until then."

"I see," said Maggie.

"I will make sure you are not disturbed."

"Thank you, Major," she said. "I will have Hettie make up the bedroom for you and the library is yours to use as before, but I suggest you avoid my husband for your own sake."

"Understood and thank you," he said, standing and starting for the door.

Maggie breathed a sigh of relief, convinced they were safe....

... until he stopped.

"I do have one more question," he called back to her.

"Yes?"

"Did you get a chance to say 'goodbye' to Major André when you were in Tappan for his execution?"

Maggie froze as her body went numb.

He knew they were in Tappan...and something told her he knew his brother had been there at the same time.

"No, unfortunately, I did not get the chance," she replied.

"It is a shame when you are unable to say a final 'goodbye' to someone you love. It is a guilt that you carry around with you for the rest of your life." He left the room.

Gabe, who had been pacing outside, came back in to join her on the sofa. "Well?"

"We are so completely fucked!"

16 CHAPTER SIXTEEN

Maggie explained to Gabe what happened.

"Listen to me," she said. "Have Cora take Kat and Alastair back to her house and have her and David keep them there until further notice. This evening, I want the babies taken to John at the tribe. I want him to keep them safe until these soldiers are gone. The women of the village will help him care for them. I need all the children safe, no matter what happens to the rest of us."

Gabe put his arm around her shoulders as she leaned her head over onto him.

"Find Duncan and the others. Tell him what is going on. Make sure Duncan understands that he needs to control his temper because losing it would be the worst possible thing right now."

"I shouldn't leave you here alone," he whispered.

"Please Gabe. I need you to do this... FOR ME."

Gabe blew out a deep breath, took her hand and kissed it before going to find Duncan, leaving Maggie sitting alone trying to figure out the next move.

She tried to gather her thoughts. He knew. He may not know precisely what happened to his brother, but he knew something had, and that they were involved. Maybe it was best to head things off at the pass.

As soon as Maggie managed to get herself off the sofa, another contraction hit her; still nothing terribly strong, but a contraction, nonetheless. She made her way to the library where the Major was. She tapped on the doorframe.

"Major?" she asked.

"Come in."

He stood and came to her aid, taking her arm. "You should not be up and moving around." He helped her to sit, then leaned back against the desk, watching her.

"Major…" she said adjusting herself in the chair. "You asked me why I did not tell you about your brother and I feel as if I owe you an explanation."

He folded his arms, curious, waiting for her to continue.

"I did not want to tarnish the image of your brother that you carry."

"I appreciate your concern, but you do not need to protect me. I would prefer to have the truth."

"Are you certain? It is not pretty."

He looked taken aback. "I am."

Maggie closed her eyes and untied her blouse to expose herself just above her breast.

He watched her closely, uncertain of what she was doing... until he noticed the scar, a few inches long across her chest.

Maggie pointed to it. "Your brother did this to me."

"He what?" he asked, the blood draining from his face.

"He did it after he broke into the house we were staying at and tied me up. He was waiting for Duncan to return so he could...rape me in front of him, wanting him to see it, before killing us both, but..." Maggie stopped as she started to become emotional.

The Major pulled up a chair so he could sit directly across from her, absorbed in every detail.

"He decided that he needed a little appetizer first. He slashed me open...so he could...taste my blood. He said that he had developed an appetite for the flavor of it."

The Major's eyes widened, and he covered his mouth with his hand in utter disbelief. "I don't understand," he choked out.

Maggie wiped a tear away from her eye. "He confessed to me that while in Oyster Bay, he had been kidnapping women that no one would miss, holding them hostage for days, raping, and killing them. It was during that time that he discovered how different each person's blood...tasted. He blamed us for messing up his fun when he was arrested and was determined to make me his next victim."

The Major shook his head. "You're lying! No one is that depraved, least of all a member of my family."

"I'm not," she whispered. "I wish I was." She took his hand, pulled it up to her breast and dragged his fingers over the still raised scar so he could feel it for himself. "Look at my face. Am I making this up?"

He took a good, hard look at her, seeing the anguish on her face and the truth in her eyes. He lightly touched the scar, examining it closer.

"Oh my God!" he whispered. "What else did he do to you?" he asked, unsure if he truly wanted to know.

"Duncan rescued me before he could do anything more. Your brother was a monster, and he would have taken great pleasure in raping and murdering me."

He leaned forward in his chair, his head in his hands.

Maggie tied her blouse and adjusted it before pushing herself up from the chair. "I am sorry to have to be the one to tell you all of this, but you needed to know."

She squeezed his shoulder gently as she walked past him out of the room, leaving him to process all he had just learned.

The Major did not join them for supper that night. After they ate, Maggie gathered the babies and their things, kissed each of them and had Duncan, Gabe, and Quinn take them to John.

"I am not leaving you alone with that man," said Duncan.

"I am nine months pregnant. He will not harm me, but I need the babies safe for my own peace of mind."

He shook his head.

Maggie took his face in her hands. "If you love me, you will do as I ask."

"That is not fair, Maggie."

Maggie kissed him. "Happy wife, happy life. You will be back in no time." She hugged him and whispered in his ear. "Besides, I think it is best if they do not hear their mother screaming obscenities while in labor."

He looked at her bewildered.

She smiled and rubbed her belly. "I am very close."

"You should be in bed!" he demanded.

"After our children are safely with John and not one minute before!" she said, determined.

He reluctantly agreed and kissed her before they all slipped out of the house. "I will be back shortly. I love ye, Maggie."

"And I love you. Now go make sure our babies are out of harm's way."

After they had been gone a good while, Maggie went to the library. The door was closed, so she knocked.

"What!" was the gruff response.

Maggie pushed opened the door. "I just wanted to check on you, but I will leave you alone."

He set down the glass in his hand on the desk where he was leaned back in the chair. He had obviously had a great deal to drink, the smell of whisky hitting her as soon as she stepped inside.

"Please, forgive me and come in," he said, the anger gone from his voice. "It has been a difficult day to say the least."

She moved to stand next to the desk and planted her hands flat on it.

"Are you alright?" she asked, compassionately.

"Pretty far from it," he replied. "I just found out that my brother is an abomination. I do not know what happened to him to turn him into such a thing."

"I'm sorry," she offered.

He slowly turned his gaze to her before he laid his hand on top of hers.

"I am the one who is sorry for what he did to you. You, of all people, did not deserve to be subjected to the wrath of a madman."

"I was the lucky one," she stated. "I survived."

Maggie leaned in harder on the desk as a stronger contraction caught her and she groaned in pain.

He immediately stood. "What is it? What is wrong? Is it the baby?"

"Nothing," she said. "I just need to sit for a bit."

He pulled his chair around for her and helped her into it then knelt in front of her. "What can I do? Can I get you anything?"

"No, thank you. I am fine."

He raised his hand to gently tuck a piece of loose hair behind her ear.

"You are such a beautiful woman," he said, touching her chin. There was no doubt that he was very drunk. "I wish I had been the one to be there to protect you. I SHOULD have been the one there to protect you. I never would have let him touch you, much less lay a blade to your breast to leave such a terrible mark on your perfect skin. If you were mine, I would never let you out of my sight."

He swallowed hard as he used his finger to trace the outline of her lips before he leaned over and lightly pressed his to hers.

Maggie was stunned by the unexpected action. She pushed back against him. "Major, I think you have had entirely too much to drink and you forget yourself. I am a happily married woman, and I will never betray my husband."

Pennington looked down and smiled. "Of course, you won't. You are a good and faithful woman. You are the perfect wife for...someone like me."

"I think I should leave." Maggie went to get up, but he held his hands on both arms of the chair and prevented her from moving.

Another contraction hit her, this time a great deal stronger. She leaned forward and grunted in pain. He slipped his arm around her waist and pulled her closer to him so that her head was on his chest while the pain held her in its grasp.

"Shhhh!" he whispered. "I've got you. I am here for you, and I will never leave you."

Maggie tried to free herself, but he held firm. "Let go of me!" She began to panic when it dawned on her that she was alone and in labor with a man who had lost his mind. She started to struggle and cry; screaming out as another contraction hit. They were suddenly coming a great deal faster and much stronger.

"It's alright," he said. "If Gerald comes back, I will keep you and your children safe, as if they are my own blood. You never have to fear my brother or anyone else ever again."

"You are crazy if you think I will ever leave my husband for you!"

"She never has to worry about your brother coming back for her," spat Duncan, seething, from the door. "I made sure of it when I snapped his neck in half, just like I am about to do to yours."

Duncan jerked the man back and hurled him against the wall, knocking the books on the shelves to the floor. Pennington floundered on his back and was trying to get his bearings when Duncan fell upon him. He picked him up by the collar and slammed him repeatedly against the floor.

"How dare ye put your hands on my wife, ye filthy bastard? Ye are no better than that fecking brother of yours." Duncan pounded him in the face with his fist; his nose shattered with an audible crack and it sent blood flying in every direction. He was about to do it again when Maggie screamed.

"Duncan! I need you!" He dropped the man in disgust and went to her side.

"The baby is coming!" she bawled.

He gathered her up in his arms and carried her upstairs, calling to Hettie. When he laid her down, she cried out again. He helped her get everything off but her shift.

Hettie appeared. "I sent for the midwife," she said before going to gather supplies.

Maggie grabbed Duncan's shirt. "There's no time! The baby is coming NOW!"

He lifted her gown to see that the baby was indeed crowning. "Oh Christ, ye are right! There is no time at all!" Duncan heard Quinn calling from downstairs. "The bedroom! Now!" he yelled.

Quinn and Gabe rushed in. "What is it?"

"The baby is coming, and the midwife is not going to make it in time."

Quinn took over as Duncan moved to hold onto Maggie. When the next wave hit, Quinn told her to push. Duncan held onto her as she screamed out...and the next MacGregor child was born into the world.

"It's a boy!" announced Quinn.

Maggie and Duncan looked at each other, tears streaming down both their faces as Duncan craned to get a better look.

He kissed her. "You have given me another son, my love!"

Hettie came around the corner with hot water and towels. "Lord have mercy! That was fast!" she said and took the baby to clean him up. When she was done, she handed the tiny newborn to his parents. As they made over him, Gabe spoke up.

"Umm...you might want to hand me the baby."

"Why?" asked Maggie, and she answered her own question by curling up with another contraction.

Duncan gave the baby to Gabe before turning back to Maggie. "Another one?" he asked.

Quinn nodded, a huge grin on his face. "Ye have to outdo everyone, don't ye brother?"

Maggie leaned in with her head down and groaned. Duncan held her tightly, while whispering in her ear.

Gabe stood on her other side, cradling and rocking the newest addition in his arms as he looked on.

A few minutes later, Maggie and Gabe welcomed another baby boy.

"We have two more sons," said Duncan excitedly and completely overjoyed.

The midwife finally came rushing in. "What did I miss?"

"Two boys," replied Quinn. "And I will happily turn the reins over to ye. I have seen far more of my sister-in-law than I ever wanted or needed to."

The midwife checked Maggie over. "That's all...this time!" She grinned.

"We officially need a bigger house," said Duncan.

Maggie leaned back, exhausted.

Duncan kissed her. "Rest, my love. Ye have earned it."

She shook her head. "We have a whole situation downstairs to deal with."

"What situation?" asked Quinn, a troubled look on his face.

Shouting from the first level of the house interrupted their newfound bliss. They could hear men rushing up the staircase. Maggie looked to Duncan fearfully as the door to the bedroom was flung open.

"Take all the men into custody!" ordered the Major as several men rushed in. He held up a pistol to Duncan.

"This one will be charged with the murder of Captain Gerald Wilson. He confessed it to me," he said, wiping the still fresh blood from his nose.

"No!" screamed Maggie. "You cannot take them!"

"How dare you come into our bedroom while I am giving birth to do something as despicable as this?"

Gabe handed the baby to Hettie and the midwife took the other.

The men rushed around to take Duncan, who shoved two of them backwards. The Major moved the gun barrel to Maggie's heart and watched Duncan.

"Go quietly or your wife pays the price."

Duncan stopped and allowed them to take him, a murderous look on his face. "I will go, but I will tell my wife 'goodbye'."

The Major nodded and the men lessened their grip.

Duncan moved to Maggie's side and took her face in his hands lovingly. "I love ye so much and I always will no matter what happens here. Ye carry half of my soul, and I will always find my way back to ye, whether it be in this world or the next. Nothing will keep us apart, not even something as immeasurable as death."

He tenderly kissed her, and Maggie broke down sobbing, trembling while his lips were still upon hers.

"I cannot live without you, Duncan," she bawled. "I love you too much," she whispered, tracing his face and committing every precious detail to memory.

"Aye, ye can," he said tearfully. "Ye will raise our children well and never let them forget how much I love them."

He kissed her passionately one last time before the soldiers dragged him out of the room.

The Major stopped him, leaned in, and whispered. "I will take good care of her and your children will never grieve you because they won't even remember you. I will be the only father they will ever know."

Duncan spit in his face before he was taken away, along with Gabe and Quinn.

As soon as they were gone, the Major went to Maggie and sat on the edge of the bed.

Maggie stared straight ahead, consumed with rage, wishing she had her sword close enough to run him through.

He touched her face and she jerked away. "You are still emotional from the birth. I understand. You will come around soon enough."

He looked over at the babies and smiled. "Boys or girls?"

"Two boys," muttered a terrified Hettie, cradling the baby tighter to her and eyeing him warily.

He stood and walked around to see them. "I have two new boys to raise," he said proudly. "That is good news indeed."

"YOU have nothing!" corrected Maggie.

He turned. "Of course, I do. The children will need a father as soon as your current husband is dead, which will be very shortly. A widow with five children needs a man to take care of her." He moved back to the bedside. "You and I will raise them well together and I will be a good husband to you...in each and every way." He stroked her arm. "And if I am truly fortunate, we will be blessed with a child of our own making. Now, get some rest because as soon as you are fully healed, I will take you as my wife. I want to wait until you are completely well so our wedding night will be something special."

He grabbed her hand and kissed it before leaving the room. "I will be counting the days."

As soon as he was gone, Maggie motioned for the babies. She closed her eyes as tears streaked her face, willed Onyx to the back door and sent him a message.

Get my babies to John and protect my children at all costs. Let nothing in this world stop you. Destroy anyone who gets in your way!

Maggie took the first baby from Hettie, smiling as she touched his little face.

"Maggie, that man!" said Hettie.

"That man is a rabid dog and I will see him put down if it kills me."

Maggie took the other baby in her other arm. "Your father and I love you both so much," she said and kissed them. "Your Uncle John will keep you safe."

She handed them back to Hettie and the midwife. "Onyx is out back. I want both of you to take my boys to the Indian village-to John, where the other babies are. Stay there with them and do not return to the house. There will be women there who can serve as wet nurses." Maggie wiped away her tears. "Tell John that if we do not return, that I am entrusting the care of my precious children to him."

"Maggie…" started Hettie.

"Go!" she said. "I need our children safe above all else."

Maggie sat up on the edge of the bed and hugged Hettie tightly before they left. She staggered over to the window and watched them until they were out of sight to make sure they got away safely. She managed to get herself over to the small desk in the corner and collapsed in the chair. Though weak from the labor and loss of blood, she opened the drawer and pulled out paper, a quill, and a bottle of ink. She wrote a letter to David Percy explaining her wishes in the event of her and Duncan's death. When she was done, she addressed it, sealed it with her wax seal and left it on the desk. She leaned her head down against the table and sobbed until she passed out. Her last thought before everything went black was to Duncan.

I love you so much!

She received no response.

The light from the morning sun woke her. She was sore, and still extremely weak; the chair and the floor beneath where she sat from the night before were covered in her blood. She stumbled to the bedroom door and cracked it open. The house was completely and eerily silent. Maggie slowly descended the staircase, gripping tightly to the rail to keep from falling. waves of dizziness impeding her progress.

Resting on the bottom step, she heard a loud thump on the front porch. She forced herself up, and as she opened the door, she nearly collapsed at the horrific sight before her.

17 CHAPTER SEVENTEEN

She looked down in horror and disbelief at the crumpled and lifeless body of her cherished lover on the steps of their home. She was still shaky and weak and the blood that streaked her inner thighs formed a puddle where she stood; her gown still wet from where she gave birth just a few short hours before. She took slow, deliberate steps until she reached him, fell upon her knees and took his precious face in her hands. His eyes were fixed, locked open, as if he were about to say something to her, to tell her that he loved and adored her as he had done so many times before since they had become one, but he could not; Duncan was gone.

His battered and bruised physical form remained, but his spirit, his life force, and that wonderous inner light, the thing that made him who he was, had been cruelly and needlessly extinguished. The love of her life, the father of her children, her reason for being, was no longer of this world, and nothing in this fucked up world mattered to her anymore. She traced the angle of his jaw and searched his sweet, handsome face, trying desperately to will the life back into his eyes, but he remained still. Her heart shattered, and her tears fell in a deluge, like a torrential downpour from a terrible storm on a hot summer afternoon. She gently pulled his head onto her lap, rocking him as she softly whispered tender affirmations of love and stroked his face, her own will to live rapidly leaving her.

"I am coming with you, my love!" She wept and kissed the cold, blue lips that refused to acknowledge her as they had never done before. "I will not live this life without you, not now, and not ever." She slid her hand down the length of his body and reached for the small dagger that she knew he always kept concealed in his boot. Maggie gripped it tightly, pulled it to her breast and pointed it upward to her own throat, ready to slash her own jugular vein, just to be with him; ready to join him in the next world, whether it be Heaven or Hell—it did not matter, as long as they were together...it was a fate she had already willingly surrendered to without giving it a second thought...

...until that British, son of a bitch, opened his mouth.

He rushed to her side when he realized what she intended to do, caught her by the wrist and peeled her fingers away one by one from the hilt. Once he had taken the weapon away from her, he looked down at it and shook his head disapprovingly. "I am afraid I cannot let you do that, my dear. The children need their mother and a dead bride is of no use to me." He tossed the blade into the yard, went back down the steps to his horse and shouted, "Kill the men, take the supplies, burn the house and do what you will with the slaves. That Scottish bastard is dead, and there is no one here left to stop us."

Infuriated by his words and actions, and even more enraged that he had kept her from joining her love, Maggie closed her eyes and slowly lifted her chin. The utter devastation and rage washed over her like a tidal wave, the contempt came forward, and seized control of her mind and body. She rose from her knees and clenched her fists tightly, as her face contorted in unadulterated hatred aimed at the one man standing before her that had taken away her entire world.

The gold in her eyes flashed red and she spat, "I wouldn't be so sure about that!"

The Major's soldiers started to make their way towards the tenant homes in the direction behind the house as he got on his horse. Gabe and Quinn laid on their sides on the ground, not far from her, both with their hands tied behind their backs. Quinn was unconscious, his face bloody and bruised, and Gabe was not in much better shape; both having taken tremendous beatings.

Maggie held her right arm straight out beside her, and a thick, dark fog rolled up from the palm of her hand. She aimed it in a straight line, forming a wall in a line from her body across, to directly in front of the soldiers. It was so thick; they could not see their own hands in front of them. The frightened horses reared up, throwing many of the soldiers to the ground, sensing the danger that surrounded them, and running off, leaving their riders alone to fend for themselves. Maggie repeated the same with her left arm, a solid line formed, now preventing any outsiders from reaching the beloved people on her estate. Maggie turned her head to glare at Major Pennington who watched her carefully.

"You bastard! You murdered my husband, the love of my life, and you took away my only reason for living!" she cried out, furious, seething. "And now you will pay the price."

Pennington dismounted, confused by what he had just witnessed, but more upset by the words from her mouth, as he moved to stand in front of the steps.

"He was not the right man for you. I know you can't see it now, but in time you will come to understand that he could not possibly have loved you as much as I do." He looked over at Duncan's body. "He is gone and there is no one to stand between us now."

"You know nothing of our love, and you know nothing about me!" she hissed.

He took a step up towards her and held out his hands. "I know I will take care of you, protect you and your children, and soon, you will forget all about him. We will be happy together, you will see."

Maggie could not believe what she was hearing. This fucking bastard that just took away her beloved Duncan, expected her to actually be with him after what he just did. He was insane. How could he possibly think that she would be with him after he destroyed her reason for being? In his own way, he was as psychotic as his brother was.

He slowly moved to the step just before the one she stood on and reached for her. She moved sideways away from him and glared down at his hands as if they were poison, diseased, an abomination to behold.

"I am afraid that is not possible," she said, her eyes still cast downward.

"Why not?" he asked. "I don't understand. I will treat you well and we will have a good life together."

"That is not possible, she said, lifting her eyes to look into his. "Because today...you die."

Maggie lifted her hands as the fog, once again, started to roll from her palms. Only this time, she directed it at him, straight into his eyes, mouth, and nose. As he started to cough, Maggie hastened the flow, and willed it with every part of her being, making it thicker and stronger. In her mind, she envisioned it going into his lungs, his bloodstream, and every inch of every cell inside his body.

His coughing worsened and he collapsed backwards off the steps to the ground in front of her, still holding out his arms to her as his face turned red, then blue and started to swell. He writhed in agony, gasping for a breath of air that would never come. He struggled as his body convulsed, using his eyes to plead for mercy while clutching his hands to his throat. It was not long before the blood poured from each orifice of his body and his organs gave up. He finally went still, his eyes fixed, staring towards the heavens...gone from this world.

Maggie heard the men to her side. She turned, her agony still very much raw and nowhere near being sated. When they saw the bloodlust and hatred in her eyes, they started to scramble away in fear, but she would not let them get away so easily. She raised her hand, and forced the fog into each one of them, the same way she had Pennington until they all lay dead as well...all save one.

One soldier was left, a young man, no older than twenty, who looked terrified. He began to alternately pray and beg for his life. "I....I... am... sorry," he stuttered, trying to get off the ground. "I didn't have any part in what they did to that man. I told them it was wrong. Please, don't kill me."

Maggie moved to stand over him. "Leave this place and tell everyone it is cursed. Anyone who steps foot on it will die a horrendous death. Spread the word and repeat nothing of what you have seen here today—or I will find you and grant you the same painful death as the others."

"I won't!" the boy sobbed before he scrambled off and was out of sight before Maggie reached Duncan.

She collapsed beside him, touching all that was left of him as the pain slammed into her again. An agonizing wail escaped her and the very ground beneath them shook.

"He can be saved," a voice spoke softly from behind her.

Maggie turned, her face red, swollen, her body wracked with misery, to see Finn standing before her.

"Bring him back to me," she begged, pitifully.

He laid his hand on her shoulder. "I do not have the power to do that," he knelt down beside her and placed his hand on her back, "but Danu does. Say 'yes', accept my gift, let me make you a full goddess and ye can raise your husband from the dead."

"I can?"

He nodded. "The power to bring back the dead will be yours. All you have to do is say 'yes'."

Maggie took Duncan's face in both her hands, tears streaming down her own. "I cannot be without you my love, no matter what price I have to pay." She did not have to think, her emotions now the only thing that ruled her actions.

"YES!" she whispered. "YES! A million times, YES! Just give him back to me! I do not care what the price. I need him more than the breath I breathe!"

Finn looked down and smiled. "So, it shall be," he said.

He whispered a few words in a long-forgotten language and touched her shoulder. A bright white light entered her body from his hand, filling in every part of her and she fell forward, the power surging throughout every cell of her being. She lay face down, panting as it took over, spreading into every inch of her.

She heard Finn's voice. "Rise up, Maggie! Breathe life into your husband and bring him back from the dead so ye may be together."

Maggie raised her head and leaned over Duncan. She touched his face, tenderly. "I will not live an eternity without you, my love. Come back to me and take your place by my side," she said and kissed him.

The same bright white light left her mouth and flowed into his. His body lurched as the air filled his lungs and his heart began to beat once more. Her lips were still on his, when she felt his hand on the back of her head and his tongue came to life in her mouth, kissing her as passionately as he ever had.

"Maggie!" he groaned.

Tears of joy and relief streaked down her face. "You are alive!" She cried and laughed at the same time.

"Aye, it seems I am," he whispered, blinking his eyes, his mind trying to catch up with the rest of him.

Maggie kissed him again before he sat up. She ran her hand over his wounds, but they had all miraculously healed. She pulled him tightly to her.

"All is as it should be," whispered Finn, from behind her before he disappeared into the fog.

Duncan pushed up on his elbows and slowly looked around at Pennington and the other dead men on the lawn.

"What happened?" he asked.

"They killed you, and they were going to destroy our home. I disposed of them," she said as she looked at Pennington's body in disgust.

He looked at her, alarmed. "You killed them? And I was dead?"

Maggie nodded.

"How did you bring me back, Maggie?"

She closed her eyes and a sudden realization hit him. "Ye said 'yes' to Finn?" he asked, horrified. "Maggie! What did ye do?"

Maggie opened her eyes and cupped his face. "I will not live without you. It was this or kill myself to join you, which I had every intention of doing."

Duncan stood and took her into his arms. "Where are the others?" he asked, taking a better look around. He caught sight of Quinn and Gabe, lying on the ground barely a stone's throw away.

He pulled back, took her hand and picked up his dirk from where it lay, and they went to check on the others.

"Quinn?" he called, cutting his brother free and rolling him over onto his back, but he did not respond. Duncan patted his face frantically. "Quinn!"

"He's hurt badly," groaned Gabe, blood dripping from his own face.

Maggie took the knife from Duncan, and freed Gabe.

Gabe crawled over to Quinn and checked for a pulse. It was there, but very faint.

"We need Kat," he croaked.

They heard someone clear their throat from behind them. Maggie and Duncan turned to see Finn standing there with Kat and Alastair.

"I thought ye might need some assistance," he said.

"Kat, come here," said Maggie and she bent down. "Your father needs healing."

Kat ran to Quinn and laid her hand on his chest; a white light came out of her palm and moved to his wounds and they slowly disappeared.

His eyes flew open and he gasped for breath as he rolled to the side coughing.

As he lay panting, Kat touched his face with her little hands and smiled. "All better, Father."

"Aye, I am," he said, and he hugged her. "Thank ye, sweetheart. Now, help your other father."

Kat turned and repeated her actions on Gabe's chest.

Gabe sat up slowly, pulled her to him and kissed her. "Yes! Thank you, princess."

She lay her hands on each side of his head and sent her healing powers into his facial wounds. "You are all better too!" She grinned and kissed his nose.

"Yes, I am!" he said and laughed.

He turned her loose and she happily skipped over to Alastair.

Quinn looked over at Duncan, and hugged him, astounded.

"How are ye alive, brother?" He choked up. "We watched them kill ye." Quinn touched his face. "Ye were gone from this world."

Duncan looked back at Maggie. "The goddess Danu brought me back."

"Goddess?" asked Gabe. "As in, full goddess?"

Maggie nodded and wiped her nose with the back of her hand. "I could not let him go. God help me, I couldn't."

Duncan pulled her to him tightly.

They all sat there and stared at each other, too stunned to speak.

Gabe looked around. "We need to get rid of these bodies. Someone will be looking for them."

"Allow me," said Finn, and he stepped forward. He waved his hand as all the remains disappeared.

They observed the now-empty lawn, to see that nothing indicated that an army encampment had ever been there.

"The children!" exclaimed Duncan, suddenly.

"I sent them to John so they would be safe. We should go get them."

Duncan took a good look at her, still covered in blood. "You should be in bed," he said suddenly, worried. "You just gave birth."

"I feel fine now," she said, as if surprised herself.

"Becoming a goddess healed ye," explained Finn. "Ye will never be weak or sick again."

"Maybe you should clean up a bit, so you don't terrify your own children," pointed out Gabe.

She looked down at all the blood and remembered she was still in her shift. "Yeah, that might be a good idea." She and Duncan turned towards the house.

Gabe and Quinn joined their children, hugging them tightly while Finn slipped away without notice.

An hour later, Maggie and Duncan arrived at John's house in the village. John was furiously pacing the floor when they came in.

"Oh, thank God!" He rushed over to embrace Maggie and Duncan. "What happened?"

"We will explain later, but right now, we need to see our children."

"Of course, you do." John smiled and waved them to his bedroom. He pushed open the door and all five of the babies were fast asleep on his bed, surrounded by rolls of deerskins to keep them from tumbling off. Hettie was watching over them. She came around the bed and hugged Maggie tightly.

"Thank the good Lord," she said and touched Duncan's arm. "Y'all alright?"

"We are perfect," replied Duncan, moving to see his two new sons, who had started to stir. Duncan picked up one as Maggie took the other.

"Look what we did." She smiled at him and turned to John. "Still want to have children after watching these five at once?"

"Absolutely!" he said as he came to look over her shoulder at the newborns. "What are you going to call them?" he asked.

Maggie and Duncan exchanged looks.

"Good question," she replied.

"Well," said Duncan. "I think it is past time that we named one after your father."

Maggie leaned her head against him. "Dad would like that," she whispered.

Duncan looked down at the son he was holding. "What do ye think, Steven MacGregor?"

"So, what about this little guy?" she asked. "What are we going to call you?"

Duncan looked over. "Any ideas?"

"Maybe one, but you might not care for it." She leaned over and whispered in his ear.

Duncan made a face and groaned. "I don't hate it as much as ye might think. I have a slight confession to make."

Maggie looked at him oddly.

"It may or may not be my middle name."

Maggie's mouth dropped. "That is your middle name, and you never once mentioned it?"

"It is not an uncommon Scottish name and, well, after he appeared in our lives, I just never brought it up."

"Well, I guess we have our son's name." Maggie looked down. "Welcome to the world, Finley MacGregor."

18 CHAPTER EIGHTEEN

With a little assistance, they were able to get all the children back to the house. Maggie finally got to nurse her newborns for the first time with Duncan by her side. Quinn and John resealed the entrance to the house with the fog to prevent any more unexpected visitors. Hettie, Cecile, and a few of the other women from the estate jumped in, getting the house cleaned up and back in order in a short amount of time.

Later that afternoon, they all gathered in the drawing room with the doors closed to discuss what happened. Maggie clung to Duncan, his arm around her, still afraid to let each other out of their sights.

"So, you are a goddess now?" asked John.

Maggie shrugged. "So, it would seem."

"How do ye feel?" asked Quinn.

"I feel great. No aches or pains, no soreness from the birth, nothing."

"So, what's next?" asked Gabe.

"I dunno," replied Maggie. "You are asking the wrong girl. I know nothing about this goddess stuff."

"We know she can raise the dead," said Duncan, squeezing her tighter.

"Do you remember anything...from being gone?" asked Quinn.

"Not much. I remember thinking that I did not want to leave Maggie and our bairns, how much I would miss them. I felt the breath leave my body and a sensation of floating. There were bright colors, a sense of warmth and love, but I fought against it. All I wanted was to be back with my love."

He kissed her forehead and she snuggled even closer.

"I would not have stayed here without you," she said, "I had the blade from your knife against my neck and I was going to do whatever it took to be in your arms again."

The room went grimly silent for a moment after her confession.

"Well, we are extremely grateful you are both still here," said Gabe.

"We could also use a few answers to all of this," added Quinn.

Maggie sat up. "I know who has them and there is no time like the present." She stood, walked over to the liquor cabinet, poured a whisky and called out. "I know you are lurking around. Come on out."

Nothing happened. Maggie looked around and rolled her eyes.

"We named one of the babies, Finley," she called, sweetly.

"Well, why didn't ye say so?" asked Finn, appearing next to her, causing everyone to jump. He took the glass. "Where is my namesake?"

"Actually, he is MY namesake," said Duncan, dryly. "Finley is my middle name."

"How do ye think YE got it?" said Finn with a certain look in his eye.

Duncan went on to say something but closed his mouth and wondered what he meant by that.

Finn looked around. "Well! Well! The gang is all here. I am Finn," he said as he held up his glass and bowed, "and all of ye, I already know."

He took a sip of the drink, looked down into the glass, and winced. "Yuck! Remind me to send ye some of the good stuff."

He took a seat in one of the leather chairs, leaving the glass on a table. "What can I do for all of ye?" he asked, leaning back comfortably.

"Don't give us that," said Maggie. "You know we want some answers."

Duncan stood. "Ye wanted Maggie as the goddess Danu, and now ye have her. I have a feeling that you have had a hand in this all along, so why don't you just enlighten the rest of us?"

Finn stroked his chin. "Ye are correct and I suppose I do owe you an explanation."

Maggie sat down. "That would be nice for a change." Finn smiled at her. "You look so much like your mother, do ye know that? Ye have the same smile, the same tilt to your head, your eyes even crinkle just like hers when ye are annoyed."

"Are they crinkled now?" she asked, pointing to her face.

"Just a little," he teased.

He waved his hand and another glass appeared in his grasp and five other full glasses appeared on the table before them.

"Please, enjoy!" he said.

"I can't drink that," said Maggie. "I'm nursing."

"Oh, it won't affect the babies," he said. "They have enough magical blood to protect them. Didn't I tell ye that with the triplets?"

"No! You did not!" she exclaimed, perturbed as she picked up a glass. "You seem to forget to tell me a great many things."

She took a sip. "Oh! That is so good," she said, savoring it.

The others picked up the glasses and settled in as Finn began his story.

"Before today, I was the only full Fae left. Danu, your mother, and I were the only ones up until now who gave a shit about this world, the others were always too absorbed in themselves and their own games with mankind to see what was really happening around them. They became bored with living and, one by one, they each chose to take the eternal slumber, damning this world to its own fate. When your mother decided to leave me, to leave behind her life as a Fae to be with your mortal father, I was devastated, beside myself and ready to move on as well, but I knew that would doom this world to a future that I would not wish upon anyone. So, when ye came along, I had a grand idea; a way to save mankind and to give myself a break in the process. Ye see, after today, I plan to slumber."

"You are leaving...forever?" asked a stunned Maggie.

"Nay, not forever, but I do need a good long nap. Being as old as I am tends to make ye a little tired of living and I am in need of a nice, long vacation."

"But Finn, you can't leave me here alone with all of this. I don't know what I am doing," she protested.

"My dear, ye will not be alone. You will be raising a royal race that will be by your side always, and the things all of ye will do will be nothing short of astounding."

"The children," whispered Duncan, sitting down next to Maggie. "It has always been about the children."

"They were born to be gods and goddesses and with the two of ye as their parents, how can they possibly go wrong?"

"They already have their full powers?" asked Maggie. She punched Duncan's shoulder. "I told you we were screwed when they became teenagers."

"Nay, I would not do that to ye!" Finn chuckled. "They have some natural inclinations now, but they will not be fully 'charged' until YE decide they are ready. There is a spell in my book downstairs, that only ye can perform, and it will make them whole when the time is right."

Finn sipped his drink. "I would advise you waiting until the children are of a mature age before granting it though. After all, you wouldn't want toddlers having a disagreement with each other resulting in leveling the house and everything within a hundred-mile radius in the process."

Maggie grimaced. "You may have a point there."

"They need their parents to raise them, to teach them right from wrong before they are given so much power." Finn looked around the room. "I would advise making everyone in this room a full god to ensure the children are raised well."

They all looked around at each other.

"Us? Gods?" asked John, stupefied.

"Can you do that?" asked Maggie.

"My dear, I have granted YE the ability to do that," he said and smiled. "I know you will make the right decisions and you can gift it to anyone that carries even the slightest Fae blood."

"But not everyone in this room carries Fae blood," whispered Quinn, turning to Gabe and laying his hand on his knee.

Gabe smiled sadly, as he took his hand. "I plan on being around for a few more years to come, and when I am gone, I know they will have you to look after them."

"Nay!" said Quinn and pulled Gabe tight to him. "I will not accept it if it means that I will not be with ye. I cannot imagine living that way, ever."

"Ye two are adorable, do you know that?" asked Finn and waved his glass around. He took a sip and stared at them, as if lost in thought. "There may be one obscure way to grant the gift to a human."

"What way?" demanded Maggie.

"It has never been done before because it requires such an enormous sacrifice; one that no one was ever willing to make before."

"Go on," said Duncan, as he folded his arms curiously.

"A Fae god or goddess can give their abilities and immortality to a human if they are willing to give up everything. They would become human themselves, destined to live and die as one would, and their memories would be taken away, so they would never even remember who or what they were."

"Like my mother did for my father," said Maggie, softly.

"Exactly!" he replied.

"But my mother is not here, and she has already given everything up," Maggie said, disappointed.

Finn shrugged and leaned to one side. "Eh...well then, I suppose it was a good thing that I had the foresight to 'bottle' her Fae essence, if ye will."

"You did what? You have it?" asked Maggie.

"Nay, I don't," he said and sipped his drink, feigning ignorance.

Maggie narrowed her eyes at him and gritted her teeth, annoyed. "Really? Why did you even bring it up then?"

"I don't have it," he smiled, and pointed at her, "but, ye do. It has always been with ye."

"I don't have anything like that!"

Duncan shook his head and sighed. "Aye, ye do! Your mother's necklace. I thought that stone looked a little too 'unusual'."

Maggie touched it. "This? Wait! This holds my mother's Fae essence? It has the power to turn a human into a god?"

"Yes!" replied Finn, matter-of-factly.

"Oh, for fuck's sake, Finn! I gave this necklace to Anna Strong. It could have ended up anywhere with anyone!" she shouted.

"Well, in hindsight, I admit, I probably should have been keeping a closer eye on ye," he said with a wave of a hand. "But I can't be everywhere at once. I do have a life, ye know?"

Maggie closed her eyes and bit her lip, trying hard to compose herself. "How would that work exactly?"

"Well," said Finn, "the human would hold it, ye would say a small incantation over it, mingle your blood with his, and break the stone. The person would absorb it."

Maggie rubbed her face. "So, Gabe would gain my mother's abilities? The same ones I have?"

"Nay, that is not how it works. The Fae essence latches on to what is already inside the person. For instance, Kat is a natural born healer, as was her great-grandmother, so she will become her own version of Brigid, the goddess of healing."

"And Alastair?" questioned Quinn.

"That boy lives to protect others. He would become the equivalent of Toutatis, the protector of the tribe, or all of ye, in this case. It is what he was born to do. Have ye not been listening to him? He keeps trying to tell ye!"

"What about our children?" asked Duncan.

Finn stroked his chin. "There are so few real surprises in the world; wouldn't ye just like to wait and find out?"

"NO!" exclaimed Maggie and Duncan in unison.

"You will not be here to give us any guidance," said Maggie, "so, cough it up, Grandpa, and don't leave out any important details while you are at it."

Finn rolled his eyes. "Very well! Kendric, like his parents, will be a warrior as was the god, Lugh. Morgan will be the female version of her brother, as in the goddess of war, soldiers, and fate, Morrigan; and Alanna will balance the two, much as Aine, the goddess of love and light did. As for your two newest additions, Steven will be the male sun god, Belenos, and young Finley will be the god of youth and love, Aengus. Each will inherit the Fae books of their predecessors to guide them along their path."

Finn cocked his head. "As ye well know, ye are your mother's daughter, Danu, and by your side is the father god of knowledge, wisdom, and lover of..." he smirked again, "good sex, the Dagda. The two of ye will now be the leaders of the next generation of Fae."

A thought occurred to Maggie. "Onyx? What about him?"

"He is a part of ye. As long as ye are alive, he will always be with ye, keeping watch, as will all of the ones he sired for the future gods and goddesses."

Maggie covered her face with both hands. "This is a lot to take in," she mumbled.

Finn leaned forward. "My dear, YE are the granddaughter of the King of the Fae. It is your birthright and ye will do me proud."

"There is so much more we need to know," she said.

"Ye have the books and each other. Ye will figure it out, as ye do everything. The spell to turn the rest of the ones in this room into gods is in my book that I am bequeathing to ye since you will be the leader of this motley crew. There are many in it that will be of use to ye. By the way, I wouldn't waste any time on turning the rest, but, please, do it with a little pomp and circumstance in the collection room, which, by the way, I redecorated a little, to make it a little more befitting the new leaders of the Fae."

"You? Redecorated?" asked Maggie dryly.

"Yes! That cute little couple in the future, the ones with all the children, that remodel homes on the television set, I am quite fond of their show. They inspired me to do something 'grand' as a going away gift."

Maggie broke into laughter that was part amusement, mostly hysteria.

"I should be off," he said as he went to stand.

"No, you will not…not just yet," said Maggie. "You have one more thing to do."

He looked puzzled.

Maggie got up and took his hand. "I must insist that you stay for dinner with the entire family, including all the children. I want one sit down meal with my grandfather."

Finn smiled and nodded. "I would like that very much," he said, and his eyes became a little watery.

That evening, they took their time eating, drinking, laughing, and enjoying each other's company. Finn regaled them with stories from the earlier days and with several about Maggie's mother. At the end of the evening, Finn raised his glass in a toast to his family. Afterwards, he bid them farewell and started towards the door. Maggie walked with him, pulling him into a tearful hug.

"What if I need you?" she whispered and held on tightly. "I am just getting to know you?"

Finn placed his hand on her face. "If ye truly need me before my nap is done, and I doubt ye will, there is one additional spell in my book downstairs that I left for ye. Merely perform it, and it will wake me instantly."

Maggie kissed his cheek, as the tears flowed. "I will miss you," she choked.

"Ye will be too busy to even know I am gone, and I will be back before ye know it. I want to see this wonderful world ye and these children will create."

He kissed her cheek, opened the door and disappeared into the fog.

Duncan came up behind her and wrapped his arms around her.

"He is gone," she whispered.

"He will be back," said Duncan, wryly.

19 CHAPTER NINETEEN

After all the children were asleep, they gathered to go downstairs. They stared in awe at the new collection room.

"He was not kidding!" whistled Maggie.

"It looks just like the one in Scotland," said Quinn, "only a great deal bigger."

Finn had left them with, not only the books, but a collection of artwork, armor, and weapons, including enough swords for everyone. He had also expanded it to include a comfy, cozy area with fireplaces, sofas, armchairs, and a separate bar room full of an array of liquors and a great deal of rum. There was a room for giving the mark, another one with an altar, and a special chamber with an enormous bed and a large fireplace for Maggie and Duncan to sneak off to whenever they wanted to be alone.

On the table next to Finn's spell book were several champagne bottles and crystal glasses with a note that read, 'A toast to the next generation. Guard it well.'

"This is…." marveled John, taking it all in.

"Yes, it is," added Gabe, grabbing him by the shoulder and looking around.

"Where does this go?" asked Maggie after finding a hidden opening off to the side of one of the rooms.

"Holy fuck!" she exclaimed. "All of you have to see this!"

Everyone came to see.

Duncan's face lit up and his face broke into a broad grin.

Before them was an underground hot spring, complete with rocky outcrops and a waterfall, looking much like the one in Scotland. The water was as blue as the water in the Caribbean.

Maggie found a note on a rock. 'I know how much ye and Duncan like the water. I hope ye enjoy this little gift- Finn.'

Duncan read over her shoulder. "Oh aye, we WILL enjoy this!"

John's eyes were alight with amazement. "How is this even possible?"

"Don't ask, just appreciate," said Quinn.

After they were done exploring, they moved to the altar room. Maggie laid her hands on and said the spell over Duncan first. The same white light that she had received from Finn left her hands and settled into him.

"Are you good?" she asked, nervously when she was done.

He held out his hands, flexing them and feeling the power. "Aye, I think I am!"

"We will be together always, my love," she said, and kissed him passionately.

His eyes glittered gold as he gazed at her. "As we were meant to be!"

Duncan stepped to the side and Quinn came up next.

Maggie repeated the procedure, Quinn grinning through the whole ritual. He shook his head as the surge flooded his body. "I have never felt anything like that before," he said as he laughed and embraced Gabe.

John was next, a little unsure, but trusting enough of Maggie to go through with it. When the light entered him, he jumped a little.

"Are you okay?" she asked.

"I think so," he replied. "I just wasn't expecting to feel it 'there'."

"Feel it where?" asked Duncan, curiously.

John cleared his throat and covered his mouth with his hand, giving Duncan a certain look, before looking downward. "There!"

Duncan looked at him strangely when he took his meaning. "Oh!" he said, confounded. "Really? Was that supposed to happen?"

"Is this something we should be concerned about?" asked Maggie, nervously.

"Nay!" said Duncan. "THAT is no concern of yours."

John chuckled softly to himself.

Finally, Maggie stood before Gabe. She took off her necklace and placed it in his hand. He looked down at it.

"I really hate to destroy this," he said. "I know what it means to you."

"It is worth it," said a smiling Maggie, hugging him tight. "I would rather have my best friend than that necklace any day."

Maggie borrowed a dagger from Duncan and used it to slice open her hand. "Your turn," she said and handed it to Gabe.

He hesitated for a brief moment before gripping it tightly and cutting his own palm.

Maggie took his bloody hand in hers and smiled, mingling their blood as she recited the incantation.

Gabe then smashed the stone against the table, releasing the essence to settle into him.

"How do you feel?" she asked.

"Strong...and a little strange at the same time!"

Maggie said the same spell over him as she had the others, just to be sure.

When they were done, Duncan came over with three Fae books. "It seems that Finn marked one of these for each of ye with these strange little yellow squares," he said, holding one up. "They are sticky on one side for some reason."

Quinn took it from him, examining it closely. "What kind of strange magic is this?"

Maggie snatched it from Quinn and wrinkled up her nose. "Sticky notes? Really, Finn?" she said to the air.

"You tell us to go through the trouble of performing formal ceremonies, and then you tag the books with these damn sticky notes. Classy!"

Duncan laughed at her and sorted the books. He handed the first one to Quinn. "Quinn, ye receive the book of Grannus, god of healing."

"That makes sense," his brother said. "I look forward to reading this and sharing it with Kat when she is older."

The next book went to Gabe. "Gabe, ye get Camulos, the god of war."

"War?" he asked, confused.

"Also, a swordsman...and ye were a soldier, so, it fits ye perfectly," assured Quinn, putting his arm around him. "Ye will be wonderful at it."

"I will do my best," he said and accepted it.

Duncan looked back at Maggie, then to John, a huge, stupid grin on his face. "And last, but not least, is the one for John. The book of...Cernunnos."

Duncan and Quinn exchanged rather odd looks and burst into laughter.

"What was that look?" asked Maggie, moving her finger back and forth between the two of them.

"Well, it explains why John felt the jolt 'there'," chuckled Duncan. "Cernunnos," he continued, "is the protector of the forest, the master of the hunt, and the god of...lust and sex."

John looked down at the book, and broke into laughter, as did everyone else around him. "Well, it is a dirty job, but someone has to do it," he smirked. "I will give it all I have."

Maggie hung her head, shaking it. "I am sure you will, but you had better be careful with that 'all'," she teased, "you have been made fertile, remember?"

They all turned to John, astonished.

"Ye let Maggie lay hands on ye to make ye able to sire?" asked Duncan.

"I did!" He smiled. "I thought it was about time, although, I seem to have a great deal more time on my hands now."

"Ye will make a wonderful father," said Duncan and gripped his shoulder.

Maggie walked over to the table and opened the bottle of champagne. She popped the cork, pouring when Duncan held out the glasses. After they all had been served, Maggie held up her glass.

"Here's to us and the next generation. Let's really hope we don't fuck this up."

They all toasted and finished off the champagne in front of the fireplace.

After a while, Duncan took Maggie's glass and set it down on the table. "If the rest of ye will excuse us, there is a new bedchamber that needs christening and my wife and I are in need of each other."

"For God's sake!" fussed Gabe. "The woman just gave birth yesterday. Let her have a day off."

"Truly, brother," added Quinn. "Pace yourself. Ye do have all of eternity."

Duncan chuckled. "We bid ye all 'goodnight'."

He picked Maggie up and threw her over his shoulder, making her giggle aloud. Taking her to the chamber, he laid her on the bed, stretched out over her and kissed her. "How lucky am I that I get to spend forever staring into these lovely eyes, and making love to my beautiful wife?"

"You might get tired of me after that long," she teased.

"Never! I am not sure eternity is long enough."

She pulled him into a kiss. "You know, this is only the beginning, right. The past few years will seem like a piece of cake compared to what the future holds for us."

"Doesn't matter," he said and started to help her out of her clothes. "We have each other, we have our family, and there is nothing we cannot handle together."

He removed her top with a wicked smile.

"There is much to be done." She tugged his shirt over his head and tossed it aside.

"Aye, there is," he growled, running his tongue over one of her breasts. "THIS needs to be done."

He moved to the other. "And THIS needs to be done."

He kissed her lips. "And THESE definitely need to be done."

"You know what I mean," she groaned as he worked his way down.

"That is tomorrow's problem," he growled, as he took her to bed, and they enjoyed their first night of eternity together.

TO BE CONTINUED…

Epilogue

December 1783
New York

Maggie and John peered out from behind the heavy, blue-velvet curtains. The room was packed with people celebrating the American victory over the British. The war had officially ended on September 3rd, but the celebrations had continued for months.

"Which one do you think she is?" asked Maggie.

"Your guess is as good as mine," replied John. "Are you sure he is going to be here?"

"Yes! I sent him a note and asked him to meet me here tonight. He will come."

"Duncan is not going to be happy about this," he whispered.

"Well, if Gabe and Quinn are doing their part, he will never know." Maggie gave John a little push. "Now, get out there and go find her."

She grabbed him by the shoulders. "Wait! Do not get distracted, and make sure that Ben does not see you. He will recognize you instantly."

"What's he going to do? Hang me?" he asked, sarcastically.

"No, but I will if you get caught," she said, shoving him out into the group.

"How do I let you talk me into these things?" he mumbled back as he moved into the crowd.

"Oh, you love it!" she retorted.

He responded with a wink and a mischievous smile over his shoulder for her to see.

Maggie shook her head, watching the women flock to him. Ever since he had become the god of lust and sex, women could not keep their hands off him. The man dripped sex appeal everywhere he went. She had even noticed Hettie, Cora, and Cecile's lingering looks. Maggie chuckled to herself, remembering the time she caught Hettie brushing her breasts up against him while putting a plate in front of him. She was not sure which one enjoyed it more.

The situation had become so bad at the tribe, that he had to start limiting his time there. Women had no taste for their husbands when John was there and the village already had several of John's 'mini-mes' running around, much to Mingan's delight.

She watched John work his way through the crowd, rolling the potion bottle back and forth in her hands, hoping this was not the worst idea she had ever had.

"Boo!" whispered a voice in her ear. Maggie jumped, startled, turning to see Duncan standing behind her, his arms folded with a scolding look on his face. "Just what the hell do ye think ye are doing?"

Damn it!

"Who ratted me out?" she demanded.

"Ye forget. Quinn is my little brother. He cannot keep secrets from me. I have been worming information out of him since he came into this world."

Maggie rolled her eyes. "He kept the fact that he preferred men from you forever, but he couldn't keep his mouth shut about this for one stinking day?"

Duncan scrunched up his face. "Exactly, what ARE ye doing?"

Maggie wrinkled her nose at him. "Giving Ben his happy ending. He has not been able to move on from what happened between us, and I cannot in good conscience continue to let him be alone. He deserves to be happy after all he has done for this country."

Duncan sighed and took her in his arms. "Aye, he does. What can I do to help?" He kissed her before they turned to face the crowd.

"Help John find Mary Floyd. That is the woman Ben is destined to marry." She held up the bottle. "We are just going to help it along a little bit to make sure it sticks…literally."

"What is that?"

Maggie grinned. "A love potion that Quinn brewed up from one of the books. That, along with a little 'lust-dusting' from John, should put things right back on course."

"I hope ye know what ye are doing," he said, cautiously.

"You and me both," she mumbled. She nodded her head to her left. "Why don't you ask around over there and see if we can figure out which one she is?"

"Whatever ye say," he said and headed off.

Maggie caught sight of John, who now had seven women surrounding him, and he was liking it a little too much. She waved until she got his attention, pointing around the room to remind him of the business they were there for. He grimaced and turned his focus back to the ladies. She could see him asking them questions.

Duncan had taken up with a couple of the men near the fireplace trying to get information out of them. She was so absorbed in the scene before her, that she never noticed his approach.

"It looks like you are hiding over here."

She turned and smiled. "Hello, Ben."

He leaned over and kissed her cheek. "Hello, Maggie."

The stress of the war did not show on him. He looked older, yes, but in a handsome, rugged way.

"I must say, I was surprised to get your note," he said. "I had no idea you were in New York."

"Yes, I just had some business to attend to and how could I resist a celebration like this."

"It has been a long, hard road; one we would have never succeeded at if not for your help."

"Ben, you give me far more credit than I deserve. There are many others that did a great deal more than I did and they are the ones who deserve the praise."

"Are you here alone?" he asked.

"No, Duncan is here, and an old friend is with us."

"I...um...should like to officially meet him," he said, looking down.

Maggie noticed John headed her way with a broad smile on his face. As soon as he saw Ben, he made an abrupt U-turn and went back the way he came.

Duncan sent Maggie a silent message.

She is by the refreshment table, in a blue dress.

Maggie smiled at Ben and patted his chest. "I think it is past time the two of you meet." He offered his arm and she accepted.

"What will you do now?" she asked, as they walked.

Ben shrugged. "I'm not sure. I have given some thought to opening a store in Litchfield. Maybe live the quiet life for a while?"

"Settle down? Marry?" she asked, hopefully.

"I don't think so," he said, softly.

We will see.

Nearing the table, Ben picked up two glasses from a tray, and handed one to Maggie.

"Good evening," said Maggie to Mary, as they approached. "I don't believe we have met. I am Maggie MacGregor, and this is my friend, Major Benjamin Tallmadge."

"Actually, it's Colonel now," he said with a sheepish smile. "I was promoted."

"Congratulations," she said holding up her glass.

"Yes, congratulations. I am Mary Floyd."

"It is a pleasure to make your acquaintance," he said and bowed.

Maggie downed her drink. "I think I need a refill," she said as she went to take Ben's glass. "And I will top yours off too while you keep Miss Floyd company for a moment."

Ben looked down. "My glass is still full."

Maggie took it out of his hand and downed it in one shot. "Not anymore," she said, shaking her head from the rush. "I will be right back, and I will get one for Miss Floyd as well, so she can celebrate with us."

Ben gave her a puzzled look, but his manners stopped him from asking what was going on in front of Mary.

Maggie turned to see that John had joined Duncan and was giving him instructions and a potion bottle. She took the glasses over to the table with the drinks as Duncan met her there.

"Are you sure about this?" he asked, mixing the punch for Mary with the potion.

"Not really," she said, making one for Ben with the bottle she had. She poured two more drinks for her and Duncan, then took a swig from a nearby bottle.

"You take that one to Mary and DON'T mix the glasses up. The last thing I need is you and Ben falling in love!" She snickered.

Duncan shook his head and laughed. "That would be unfortunate."

"I love you," she said, gazing up at him.

"I love ye, too," he replied.

They went back to Ben and Mary, handing them their drinks.

"Allow me to officially introduce my husband, Duncan. This is Miss Floyd, and this is Ben."

Ben nodded before slowly holding out his hand to shake Duncan's. "It is a pleasure to finally meet you, sir," he said.

Duncan returned the handshake warmly with a smile. "The pleasure is all mine."

Maggie held up her glass for a toast. "Here is to the end of the war and to new beginnings. You never know what the future holds."

They all clinked glasses as Maggie watched anxiously. As soon as Ben and Mary took a sip, their eyes met, and it was if they had just seen each other in that very instant.

Maggie let out a relieved breath; by the looks on their faces, she knew they were in love.

John, who had a woman on his arm walked up behind Ben, lightly touching his back, giving him a little touch of desire. Maggie saw Ben's body shiver slightly as if he had gotten a chill...and then noticed him step slightly to the side to 'adjust' himself.

Maggie smirked at Duncan who was using his hand to cover the laugh he was holding in.

Maggie touched Ben's back.

"I'm sorry, Ben, but we must go."

"So soon?" he asked. "We haven't had time to catch up."

"There will be plenty of time for that in the future," she said, squeezing his hand. "It was good to see you, Ben."

"And you too, Maggie."

Maggie hugged him and whispered in his ear. "Be happy!"

He nodded. "You too and don't be a stranger."

"You never know where I may turn up," she said and kissed his cheek. She smiled and turned to Duncan.

Ben and Mary were already lost in each other's gaze.

"Time to go home, my love."

John kissed two women 'goodbye' before he came to join them. "How did it go?" he asked.

"I would say 'mission accomplished'," replied Maggie, as they stepped outside into the garden and then into the fog, arriving back at their home in Virginia in a matter of moments.

BOOK SIX IS COMING SOON!

ABOUT THE AUTHOR

Tempie W. Wade is the award-winning author of The Timely Revolution Book Series. She is a lifelong resident of Virginia and currently resides in Williamsburg. The author's writing style incorporates Celtic lore and fantasy with historically accurate events, often bringing to light lesser-known details from the past.

The Timely Revolution Book Series
(In Order)

www.ingramcontent.com/pod-product-compliance
Lightning Source LLC
Chambersburg PA
CBHW050553260626
47157CB00002B/548